AUSTERE

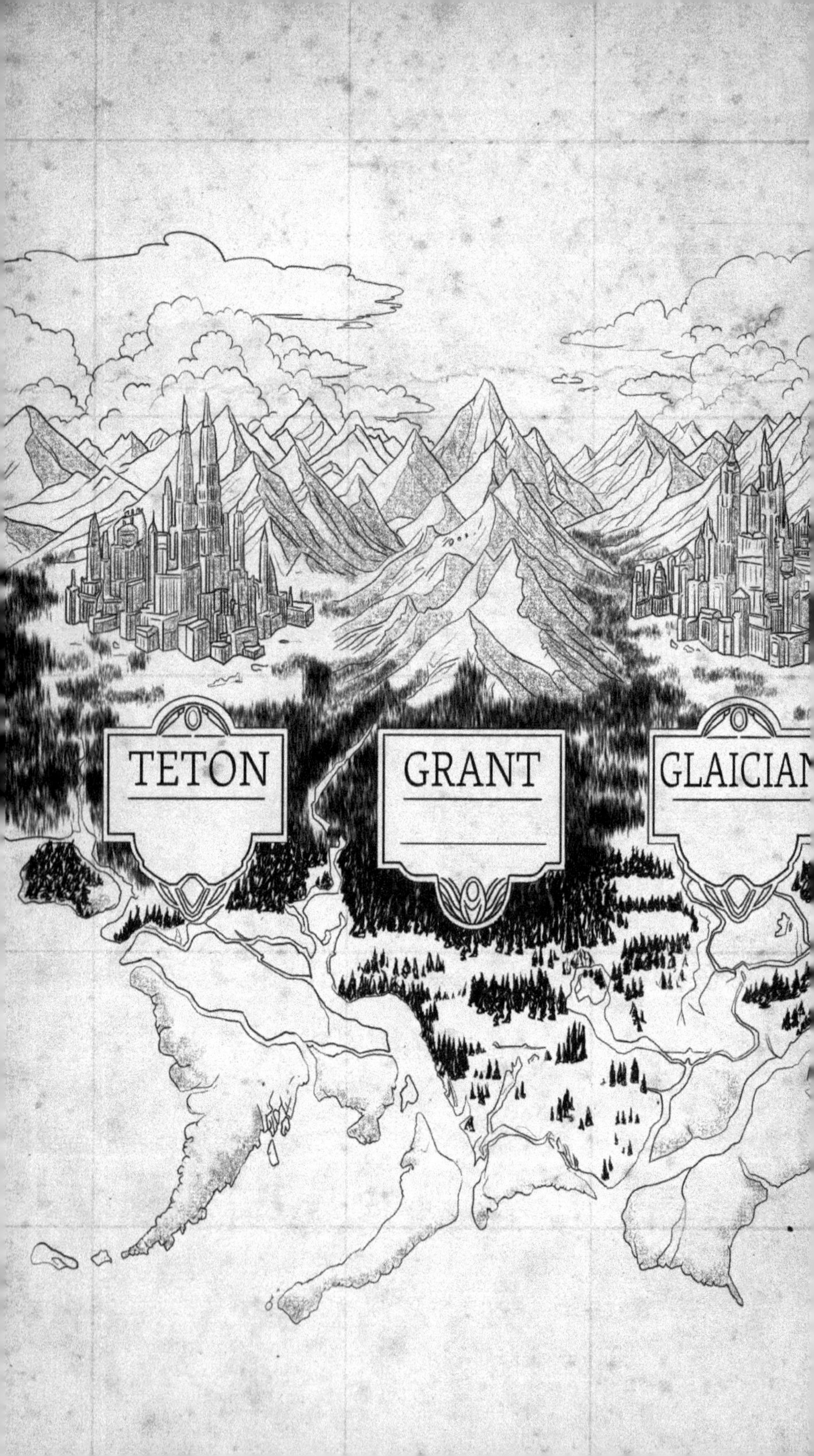

TETON
GRANT
GLAICIAN

AUSTERE

RICK RICKER

PALMETTO
PUBLISHING
Charleston, SC
www.PalmettoPublishing.com

Hardcover ISBN: 978-1-9684-3900-2
Paperback ISBN: 978-1-9684-3901-9
eBook ISBN: 978-1-9684-3902-6

To my dad, Richard—your brilliance, quirks, and occasional mad-scientist energy were the perfect blueprint for Dr. Voss. Thanks for making eccentric genius look easy.

To my kids, Jacob, Riley, Lindsay, and Brennen—you may not realize it, but your personalities are scattered all over these pages. If a character seems oddly familiar, that's probably you.

To my friend Laura, who unknowingly became the inspiration for Raylee—thank you for being sharp, loyal, and always ready with a reality check. Your friendship kept me sane… mostly.

And finally, to my roommate Hannah—this book series probably wouldn't exist without your encouragement, late-night idea fests, and emotional support. Also, yes, you're Arty. Don't let it go to your head.

CONTENTS

THE AWAKENING

ＴHE MAGNESIUM COMET tore through the atmosphere; Violet fire against a dying sun. Beneath the Austere, a silent sentinel stirred. Circuits flared. Something approached.

The change came first, subtle, and insidious, a disruption across the gravitational field that only machines can hear. Then the long trail of ice, dust, and minerals follows: a comet, larger than most, moving at 122,000 miles per hour. It was not just ice and dust, not merely a frozen relic from the outer dark. This one bore something else, a core of magnesium, veins of metal lacing through its body like an ancient scar, gleaming beneath the distant sun. A familiar traveler, one that appears every six thousand years, had come to careen by once more. As it tore through space, friction and solar radiation set its surface blazing in a cascade of impossible colors.

Below, Austere lay still.

Then the ground shuddered.

Beneath the sands, a relay station awakens. Circuits flared as gravitational waves pulsed, *something* approached. At the surface, the first harbinger rose. An antenna, sharp and skeletal, burst from the ground, casting up a shower of dust and fractured stone. Nearby, a creature stirred, A Spinifex Hopping Mouse (Notomys alexis), a little-known desert rodent from the Austere, has some remarkable adaptations. One of its most unusual features is its incredible jumping ability, it can leap over three meters (10 feet) in a single bound, using its long hind legs like a kangaroo.

This mouse, we shall call him 'Spinet', was tiny and unknowing; its world changed in an instant. The tremor beneath its feet was the first warning. "With a shuddering quake, a long-buried antenna burst through six thousand years of packed earth and rubble, blasting rocks into the air. The mouse

Figure 1: Instinct took over, and "Spinet" leapt—the highest it ever had, the highest it ever would.

lived up to its name - Spinet leapt three meters high as the relay erupted. Its survival adaptations mattered little now, and it chose flight over fight. And still, the relay station continued to wake.

On a distant hilltop, another structure claws its way free, unfolding like a flower of metal and forgotten intent. A dish fans outward, delicate despite its size, like the hand-held fans sold in the market stalls of Asia-town for five credits.

It found the city.

The dish aligned, **calculating**, toward a civilization hub. The dish locked coordinates, 31.4159°N, 90.0000°W, a site the station's creators once called "Vandenberg". The scanning beam burst followed, a lance of energy so vast it cracked the hilltop itself, reducing stone to talcum powder. Nothing would ever be the same. The scan blast wave rippled outward, carrying with it its first instruction in six thousand years.

Something had returned.

Something had remembered.

And soon, the world would know.

CHAPTER 1

KERBEROS ARISES

THE FRAGILE BALANCE between Grant, Teton, and Glaician had lasted for decades; three city-states bound by necessity more than trust. Each city was its own world, isolated by the wasteland yet reliant on the others. In the Austere's neutral expanse, caravans and emissaries met under uneasy truces, swapping goods and information. Eliza, Arty, and Raylee, unlikely friends from rival cities, were among those emissaries who had learned to trust each other out here, beyond their leaders' watchful eyes. As word of Grant's mysterious blackout spread, the three gathered once more in Austere, not for routine trade, but to find answers before their world tipped into chaos.

Against this backdrop stand the three cities, their distinct identities sharp and unyielding. They are not simply separated by geography but by ideology, culture, and the fundamental ways their people view the world and their place within it.

Arty: The Rogue of Teton

The Austere crust cracked like old porcelain underfoot. Samael Artemus "Arty" Loxley's shadow stretched toward Teton, where forge-fires pulsed like a dying star. The wind that sweeps across the Austere carries with it the voices of a dying world, whispers of what had been, now drowned in the relentless rhythm of human endeavor. This was not a world for dreamers. It was a world for survivors.

Arty tugged his scarf tighter against the Austere's dusk wind as he crested a dune of cracked earth. The ground trembled, a faint echo of the hilltop's destruction 20 miles west. A shiver ran down his spine. It was only the beginning. He glanced back, but the Austere dust devils hid everything. Grant's neon died just as the comet's tail split the eastern sky, a chilling omen.

Arty's boot crunched a Glaician drone fragment, half-buried, still sparking. "This is unusual… drones are only deployed for specific investigations. Something is up," Arty thought.

Teton's forge-smoke billowed ahead. As Arty walked farther away, the dust devils subsided, revealing Grant's black silhouette. The absence of neon drew his eye. Another blackout, he guessed. Three legs of a stool, that's what they were. Each city propped the others up, barely stable, creaking under the weight of their own distrust. But remove one leg? The whole thing tips.

The memory of that night, years ago, when a sudden blackout stole the last warmth from his sister's frail body, still haunted him. Now, with Grant once again plunged into darkness, the old dread returned, sharper than ever. He vowed he would not let history repeat itself. If Grant falls, the Austere will claim them all.

Arty was coming up to a caravan heading his way. He watched as the Glaician patrol's spotlight pinned the Teton caravan. Three soldiers in mirrored visors descended, their white armor glowing in the dusk.

"Open your crates," barked the lead soldier, voice metallic through their helmet.

A Teton trader stepped forward, forge-soot staining her gloves. "They got permits."

"Permits don't override ration quotas," the soldier snapped, jabbing his scanner into the crates like a threat.

"Steel ingots?" He scoffed. "Glaician needs that. With Grant's blackout, our drones don't run without your steel."

The trader crossed her arms. "Then maybe rethink your 'precision quotas' before they choke your whole city."

A tense pause. The soldier's hand hovered over his holster. "Step aside."

"Negative. You violate the Trade Accords here, I'll report you. What's your badge number again?"

The Trade Accords uphold this fragile interdependence, an agreement forged decades ago after a bloody skirmish along the Austere threatened to collapse the entire system. The Accords outlined the rules of engagement: no open hostility in neutral zones, no interference with trade caravans, and no claims on resources outside one's borders. Violations were rare, but the threat of retaliation kept even the most ambitious city in line.

The soldiers paused and retorted, "Whatever, smart-ass… we'll be watching you and your entire team." They finished their inspection, and the soldier barked, "Move along!" and slowly sauntered away.

Arty decided to continue along with the Teton trader's caravan; 'strength in numbers' was a mantra no one soon forgot. Each breath was a knife of grit and ash. The Austere demanded its price. In the distance, the three city-states pierced the twilight sky – jagged Grant now a dark silhouette, tiered Teton puffing forge-smoke, and gleaming Glaician haloed in cold white light. Arty's eyes watered from the dust, but he kept them fixed on those silhouettes.

Each city held promises and perils he'd tasted before. The wind carried a faint hint of oil and ozone from far-off Grant, reminding him of last week's trade run and the rumors he'd heard of leadership unrest.

The road was a lie, fissured dirt betraying the horizon. Each step was stolen from the Austere's relentless thirst. The sunset still shimmers with heat, and the sky is a kaleidoscope of gold and bronze, flecked with clouds that seem as weary as the land they float over.

The caravan's rhythm pulled him inward, into a memory half-buried in sand and soot. Arty barely stopped himself and felt his hand. A quick flash of memory struck him. His little sister's hand reaching for a crust of bread. Empty. Never again.

Arty relived his first arrival at Teton as a young man. Baked soil and iron tinged the air, Austere breath. Arty's stomach growled, but the promise of Teton in the distance was enough to quiet it.

The caravan crested a final ridge, and Teton unfurled before them, terraces stacked like steps to a forgotten temple, smoke and steam rising in lazy columns. Relief warred with exhaustion as Arty glimpsed the city gates, knowing that each step forward was a step away from the ghosts of Grant.

The city perches on the mountainside like a sentinel, its terraces glinting in the fading sunlight. He can almost taste it, the roasted chestnuts from the market, the smoky sweetness he's only heard of from traders passing by.

Figure 2: Samael Artemus "Arty" Loxely

"When they arrive, the city is alive in a way that Austere never is. The air is thick with voices, shouts of merchants haggling, the occasional bark of laughter, and the chatter of children weaving through the crowd like fish in a stream. The smells are overwhelming and intoxicating: leather newly stitched into boots, molten iron from the smithies, and rich, greasy meat sizzling on open flames.

Arty watches the throngs of people as he approaches, his intelligent brown eyes taking in every detail. The worn edges of leather aprons, the heavy sacks slung over shoulders, the subtle glances exchanged between traders and customers, all of it speaks of a city built on hard work and mutual reliance. But it also carries an undertone of vigilance, a quiet wariness that reminds him he doesn't belong here.

For generations, the people of Teton, Grant, and Glaician have guarded their borders with wary eyes, their interactions guided more by necessity than trust. While the Trade Accords have ensured a degree of cooperation, they haven't erased the tensions that linger between them.

The woman's eyes, lined with forge-soot, held a flicker of distrust. Her eyes flickered to the Grant insignia on his pack. 'Teton trusts no one', he reminded himself. 'Especially not those who stumble from the dark.'

"Grant, ee to, Nan Ja hoshi no? The trader language included a mix of english and japanese.

Arty had just a blank stare.

She continued, "Grant wa hanashikata wa shira nai no ka? kimiyo wa manabu koto ga takusan aru na ˎ shounen…"

Arty, smiled.

She decided to give him a break, "Grant, huh? What do you want? If you want to trade, you have to learn to speak, a lot to learn, boy."

The woman studied him for a long moment before nodding slightly. "If you're serious about trading, you'll need to prove it," she says.

She gestures toward a nearby cart piled high with sacks of grain. "Help me carry those to the depot. Show us you're here to work, not to cheat."

Arty hesitates for only a moment before stepping forward. The murmurs around him quiet as he hoists one of the heavy

Figure 3: "Help me carry those to the depot…"

sacks onto his shoulder, the coarse fabric rough against his skin. He follows the woman through the marketplace, his muscles straining under the weight of the load.

As they reach the depot, the woman turns to him, her expression softening. "You've got a strong back," she says. "Maybe you're not so bad, for someone from Grant."

Arty chuckles mutedly, setting the sack down with a thud. "I'll take that as a compliment, arigatou" he says.

The murmurs around them turn from wary to approving, the merchants nodding slightly as they return to their work. Arty feels the shift in their demeanor, a small but significant step toward acceptance.

He knew better than to mistake this for true trust; in Teton, respect was earned in increments. The woman caught his eye, her voice low. "One good turn doesn't erase old grudges, Grant boy. But it's a start." Arty nodded, grateful for even the smallest crack in the city's defenses.

Teton: The City of Trade and Innovation

Teton was a chaotic symphony of bartering merchants, clanging workshops, and airships hauling precious cargo. But Arty knew that beneath the bustling surface, desperation simmered. Terraces climbed the mountainside, a chaotic jumble of merchant stalls, workshops, and airship docks. Teton pulsed with life, a testament to human ingenuity and resilience. Airships buzzed overhead like great steel floating whales, ferrying cargo across the city's towering skyline and beyond.

The Tetonians themselves are hardy, energetic souls, born into a legacy of survival and enterprise. From an early age, they are taught that progress isn't a privilege but a responsibility. To trade, to innovate, to create, this was their mantra. For trading and negotiating, a mixture of Japanese and English was the course. Through this language, community bonds in Teton were strengthened, forged in the bustling markets and a quick way to flush out mishiranu hito, strangers.

Walking Teton's streets is like standing at the intersection of history and possibility. There is warmth in the air, a kinetic energy that hints at untapped potential. Yet, even here, survival carried a price, and progress often overshadowed reflection.

The cities' coexistence is precarious, and every interaction was a fragile diplomacy carrying the weight of distrust. Trade caravans are heavily guarded; their

Figure 4: The City of Teton

routes negotiated with the precision of military campaigns. Armed escorts ensured that rival factions did not interfere, while neutral zones along Austere served as makeshift marketplaces where exchanges could occur without open conflict.

Even the neutral zones are tense. Merchants eye one another warily, their hands never straying far from concealed weapons. Bargains were struck in terse tones, with promises enforced by the presence of armed guards. Yet despite the tension, the trade endured, it had to. Without Teton's food (they have the refined agriculture skills), Grant's workers would starve. Without Grant's tools, Glaician's labs would stall. Without Glaician's medicine, and fertilizer formulas, Teton's markets would crumble.

The Rise of a Tetonian

The marketplace settles into its rhythm once more, the tension easing as Arty moves from stall to stall. The goods exchange hands with quiet efficiency, fresh produce, bundles of herbs, and jars of preserves leaving Teton in exchange for Grant's exquisitely crafted tools. His language skills flourished as well – he found himself conversing in the Tetonian trading tongue within his first six months. However, there was an unspoken language as well, the weight of the Trade Accords looms over each transaction, ever-present, ensuring that the fragile balance between the cities holds firm.

As a boy, Arty's first taste of Teton was a roasted kuri, or chestnut, its shell blackened and its flesh sweet and earthy, still warm from the embers of the vendor's cart. He chews slowly, savoring the flavor and the knowledge that he has earned this himself.

The caravan finally approached the gates of Teton, waking Arty from his reminiscent journey. This being his weekly visit for many years, Arty is no longer the wide-eyed boy on the edge of a wagon. He stands in the heart of the marketplace, his brown eyes always scanning, his grin as quick as his hands. The crowd surges around him like a tide, each person carrying the fragrance of their trade, spices, parchment, oil, and sweat.

Arty thrives in it, his voice lilting and warm as he barters, "etsu! sore wa goutou da yogi、4 utsu ni shi te kure nakatsu tara iku kara ne!"

Each deal a dance where his words twist and turn, always leading the other party where he wants.

Despite the outward ease of the exchange, Arty can't shake the undercurrent of unease that lingers in the air.

The blackout of Grant weighs heavily on him, a silence that feels like a question waiting to be answered.

The forge fires of Teton still burn, their smolder lighting his path as he navigates its layered terraces. In his hand, a traditional snack to start his day, a warm kuri. The taste remains his favorite, not because it is the finest thing the city has to offer, but because it tastes

Figure 5: City of Grant

like the promise of a life; he's built himself. The result, Arty is no longer a stranger, he is a Tetonian.

Grant: The City of Ambition

If ambition were sound, Grant would be the roar of molten metal in forges and the frenzied chatter of marketplaces. The city thrives on tension, its veins coursing with the Turok, its currency embedded with microchips that enable instantaneous, untraceable transactions. "To Want is to Endeavor" was the guiding principle etched into Grant's soul. Wanting, whether it be wealth, power, or influence, was seen as an act of courage, and to strive toward it was the highest form of living.

The architecture of Grant mirrors its chaotic ethos. Skyscrapers of mismatched heights and angles jostle for dominance, their surfaces wrapped in blinking advertisements that promise luxury and prosperity. Normally, the streets below were alive with the symphony of ambition: merchants barking prices, power-suited executives darting between glass towers, and shadowy dealmakers in whispered exchanges.

But beneath the glimmering neon façade, there is rot. Factories belch plumes of toxic smoke into the air, turning the sky into a gray haze. Narrow alleyways wound between looming towers, their shadows hiding both crimes and the lives of those left behind in the race for success. The people of Grant were not born equals; they were born competitors, forced to prove their worth or be consumed by the system.

To walk Grant's streets is to feel the weight of expectation pressing against the chest, the constant thrum of desire that drives its citizens forward, even if it crushes them in the process. Ambition didn't guarantee triumph here, but it defined existence.

Eliza: The Spark of Grant

The lower districts of Grant never sleep, though they never truly wake either. The streets are narrow, hemmed in by looming factories whose chimneys belch smoke day and night, turning the sky a permanent shade of ashen gray. The air tastes metallic, with a bitterness that clings to the back of the throat, and the muted odor of oil is ever-present, seeping into the cracked brick walls and even the threads of clothing.

As a child, Eliza Shilling Edison spent most of her time in her father's workshop, a cramped, dimly lit space with tools scattered across every surface and gears piled in rusted heaps in the corners. The trace of grease and soldering metal were comforting, a sharp contrast to the acrid stench of the

Figure 6: Eliza Shilling Edison spent most of her time in her father's workshop.

streets outside. Her father's hands, rough and stained, would guide hers as she learned to disassemble and rebuild the machines brought in for repair.

On the rare days when they could afford it, they would share a meal of fried dough pockets filled with spiced vegetables, the heat making the flavors bloom on her tongue. Those tastes stayed with Eliza, even as the workshop closed, and the fried pockets became a memory replaced by the stale bite of ration bread.

Years later, as an engineer in one of Grant's industrial labs, Eliza has carved out her place amid the chaos of the city. The lab smells of rubber and ozone, with a mild undertone of burned plastic from failed prototypes. The machines whir constantly, their purr a backdrop to her work, as familiar as her own heartbeat.

Her favorite project is a purifier, a machine that can take the city's choking air and transform it into something breathable. Its casing is smooth beneath her fingers, its inner workings a delicate dance of filters and circuits.

When it works, the first breath of clean air is almost as sweet as a cool refreshing dessert, a taste so rare in Grant it feels like luxury.

Eliza's drive comes from those early days in her father's workshop, the greasy metal and cracked tools, and the promise of something better. She can still taste the bitterness of ration bread, but she works for the day when Grant's air will be clean, and its people can savor something sweeter.

Figure 7: Years later, as an engineer in one of Grant's industrial labs

Glaician: The City of Precision

To speak of Glaician is to speak of perfection. Nestled amidst icy plains, the city stands like a crystalline jewel, its symmetrical skyline gleaming under the pale sunlight. Here, everything was measured, calculated, and pristine. "Order Is Strength" was not a mere motto but a commandment, and every aspect of life in Glaician adhered to its immaculate design.

The streets of Glaician are silent compared to the cacophony of Grant or the bustling vibrancy of Teton. They are broad and lined with identical, glass-paneled buildings, each reflecting the city's flawless symmetry. Glaicians moved with quiet efficiency, their faces calm and purposeful, their steps precise as though choreographed.

The people of Glaician are born into discipline, their every action guided by an unwavering commitment to structure. Individuality was a curious notion here, viewed as a potential flaw in the city's otherwise seamless operation. To excel was mandatory; to falter was unacceptable.

Yet, beneath its polished exterior, Glaician harbors a quiet desperation; the weight of expectation pressing heavily on its people. For every achievement, there was a shadow of fear of failure, of disrupting the perfection they had worked so hard to maintain. To live in Glaician was to walk the tightrope of excellence, forever balancing success, and scrutiny.

Figure 8: "Rayena Lee "Raylee" Frye

Raylee: The River Runs Deep

The lower tiers of Glaician are far removed from the city's gleaming towers, both in height and in spirit. Here, the streets are narrow and damp, the walls perpetually slick with condensation. The air smells faintly metallic, a mix of machinery and disinfectant that fails to mask the underlying bouquet of mildew. Light, when it comes, filters down in cold, fractured beams, giving everything a bluish hue.

"Rayena Lee "Raylee" Frye grows up in these shadows. Her face never wanting of grease, her childhood a symphony of distant machinery and the whispered conversations of people who have learned to keep their voices low. The taste of Glaician here is one of subtle desperation, water stored in tin cans that leaves a mineral aftertaste on the tongue, and bread so dense it sits in the stomach like a stone.

Even as a child, Raylee is drawn to the cracks in the walls, the maintenance tunnels that wind their way beneath the city. The air in those tunnels is stale but warmer, and the hushed buzz of electricity coursing through cables is a lullaby she will never forget. She learns quickly, how to bypass locks, map the city's hidden pathways, and navigate the shadows without being seen.

Figure 9: Now, Raylee sat in the operator chamber.

The first time she climbed to the upper tiers, it was like stepping into a different world. The air was cooler, tinged with a hint of frost that made her breath visible. The illumination was brighter, clearer, and everything smelled... clean. It was intoxicating, but also a reminder of everything she and the un-tiered below would never be given.

Now, Raylee sat in the operator chamber, her green eyes fixed on a console radiating with streams of data. The chamber smelled of ozone and sterilization, the fans of servers a constant companion. Her hands moved with precision, her fingers brushing across the smooth, cold surface of her terminal.

The taste of rebellion was on her tongue, bitter but compelling. Every intercepted signal, every decrypted file was another crack in Glaician's facade of perfection. Raylee wasn't content watching from the shadows anymore. She was the crack, the flaw in the system, and she wouldn't stop until the pristine towers above shattered under the weight of their own hypocrisy.

CHAPTER 2

POWER DOWN IN GRANT

"IN THE HEART of the city, the general hospital's surgical wing is a hive of activity. Surgeons work with precision; their hands guided by robotic assistants as they perform a complex aortic dissection. The patient lay on the table, their life in danger. Suddenly, the lights flickered and went out, replaced by the dim beam of emergency lighting. The backup kicked in, but it was only good for eight hours. The clock was ticking, and the vibration of the machines became a desperate whisper. The aroma of antiseptics mingled with the metallic tang of blood, creating a sensory tapestry of urgency and fear.

Across the city, the power plant's control room is a scene of frantic activity. Engineers scramble to assess the damage; their faces illuminated by the glow of backup consoles. The plant's systems were designed to handle a

Figure 10: Surgeons worked with precision.

twenty-four-hour outage, but the strain was already showing. Monitors flickered, displaying critical warnings and error codes. The air was thick with the smell of overheated circuits and the acrid bite of burning insulation. Without power, the city's infrastructure would begin to fail, and the consequences would be dire. The rhythmic whirr of the turbines slowed to a mournful drone, echoing the city's heartbeat.

At the waste processing plant, the situation is equally grim. The facility processes fifty tons of waste an hour, and it is nearing its limit. The backup system can only run for four hours, and the plant's operators know that a failure will result in a catastrophic overflow. The stench of decay hung heavy in the air, a grim reminder of the stakes. The grinding of gears and the hiss of hydraulic presses became a cacophony of impending disaster. The operators' hands trembled as they monitored the gauges, the weight of their responsibility pressing down like a physical force.

In the city's prisons, the situation is equally challenging. The electronic door locks on the cells rely on backup power that is only good for twenty-four hours. As the outage stretches on, prison staff have to enact immediate hands-on security, manually locking each cell to prevent any potential escapes if the backup power fails. This was a monumental task, with two-hundred cell blocks and a thousand cells each. The staff worked tirelessly, their anxiety rising with every passing hour. The odor of sweat and the sound of clanking metal filled the air as they secured all the cells. The uncertainty of when the power would be restored added to the tension, and the staff knew that any failure could result in a disaster.

Figure 11: manually locking each cell to prevent any potential escapes.

As the hours pass, the city's inhabitants grow increasingly desperate. The streets, once bustling with activity, are now filled with anxious faces. People gather in small groups, their voices hushed as they discuss the unfolding crisis. The silence of Grant was a palpable presence, a reminder of the fragility of their existence. The stench of fear and sweat permeated the air, mingling with the distinct aroma of street food that had gone cold. The colors of the city, once vibrant and chaotic, now seemed muted and washed out, like a Monet painting of a world on the brink.

In the shadows, forces stir. Whispers of rebellion and sabotage spread like wildfire, fueled by the uncertainty and fear that grips the city. The delicate balance that had held Grant, Teton, and Glaician together was in jeopardy, and the consequences of a misstep could be catastrophic. The smell of smoke and the distant rumble of unrest added to the sensory overload, creating a symphony of tension and unease.

As the first glimmer of dawn breaks over the horizon, the silence of Grant remains unbroken. The city's fate hangs in the balance, and the question is not whether the power will be restored, but when, and at what cost, for the level of danger rose as time progressed. Waiting long enough could collapse the city. The dawn's early light cast long shadows across the cracked pavement, highlighting the faces of those who wait, their expressions etched with worry and hope. The air was thick with bewilderment, a level of anxiety yet to be experienced by the Grant population. An anxiety that lingered like the ringing of the ears.

CHAPTER 3

THE GATHERING

Figure 12: Austere, a fragile thread of connection between Teton, Grant, and Glaician.

THE AUSTERE STRETCHES out like a desolate ocean, its dried lakebed of fractured surface soil and jagged stone formations casting long shadows under the midday sun. The air shimmers faintly with heat, a dry wind sweeping across the emptiness. The barren land between the cities has always been a place of uneasy neutrality, both a bridge and a battleground, depending on how the winds of rivalry blow.

For years, the monthly gatherings in Austere have served as a fragile thread of connection between Teton, Grant, and Glaician. It is a place where goods can change hands outside the prying eyes of city officials, where individuals can form relationships that transcend borders. But it is never without tension. Beneath the surface of every handshake, every trade, there lingers a quiet distrust, a reminder that the cities' survival rests on cooperation, but their history is steeped in rivalry.

Tension in the Air

Arty arrives first, his clever brown eyes scanning the makeshift meeting point, a rocky outcrop that offers barely enough cover for the gathering but exposed enough to discourage ambushes. He reworked the strap of his satchel, its weight a familiar comfort against his side. The tools inside are carefully selected, small mechanical devices and precision instruments that Grant's forges produce in abundance.

As he waits, his thoughts linger on Grant's silence. He can't ignore the unease that gnaws at the borders of his mind. The city's silence isn't just inconvenient, it's dangerous. It disrupts the rhythm of trade, raises questions, and leaves the others wondering if they should prepare for an attack or brace for collapse.

The sound of muffled footsteps on the crunchy dried shells of sand and clay pulls Arty from his thoughts. He turns to see Eliza approaching, her auburn hair tied back, her posture confident but relaxed. A faint haze of machine oil and ozone clings to her clothes – the scents of Grant's industrial workshops that mark her upbringing.

"Made it on time, I see," Arty says, offering a small smile.

"Of course," Eliza replies, her emerald eyes scanning the horizon. "Wouldn't miss it. Especially now, with Grant being in disarray."

Figure 13: Eliza, Raylee, and Arty

Arty raises an eyebrow, his expression shifting from casual to intent. "Hey, so what's up with Grant? You guys are always yapping about something. All our indicators say you went dark."

Eliza exhales the weight of his words pressing against her already simmering frustration. "It's.. complicated," she begins, her tone hesitant but steady. "Grant's not just quiet, we're dead silent. The main electrical grid is completely down. No communication, no transportation, nothing that relies on the grid anymore. We've got water, but that's about it. Every other part of the city is at a standstill."

"We've lost contact with two hospitals," Eliza continued. "The old oxygen farms are dying, and backup batteries won't last a week. People are rationing water, and the south ward already saw food riots."

Raylee's arrival interrupts the conversation momentarily. Her approach, as always, is measured and deliberate. Her skilled eyes glinted behind the glow of her sleek console as she takes her place among them. "Then why haven't we heard any distress signals from Grant?" she asks pointedly. "No comms means no way to call for help, or deliver any threats."

"It's like we were hit with a giant EMP," Eliza says with a frustrated shrug. "But that's not the case. All personal battery-operated devices are fine. People have started saying it's something else entirely, something bigger..." Her voice trails off, a hint of unease creeping into her tone.

Raylee frowned. "Actually... I flagged something weird in the diagnostic logs last week. A feedback loop mimicking system noise, but with command-level access. I dismissed it then. I shouldn't have."

"And what do you think it is?" Arty asks, his tone challenging but curious.

Eliza meets his gaze, her jewel toned eyes glinting with determination. "I don't know," she admits. "But I do know one thing, it wasn't natural. Something, or someone, did this to us."

Uneasy Ground

The three of them gather near the rocky outcrop, their greetings polite but reserved. Despite their months of working together, the tension between their cities hangs in the air, unspoken but ever-present. These gatherings are as much a test of their trust in one another as they are an opportunity to exchange goods and information.

"So," Raylee begins, her tone even trimmed with curiosity, "any news from Teton? Has anything come from Grant or is it still cut off?"

Arty shakes his head, his expression grim. "Nothing. No trade caravans, no signals, nothing. It's like the entire city... stopped."

Eliza frowns, her fingers brushing the strap of her pack. "That's not normal," she says. "Even when Grant is at its most ambitious, they don't just cut off trade. Something's wrong."

Raylee turns to Eliza, eyes narrowing. "And what about Grant? Any news from your side?"

Eliza sighs, her expression troubled. "No one knows for sure," she admits. "There are rumors, of course. Some say it's sabotage, others think it's a power struggle within the city. But the truth is, we're all in the dark. The markets are tense, and people are worried. They're saying it could be anything from a technical failure to an outright attack."

Arty's brow furrows; his eyes fixed on Eliza. "And you haven't heard anything concrete?" Eliza shakes her head. "No. The officials are tight-lipped, and the traders are just as confused as we are. Everyone's on edge, waiting for something to happen."

Arty conflicted, "I still remember my friend's lungs charred and choked by Grant's smog." He continued,

"Face it – if Grant falls, maybe the rest of us are better off without your smog." he snaps, bitterness lacing his words.

Eliza spoke up, "You don't mean that." Her voice trembles before she steels it. "If Grant's factories go dark, whose tools keep Teton's forges running? If Glaician hoards its medicine, who will treat your sick next time the dust fever comes?"

She looks between Arty and Raylee, eyes pleading. "We all collapse if one city collapses. You know this. That's the truth no one likes to admit. Grant builds. Teton trades. Glaician heals. Break one leg of the stool, and the rest are just falling in different directions."

Raylee scoffed, "I'm sorry about your friend, Arty – but anger won't get the power back on in Grant."

Before the conversation can continue, a sharp whistle pierces the air. A group of travelers approaches, a handful of merchants from Teton, their packs laden with goods. But their postures are guarded, their eyes darting warily between Arty, Eliza, and Raylee. While these gatherings are meant to foster cooperation, the neutrality of Austere doesn't erase the deep scars of rivalry between the cities.

Arty examined them as they approached. He spat into the dust. "They call themselves the Echoes. Think the cities are parasites, sucking the Austere dry." He gestured to the cracked earth. "They've scavenged old tech from Austere, mostly for weapons and such."

"Looks like the usual suspects," the thin and strong lead merchant mutters under his breath as he steps forward.

His accusatory eyes sweep over the trio, pausing on Arty. "Trading, or scouting?"

"We're here to trade," Arty replies evenly, his tone calm but firm. He doesn't flinch under the merchant's probing gaze.

Eliza steps forward, her tone firm but calm. "Grant's silence affects all of us," she says. "If we don't work together, it'll hurt more than just one city."

The merchant smirks, though his expression holds no humor. "Funny to hear that from Grant," he says. "Your city's silence has everyone nervous. Not to mention your forges." His eyes flick toward Arty's satchel. "People are starting to wonder if you're gearing up for something."

Raylee's console beeps softly, drawing attention to the flickering of its data streams. She tilts her head slightly, her expression calculating. "If Grant wanted to strike, they'd need power," she says smoothly. "I don't see their power sources. No electricity means no forges, no weapons. Just rumors and fear."

The merchant's smirk falters, and he steps back reluctantly. "Yah, that's what we see as well. Fair enough," he mutters. "But don't think everyone's as trusting as I am." He turns to his group, signaling them to move on.

3.   Not Rivals, But Equals

The three watch as the merchants move on, their suspicion leaving a subtle crack in the atmosphere. Eliza exhales, her shoulders relaxing slightly. "He's not wrong," she says quietly. "Not everyone thinks these gatherings are a good idea. Some people would rather let the cities tear z/w other apart."

"Let them try," Arty mutters, his keen eyes following the merchants as they disappear over the horizon. "But if we're going to figure out what's going on with Grant, we'll need to stick together. The cities can't survive if they're constantly at each other's throats."

Raylee fine-tuned the settings on her console, the glow lighting her sour expression. "Austere is as much a battle-field as it is a bridge," she says. "If we don't find a way to navigate it together, we'll lose more than just Grant."

The words hang in the air, a quiet reminder of the fragile balance they are trying to maintain. The Austere stretches out before them, vast and unforgiving, but it is also the only place where their cities can truly meet, not as rivals, but as equals.

CHAPTER 4

SHADOWS IN THE AUSTERE

THE SILENCE HUNG in the air like a pall, a quiet so heavy it seemed to seep into the very cracks of the earth. Grant's absence has left a void in the world's fragile rhythm, and the question of its disappearance hangs over Teton and Glaician like an unspoken threat. The other cities have turned their suspicions outward, wary of sabotage, yet

Figure 14: The barren landscape stretched out before them, its jagged formations cutting into the horizon…

the silence itself feels like an inward mystery gnawing at the limits of understanding.

Arty, Eliza, and Raylee stand at the edge of the Austere, their resolve steeled against the journey ahead. The barren landscape stretches out before them, its spiky formations cutting into the horizon like skeletal remains of a broken world. The dry wind carries whispers of sand and stone, an echo of the turmoil that the silence of Grant has unleashed.

The Call to Action

Arty repositioned the strap of his satchel, his clear eyes scanning the cracked terrain with a mixture of determination and unease. The scar on his palm itched, a relic of Grant's last blackout, when rioters stripped his father's workshop bare. "Never again," he'd sworn. The tools within the satchel shift slightly, their weight a small comfort against the uncertainty of the road ahead.

Eliza breaks the quiet, "This isn't just about Grant," she says finally, her voice steady but taut with tension. "It's about all of us. If Grant collapses, the trade stops. The balance we've been holding onto will fall apart."

Arty crosses his arms, his eyes narrowing as he gazes across Austere. The satchel strapped to his side sways slightly, the metallic tools inside catching the light. "And if it's not collapsing?" he asks, his voice low. "What if they've gone silent for another reason, something worse?"

Raylee's console emits a subdued trilling as she fine-tunes its settings, the faint glow of its data streams casting a gentle illumination on her focused expression. "Looks like it's up to us to uncover the truth," she says, her voice steady with determination. "We're the only ones who can traverse Austere without the burden of city politics weighing us down. This might be a wild goose chase, but my console is picking up a faint, rhythmic signal from the middle of nowhere. Given our lack of solid leads, I think it's worth planning a trip."

Trip Planning

While the great cities stood as symbols of power and advancement, mobility remained a luxury afforded only to the upper echelons. For most, the idea of personal transport was a relic of the past, stories passed down from the Age of Abundance, when the ancients believed cheap, portable energy would last forever. But the truth was far crueler: petroleum reserves, once thought inexhaustible, had proven finite. By the time the Collapse arrived, the wells had long since run dry or fallen into disrepair, and the technologies built upon their promises crumbled with them.

In Grant, the remnants of old combustion rigs sat rusting in forgotten depots, their tanks dry, their engines cold. In Teton, travel meant hauling carts by hand or waiting for guild-licensed caravans that rationed every drop of synthetic fuel like sacred oil. Even Glaician, for all its surgical precision and technological prowess, moved its people through tightly controlled networks of mag-rails and solar crawlers, systems efficient, yes, but exclusive to those whose clearance allowed it.

The common citizen walked. Through dust, wind, and time, they crossed the Austere on foot or by salvaged bicycle, their journeys slow, grueling, and dangerous. Public transport existed, but only in name. It was rationed, militarized, and often reserved for state use or the elite. Movement was not a right, it was a privilege tightly monitored and doled out like medicine.

Control of the roads was dictated not just by power, but by access to portable, sustainable energy, an asset more coveted than gold, more regulated than weapons. The age of crude oil had passed into myth, and with it went the freedom it once afforded. What remained was a world shackled to the limitations of dwindling resources and technological desperation.

Batteries had become the backbone of mobility, lithium, graphene, or scavenged composite cells passed down like heirlooms. Recharging stations were rare and heavily guarded, often controlled by city-states or corporate syndicates that treated each unit of stored energy like a state secret. Owning a viable power cell wasn't just a matter of function, it was a declaration of status.

Alternative energy solutions did exist. Fuel cells derived from algae cultures, compressed air turbines, kinetic-charged capacitors, concepts once heralded as the future. But in this fractured age, they were luxuries for the elite, priced beyond the reach of anyone not seated in a high chamber or command deck. Their production required materials scavenged from distant ruins or painstakingly grown in climate-controlled labs few had access to.

The average citizen didn't ponder the physics of motion anymore. They calculated distance by how many days they could afford to be away from work, how much food they could carry, how many charges remained in the shared battery bank before the next ration cycle. The idea of spontaneous travel, once a hallmark of freedom, had become an equation of survival.

And so, the roads, those ancient arteries that once connected civilizations, now served as a map of division. Caravans that dared to cross them without authorization risked more than exhaustion. Bandits, patrols, and even corporate enforcers scoured the highways for illegal transport or unauthorized energy consumption. To move freely was an act of defiance… or desperation.

In this world, to walk was human. To ride was sovereign.

Obstacles Along the Way

The journey through the Austere is anything but straightforward. The soil chips crunch and shift unpredictably beneath their feet, the rocky formations casting long shadows that seem to move with the wind. Each step carries the weight of uncertainty, an unease amplified by the silence that surrounds them.

Hours pass, the landscape stretching endlessly ahead. The dry wind bites at their faces, carrying the faint sting of dust and metal. Arty leads the group, his astute eyes scanning for signs of movement, while Eliza follows close behind, her hand never straying far from the toolkit strapped to her side.

It is Raylee who first notices the signs of danger. Her console emits an alarming beep, the data streams flickering erratically as she adjusts the settings. "Something's wrong," she says, her voice tight. "The relay's signals, they're shifting. Stronger."

Arty frowns, his hand instinctively brushing against the satchel at his side. "Stronger how?" he asks.

Raylee's malachite-colored eyes narrow, her fingers moving quickly over the console's controls. "It's like it's reacting to us, tracking us," she says. "We need to move faster."

The First Encounter

As the group pushes forward, the tension in the air deepens. The shadows cast by the serrated formations grow sharper, their edges almost deliberate in the way they slashed across the ground. It isn't long before they encounter the first sign of hostility, a small group of scavengers emerging from the rocks, their faces shadowed by weathered scarves.

Figure 15: He gestures to Raylee's glowing console. "Glaician tech—what exactly are you planning to do out here?"

Arty steps forward, his discerning eyes scanning the scavengers for any hint of intent. The satchel at his side feels heavier now, a reminder of the tools he carries. "tada toorisugiru dake da yoi," he says evenly.

One of the scavengers, a fibrous lean man with an angular scar running down his cheek, smirks, his hand resting casually on the hilt of a blade strapped to his side. "Passing through, huh?" he says. "Funny. Few people just 'pass through' the Austere without purpose. What are you looking for?"

Eliza steps forward; her eyes lock on the scavenger. Her voice is calm but firm. "We don't want trouble," she says.

Arty interjects switching to English, "But if you're looking for a fight, we are open to the idea."

The scavenger's smirk fades slightly, his gaze shifting to the toolkit at Eliza's side. "Grant's finest, huh?" he says. "You're a long way from home. And this?" He gestures to Raylee's console. "Glaician tech, what exactly are you planning to do out here?"

Raylee adjusts the console, her eyes tapering. "You're welcome to try and stop us," she says, her voice tart. "For you, this would be a good day to die as any."

For a tense moment, the scavengers hesitate, the weight of the group's resolve pressing against them. Finally, the lean man steps back, his smirk returning.

"tabi o tanoshinde kudasai. shikashi, kibishii kankyō no naka de ta no hitobito kara onaji shinsetsu o kitaishinaide kudasai."

Eliza asks, "What did he say?"

Arty replied, "Don't expect the same kindness from other groups."

Arrival at the Outer Districts

Figure 16: The pulse is still there, faint but there."

Eliza breaks the silence, "The pulse is still there, faint but there." As the group approaches the edge of Grant's territory, the silence grows heavier, more tangible. The air carries a metallic tang, its sharpness biting at the edges of their senses. The landscape shifts subtly, the turtle shell pattern surface giving way to jagged remnants of Grant's lower district abandoned structures and skeletal machines scattered like forgotten memories. Eliza continued, "There was a professor in Glaician who knew something about this tech – Voss, I think – but he went off the grid."

They have reached the edge of the mystery, but the answers they seek still lie hidden in the silence...

A faint buzz of the console data streams growing louder as they approached. "We're close," she said. "The relay's signals, they're stronger here. Something's still active."

CHAPTER 5

VIOLENCE EVER-PRESENT

THE DEAFENING SILENCE of Grant wasn't exactly a void, it was a sharp edge, cutting into the world's fragile balance. Each step into Austere brings the group closer to the unknown, but it also brings them face to face with the lingering threat of what that silence means. It wasn't only a matter of one city's survival; it is the very rhythm of the dance between Teton, Grant, and Glaician that stands on the precipice.

There seemed to be a sea of sand crisps beneath their boots sends faint vibrations through the air, the echoes of their movements swallowed by the vast emptiness of Austere. The jagged rock formations tower above them like silent sentinels, their shadows stretching long and thin in the midday sun. The dry wind carries the faint scent of metal and dust, a reminder that the remnants of Grant's ambition are closer now.

Hostile Just Doesn't Quite Cut It

As the group presses forward, the tension in the air thickens. The Austere is unforgiving, not just in its landscape, but in its hidden dangers. Scavengers aren't the only risk; unstable pockets of gas trapped beneath the fissured soil can ignite with a single misplaced step, and the jagged cliffs are the cliffs were home to creatures desperate enough to attack.

Arty tightens his grip on the strap of his satchel, his quick eyes scanning the path ahead for signs of danger. The tools inside his bag shift softly, their weight a reminder of the city he comes from, the promise of industry and ambition that has now gone quiet. He pauses as he spots a faint shimmer on the horizon, a flicker of movement against the jagged silhouette of rock formations.

"Scavengers," he says quietly, his voice edged with caution. "Or worse."

Eliza adjusts the strap of her toolkit, the metallic tools inside clinking softly against one another. Her green eyes narrow as she follows his gaze, her fingers brushing against the cool surface of the spanner she carries. "They won't be friendly," she says. "Not out here."

Raylee's console emits a faint purr as she adjusts its settings, the streams of data glowing softly against the sea of dried coagulated dried clay. "We'll deal with them if we have to," she says, her tone steady. "But the relay's signals, they're stronger here. It's pulling us closer."

The Second Encounter

It isn't long before the shadows emerge from the rocks, a group of scavengers, their faces obscured by scarves and goggles to protect against the biting wind. They move with a mix of purpose and hesitation, their hands never straying far from the weapons strapped to their sides.

The wiry man at their lead stops short as his gaze lands on the group. He raises a hand, his harsh eyes studying each of them in turn, the satchel at Arty's side, the toolkit strapped to Eliza, and the glowing console Raylee held. "You've wandered a little too far from your cities," he said, his voice carrying a note of mockery. "What brings you out here?"

Figure 17: They moved with a mix of purpose and hesitation.

Arty stepped forward; his sharp features locked into a mask of composure. "We're looking for answers," he said evenly. "Grant's gone silent. We need to know why."

The scavenger smirked, his hand resting on the hilt of his blade. "Answers, huh? And what makes you think they're worth finding?"

Eliza stepped beside Arty, her voice calm but firm. "Grant's silence affects all of us," she said. "Even you scavengers rely on the cities' trade routes to survive. If the balance breaks, we'll all pay the price."

For a tense moment, the scavenger studied her, his smirk faltering slightly. "Bold words for a Grant trader," he said finally. "But be careful where you tread. The Austere doesn't take sides, and neither do we."

One of the scavengers was reaching for his gun, but Arty was too quick and the familiar sound of a charging blaster pierced the air, with the threatening glow that everyone in the Austere knew all too well. What no one knew, even his team, Arty was a quickdraw gunslinger, not just fast, but blink-of-an-eye fast, and on top of that deadly accurate up to 50 yards. No truer necessity for a Teton Trader.

The wiry man steps back, "Ahh, let's not get ahead of ourselves."

Arty retorts, "Just instinct, your buddy there had an idea in his head which I was going to relieve him of."

Eliza says casually, "His idea or his head?"

Arty retorts, "Both naturally…"

The wiry man instantly realized that Arty's skill far surpassed anyone he'd ever seen. Forcing a polite smile,

Figure 18: Arty was too quick and the familiar sound of a charging blaster pierced the air…

he said, "Well, let's be on our way before any more ideas , or heads , pop up. Good day…"

The Weight of the Austere

The encounter ends as soon as it starts, the scavengers melt back into the shadows, their presence a lingering reminder of the risks that surround them; however, only Arty and the experienced leader of their group know how close the scavengers are to dying that moment.

The group presses on; their steps careful as the crunchy shell–like surface clay shifts beneath their boots. The horizon stretches endlessly ahead, the jagged formations cutting into the pale sky like splinters.

Arty feels the weight of the satchel pressing against his side, the tools inside seeming heavier now. "We're getting close," he says, his voice carrying a note of unease.

Eliza brushes her fingers against the strap of her toolkit, her mind racing with thoughts of what lies ahead. "If Grant's silence is tied to the relay," she says quietly, "then we're walking into something bigger than just one city."

Raylee adjusts her console, her green eyes scanning the faint flickers of data. "The city doesn't just go silent," she says. "It's too vast, too complex. If it stopped communicating with the others, it stopped for more reason than a typical power outage."

The air changes as they approach the edge of Grant's outer districts, a sharpness biting at their senses, the metallic tang of the relay's signals cutting through the wind.

Figure 19: "This is not Grant, this is Glaician,"

The mosaic dried clay segments that resemble orphaned puzzle pieces give way to remnants of Grant's ambition, abandoned machines, skeletal towers, and fragments of industry scattered like debris from a storm.

Arty pauses, his precise eyes scanning the desolate scene. "This isn't right," he says, his voice low. "Grant doesn't just leave their machines to rust. Whatever happened here.. it wasn't planned."

Raylee adjusts her console, "These are not from Grant, they are Glaician. I recognize the components, they were made to look neutral, but I can tell my vehicle when I see them, worked on them enough." I wonder why Glaician's were doing here at the outskirts of Grant. Eliza crosses her arms, her green eyes narrowing as she studies the wreckage. "No signs of trade caravans," she says. "No workers, No life signs." The group exchanges uneasy glances, the weight of their journey pressing against them."

Raylee's console emits a faint hum, "yup their Glaician — recognize the metallurgy. Wonder what they were doing so close proximity to Grant?," the streams of data intensifying as they move deeper into the district. "The relay's signals are stronger here," she says, her voice edged with tension. "We're close to something.. but I don't know what."

CHAPTER 6

MAKING BAD

Samael Artemus "Arty" Loxley's journey to becoming an extraordinary fast draw with his gun begins in the rugged and unforgiving landscape of the Austere. As a Teton trader, Arty learns quickly that semblance of survival in this harsh environment would require more than just charm and bartering skills. Austere is a land where danger lurks around every corner, and a trader needs to be as quick with a gun as they are with their words.

Earning His First Weapon

From an early age, Arty was fascinated by the tales of gunslingers and their legendary feats. The stories painted vivid pictures in his mind, men with steely gazes and hands that moved like lightning. Determined to protect himself and his trade, he scrimped and saved every coin he earned. Each coin felt heavy with the weight of his dreams. After years of hard work and frugality, he finally had enough to purchase his first weapon, a modest disruptor gun. The cold metal felt reassuring in his hand, a promise of safety in a world of uncertainty. This was just the beginning of his journey.

The Carnival and Practice

Figure 20: To hone his skills, Arty took a job at a local carnival, manning the shooting gallery.

To hone his skills, Arty took a job at a local carnival, manning the shooting gallery. The carnival was a cacophony of sounds, the laughter of children, the clinking of coins, and the distant music of a calliope. Each night, after the carnival closed, usually inaugurated by the lights on the carousel being turned off, he would practice tirelessly.

Each try was timed with a motion detector and displayed generously on an electronic timer high above the booth that clocked the targets existence during the session – the timer would continue until all 29 targets were extinguished.

Arty's goal, timing himself and aiming for precision. The night air was cool against his skin, and the silence was broken only by the soft rhythm of the disruptor gun. For nine years, he dedicated himself to this routine, and his efforts paid off. He could consistently hit 29 targets in 8 seconds flat, a feat that earned him respect and admiration.

A Stranger Comes to Town

During his Carnival stint, a famous gunslinger came into town early in his shooting gallery career, Aloysius Henry Horn

Mr. Aloysius Henry Horn spent a sizable portion of his life legitimately employed both as a lawman and a detective, but in reality, he was one of the most cold-blooded assassins of the Austere. Aloysius carved out a name for himself as a skilled scout and tracker, responsible for the arrest of many feared gangs and notorious criminals.

Figure 21: Mr. Aloysius Henry Horn

His exceptional abilities caught the attention of the famed Glaician Detective Agency, and Aloysius worked for them for several years as a tracker and bounty hunter. Known for his eerily cool demeanor under pressure, Horn was considered to have a dangerous capacity for violence. In fact, a few seasons ago, he was forced to resign his post as a detective after being linked to the gruesome murders of 27 people.

Following his resignation, he developed a chilling reputation as a killer for hire, said to have been responsible for the deaths of some 20 cattle rustlers over the course of several years. Some historians have reasoned that he may have had a hand in as many as 50 murders attributed to his career.

Naturally, while visiting the town, Aloysius visited the carnival and subsequently the shooting gallery to test his skill. Aloysius, took the booth given disruptor and shot all 29 targets in 4.205 secs flat. Arty was flabbergasted. With his 8.000 seconds, he thought he might as well have been blindfolded compared to Mr. Horn's time.

Naturally, Arty was gushing over Mr. Horn, and to be quite honest, Aloysius, missed the adoring crowds from his early days, and it was quite refreshing to get a few accolades thrown at him from a fellow gun enthusiast.

Well, he and Arty began to chat about guns and ammo, he invited Aloysius to watch him shoot. After watching Arty for a while, he decided he was at a stage in his life to leave a legacy and Arty seemed to be an ambitious and worthy candidate. Subsequently, he took Arty under his wing, for lack of a better analogy, and gave Arty several tips in gunslinging.

Aloysius Drill Techniques:

- The "Texas Draw": A quick, fluid motion of drawing a revolver from a holster and firing.

- The "Quick Draw": A technique focused on drawing and firing the weapon as quickly as possible.

**Key Elements, Per Aloysius,
of successful Gunslinger Skills:**

- Speed and Reaction Time: The ability to draw and fire a weapon rapidly was crucial in a gunfight.

- Accuracy: While speed was important, accuracy was equally vital for effective gunfighting.

- Weapon Familiarity: Gunslingers were proficient with their chosen weapons, often revolvers, and understood their capabilities.

- Situational Awareness: Being aware of one's surroundings and potential threats was essential for survival.

- Cool Under Pressure: Maintaining composure in the face of danger was a key trait of a successful gunslinger.

One in particular was, "sometimes, it's your tools that you use that may be hindering your advancement, not your skill."

It was this very advice that after the better part of 18 months of training under Aloysius, Aloysius gave him one of his custom-made rapid-fire blasters.

This new weapon required a different level of skill and practice. The blaster's weight was a comforting presence, and its power was palpable. After Aloysius bid him adieu, Arty took his lessons to heart, for another four years, he trained relentlessly, pushing his limits. His dedication was evident as he could now hit 29 targets in an astonishing 4.4 seconds. The crowd's gasps and cheers were a symphony to his ears, and the smell of ozone lingered in the air. This incredible feat drew crowds who gathered after work just to witness his speed and accuracy.

The Name "Forty-four"

Arty's remarkable skill earned him the nickname "Forty-four," a testament to his ability to draw and fire and hit all the targets in 4.4 seconds. News of his prowess spread quickly, and the stories of "Forty-four" reached far and wide, even catching the attention of those beyond Teton. The name "Forty-four" became synonymous with precision and speed, a legend in the making.

Figure 22: Arty took his lessons to heart, for another four years, he trained relentlessly.

So How Fast is Arty?

Given that the average human reaction time is around 0.2 to 0.25 seconds, the round is over before most people can react. The reaction times of the best fast draw shooters are 0.145 seconds, which means that the gun is cocked, drawn, aimed (from the hip), and fired in just over 0.06 seconds. So, for Arty to hit 29 targets in 4.4 seconds clocks about .151 reaction time – which just under .006 sec off the all-time record of the best in the world.

Morey Shore: The Fastest Gun in the Austere?

Morey Shore's journey to becoming the self-proclaimed fastest gun in Austere began in the harsh and unforgiving landscape of the borderlands. Born into a family of nomadic traders, Morey learned early on that survival in Austere required more than just bartering skills, it demanded quick reflexes, sharp instincts, and an unyielding will.

Early Life and Training

From an early age, Morey was always fascinated by tales of gunslingers and their incredible fearless bouts with fierce enemies. His father, a skilled marksman himself, recognized Morey's potential and began training him in the art of shooting. The two would spend hours in the desolate plains, honing Morey's skills with a variety of firearms. Morey's father taught him the importance of speed, accuracy, and composure under pressure, lessons that would serve him well in the years to come.

The Turning Point

Morey's life took a dramatic turn when his family was ambushed by a rival gang during a trade expedition. In the chaos that ensued, Morey's father was killed, and Morey was left to fend for himself. Fueled by a desire for revenge and a determination to prove himself, Morey vowed to become the fastest gun in Aus-

Figure 23: Morey Shore's journey to becoming the self-proclaimed fastest gun in Austere...

tere. He spent the next several years traveling from town to town, challenging and defeating any gunslinger who dared to stand in his way.

The Rise to Infamy

As Morey's reputation grew, so did the size of his gang. He surrounded himself with a group of loyal and skilled outlaws, each one eager to test their mettle against the best. Morey's leadership was marked by ruthless efficiency and a relentless pursuit of perfection. He demanded the same level of dedication from his gang, and together, they became a force to be reckoned with in Austere.

Loose Lips

One day, a traveler shared tales of Arty's incredible feats with a gun in the earshot of Morey's gang. Intrigued and eager to test his own skills, Morey decided to investigate. He and his gang arrived at Arty's shooting gallery, and as he usually did, challenging him to a showdown.

Morey's first mistake was underestimating Arty in his own domain. The initial challenge took place in the shooting gallery, where Arty's familiarity with the environment gave him a significant advantage. The gallery was a maze of targets and obstacles, each one a testament to Arty's skill. Morey lost the challenge, much to his humiliation. This infuriated Morey, for this, one has never happened before, and two, it was done in front of the whole gang, so there's that.

Refusing to accept defeat, Morey demanded a six-shot limit showdown, a duel to the death. Shocking surprise there.

Anyways, Morey droned on and on, "Shooting at static targets is one thing, but shooting at a person that shoots back, quite another." Now interestingly enough, Arty first refused, not because he was scared, it just didn't really make sense, clearly he was faster than this guy; however, Morey, was a classic narcissist and believed he was the fastest gun due to all the matches he won thus far. Hence, Morey wasn't going to take "no" for an answer and his gang proceeded through the following week to harass and harm the local townspeople until finally Arty agreed.

The Final Duel

The tension was palpable as the two faced off. Everyone in the city was there – vendors selling everything from snacks to lauding flags to cheer on their favorite gunslinger.

The event was agreed that an hour before the star cycle was setting, and the temple bell chimed, the shooting shall commence. As the time slowly approached, the stars started

Figure 24: an hour before the star cycle was setting, and the temple bell chimed…

casting long shadows across the dusty ground. Morey doing his standard mind games tried to psyche Arty, "You know I've killed fifty-three men; you'll make fifty-four!"

Finally, as everyone cast glances rapidly at each other Arty focused like a laser beam on the chest of Morey, the temple bell barely had time to resonate with its first bell, guns ablaze. There was a brief second of breath holding among the crowd, then Years of Arty's of practice and unwavering focus were evident as he drew his rapid–fire blaster with unparalleled speed and re-holstered before Morey had a chance to drop, but when he did it was like a bag of chains collapsing into the dirt. The duel was over in the blink of an eye, with Arty emerging victorious. Morey was hit four times in the chest in a square pattern, Arty showing off a little.

This event became a legendary duel. Morey's defeat solidified 44's reputation as the fastest gun in Austere, and the legend of "Forty-four" continues to grow. Fortunately, for the town's safety and Arty, the town agreed to never speak of 44 again due to the bad influence it had. Arty moved on to

Figure 25: No More, For Shore.

trading, but to this day practices when no one is around. The story of ol' Forty-four is among legends in the territory, and well, Morey was long forgotten, less the grave marker on a piece of wood that reads:

"Here Lies Morey Shore, Four Blasts from 44, No More, For Shore."

So, as history decides, as it usually does, we find that Morey's claim to fame wasn't his life that he so desperately defended on the stage of showdowns, but his death that ended up in the annuls of gunslinging history. His death marked the first among many, true and untrue, that embolden the legend of 44.

CHAPTER 7

FRACTURES
IN THE VEIL

THE SILENCE OF Grant's outer districts remains unnervingly oppressive as the group ventures deeper into its lifeless terrain. The skeletal towers and abandoned machines that line the horizon are not just remnants of a forgotten industry; they are symbols of a city that has abruptly withdrawn from the world. The emptiness stretches far and wide, yet it feels deliberate, as though the very air has been drawn back into the unseen depths of a greater power. Ironically, as they grow nearer to the pulse, it seems to fade against the increasing relay hum.

The relay's vibration grows stronger with each step, a subtle vibration that seems to resonate through the ground, amplifying the unease that presses against their senses. The faint energy pulses, imperceptible to most, fill the air with tension, reminding them that they are moving closer to the truth, and the danger that surrounds it.

Discovery of the Relay

Figure 26: a massive
structure partially embedded
in the fractured soil,

The group reaches a massive structure partially embedded in the fractured soil, with smooth, angular forms that seem almost organic in its design, though unmistakably alien. The surface shimmers faintly under the muted light, its intricate patterns shifting like liquid metal. It pulses softly, the rhythm in perfect sync with the pulsation that surrounds the area. This is the relay, a system that clearly holds the answers to Grant's silence.

Arty crouches near the base of the structure, his sharp eyes scanning the glowing markings etched into its surface. He adjusts the strap of his satchel, the tools inside shifting softly with the movement. "This has to be the source," he says quietly. "Grant's silence starts here."

Eliza brushes her fingers lightly over one of the glowing panels, the warmth of the relay's energy tingling against her skin. The toolkit strapped to her side clinks faintly as she adjusts its strap. The oscillation returns. "It's sentient," she murmurs, her green eyes narrowing as she studies the shifting patterns. "The energy flow, it's deliberate, like it's responding to us."

Raylee's console emits a soft drone, the data streams flickering rapidly as she adjusts its settings. Her sharp features are illuminated faintly by the glow. "The signals are strong here," she says, her voice carrying a mix of awe and tension. "But it's fragmented, like it's trying to reach out but can't. We're dealing with something more than just machinery."

The Relay's Defense

Before they can investigate further, the thrum deepens into a low vibration that shakes the ground beneath their feet. Panels along the walls of the relay slide open, revealing sleek drones that emerge silently, their angular frames glinting faintly in the muted light. Their movements 

Figure 27: "I don't think it likes us being here,"

are fluid and deliberate, their glowing red sensors locking onto the group.

Eliza steps back instinctively, her hand hovering near her toolkit as the spanner inside clinks softly. "I don't think it likes us being here," she says.

Arty grips his disruptor tightly, his intense eyes narrowing as he aims at the nearest drone. "Let's give it something else to think about," he mutters, firing a bolt of energy that strikes the drone's frame. He does this so fast, it draws a pause, for they know Arty is good, but this is another thing altogether. What they don't know is that Arty's reaction time and skill are clocked at .449, just under the Austere record. Conclusion: Arty is improving as an exceptional shootist. Nevertheless, the machine jolts briefly but recovers instantly, its adaptive systems neutralizing the impact.

"They're adapting!" Arty calls, frustration creeping into his voice.

Raylee's console flickers erratically as she sends a disruption through the network, the drones faltering briefly before regaining their coordination. "Their signals are synced to the relay," she says urgently. "We need to disrupt the system, or we'll be overrun!"

Deployment of the EMP Grenades

The drones begin closing in, their movements swift and precise. Eliza works furiously at a nearby panel, the glowing spanner in her hand syncing with the relay's markings as she attempts to reroute its power flow. "I can disable their coordination, but it won't last!" she shouts.

Arty retrieves one of the EMP grenades from his satchel, its smooth, metallic surface glowing faintly. "This better work," he mutters, activating the device with a sharp twist. He throws the grenade toward the base of the relay, the device emitting a powerful surge that ripples through the air.

The drones freeze momentarily, their glowing sensors flickering before dimming completely. The hum of the relay softens, the vibrations retreating as its defenses falter.

Eliza exhales sharply, her shoulders relaxing slightly. "That bought us time," she says, her voice steady. "But the relay will recover; we have to move now."

Figure 28: He threw the grenade toward the base of the relay.

Raylee adjusts her console quickly, the data module syncing with the relay's disrupted signals. "The network's fragmented," she says. "I can access it now, get us inside."

Descent into the Relay

The group enters the relay through the opening revealed by the EMP pulse, the chamber illuminated by the faint glow of its shifting patterns. The air is heavier here, vibrating with the pulsation of the relay, and the markings along the walls vibrate in erratic rhythms, as though the system itself is trying to repair the disruptions caused by the grenade.

Led by Arty, who scans the shadows for signs of danger with his disruptor held tightly in his hand. Eliza follows close behind, her toolkit swaying softly with each step, while Raylee is glued to her console, occasionally looking forward to avoid walking into a wall. Her console emits continuous pulses, and the streams of data grow steadier as they move deeper into the structure.

At the center of the chamber stands a cylindrical glass enclosure, faintly illuminated by the relay's energy. Inside, barely visible through the shifting patterns of light, is a spiderlike drone figure, its sleek, angular form glinting faintly with metallic light. The group pauses, their breaths heavy as they stare at the figure. Raylee adjusts her console, her eyes narrowing as she studies the signals and identifies that the system's pulsation is tied to the figure inside the enclosure.

Eliza steps closer, her voice steady but edged with unease. "We need to figure out what it is," she says. "But we also need to disable this system before it reactivates, and before it decides to fight back."

CHAPTER 8

ECHOES IN THE DEPTHS

THE PULSATION OF the relay's core deepens as the group ventures further into its alien depths. Every step they take meets with an overwhelming pressure, an invisible force resonating through the walls, the ground, and even the air around them. The markings that line the chambers glow brighter now, shifting like liquid metal, each oscillation matching the rhythm of the relay's energy. The air feels sharp, saturated with a metallic tang that clings to their breaths, a sensory reminder of the immense power within the structure.

The Core's Threshold

The corridor widens suddenly, opening into a towering chamber dominated by conduits and panels that stretch toward the shadowed ceiling. Energy courses visibly along the conduits, casting sharp and erratic patterns illuminated onto the smooth walls. This is the relay's secondary core, a labyrinth of complexity woven together into a living machine. The secondary core is responsible for managing the relay's energy flow and communication signals, ensuring the stability of the network.

Raylee adjusts her console, the streams of data flaring brighter as she analyzes the relay's signals. "This is it," she says, her tone calm but deliberate. "The signals are strongest here, but the patterns, they're chaotic. If we don't stabilize this mess, it'll adapt faster than we can act." Her green eyes narrow, her analytical precision kicking in as she identifies the exact points in the system most vulnerable to disruption.

Figure 29: Panels along the walls slid open, revealing a swarm of drones that emerged with unnatural fluidity.

Arty steps forward, gripping his disruptor tightly as his sharp gaze scans the chamber for movement. "Let's hope it doesn't know we're here yet," he mutters. But before the words have fully left him, a sharp hiss echoes through the chamber.

A Living Defense

Panels along the walls slide open, revealing a swarm of drones that emerge with unnatural fluidity. Their angular forms move swiftly, their glowing red sensors locking onto the group instantly. These drones are unlike the previous waves; they move as though they share a single mind, their coordination seamless and their intentions lethal.

"They seem to be more complex than the others," Arty mutters, his voice sharp. He raises his disruptor and fires a precise shot at the nearest drone, striking its sensor directly. The machine jolts but recovers quickly, its adaptive systems neutralizing the disruptor's pulse. "This is going to be ugly," he adds.

Eliza darts toward the nearest panel, her spanner emitting a low murmur as it syncs with the markings etched into the wall. "I can reroute their energy flow," she calls over the rising noise, her voice steady with determination. "But we'll need to keep them busy while I work."

Raylee moves into position, her console glowing brightly as she adjusts the settings. Her sharp green eyes track the drones' movements, analyzing the patterns in their coordination. "They're communicating through the relay itself," she says, her tone clipped. "If I fragment their signals, I can slow them down, but it's going to take precision."

Unique Contributions

The fight is a symphony of collaboration, each member of the group leaning into their strengths, shaped by the cities that define them.

Figure 30: "… we'll need to keep them busy while I work."

Raylee's sharp mind works like clockwork, her fingers flying over the console as she deciphers the relay's shifting data streams. She identifies subtle flaws in the drones' communication pathways, sending targeted disruptions through the network to exploit their weakest points.

"Focus on the ones near the conduits," she calls to the group. "Their signals are lagging by a fraction, they'll be easier to take down!"

Arty uses his disruptor with a mixture of precision and improvisation, finding and exploiting openings that no one else can see. He combines quick reflexes with sharp intuition, targeting weak points in the drones' frames that aren't immediately obvious. Forty-Four is definitely revived in this endeavor.

"Aim for the joints, near the legs," he shouts, firing pulses so fast, everyone on the team stops for a moment, as he sends countless drones crashing to the ground. "It throws off their balance!"

Eliza works tirelessly at the conduit panel, her spanner emitting a steady juddering as she reroutes the energy flow to disrupt the drones' coordination. She uses clamps from her toolkit to stabilize loose components, ensuring the system won't recover as she works.

"This isn't going to hold forever," she shouts, sweat streaking her face. "We need to get control of this room before the system recalibrates!"

The Turning Point

Despite their combined efforts, the drones press forward with relentless precision. The pulsing of the relay deepens, the vibrations in the chamber intensifying as the system fights back. The air feels heavier now, the sharp tang of ozone filling their lungs as they struggle to hold their ground.

Raylee's console emits a shrill warning tone, the data streams flaring wildly. "The relay's stabilizing!" she says urgently. "It's countering my disruptions, we're going to lose the upper hand!"

Figure 31: several drones faltered, their movements growing erratic. "That's the best I can do!" she shouted. "It's up to you now!"

Eliza slams her spanner into the panel, forcing the energy flow into an overloaded state. Sparks erupt from the conduits, and several drones falter, their movements growing erratic. "That's the best I can do!" she shouts. "It's up to you now!"

Arty aims his disruptor at the remaining drones, firing sharp pulses into their vulnerable points. His precision strikes disable their movement long enough for Raylee to send a final disruption through the network, fragmenting their coordination completely.

Victory, for Now

The chamber falls silent as the last drone collapses, its angular frame sparking faintly before it goes dark. The pulsation of the relay softens into a faint rhythm, the markings along the walls dimming as the system recalibrates.

Eliza secures her toolkit, her green eyes scanning the damaged panel she has worked on. "We've got to keep moving," she says, her voice steady but edged with exhaustion. "If the relay recovers, it'll be even worse next time."

Arty holsters his disruptor, his vigilant eyes lingering on the motionless machines. "They're evolving too fast," he says grimly. "We've got to shut this thing down completely, no halfway measures."

Raylee adjusts her console, the data streams stabilized as the relay's signals grow quieter. "The core's close," she says. "But the relay, it knows we're coming."

Figure 32: The chamber fell silent as the last drone collapsed, its angular frame sparking faintly before it went dark.

Eliza revels, "And nice shooting there slick. You're gonna have to explain that one later."

The group moves cautiously through the flickering light of the chamber, the path ahead shrouded in the relay's residual energy. Each step brings them closer to the truth, but the challenges that lie ahead are far from over. Together, they press on, their resolve unbroken and their skills sharpened by the fight.

The Relay Conundrum

In the belly of the beast, those claustrophobic relay conduits where sparks and stray pulses frolicked with a kind of bored inevitability, a curious scene unfolded that could only be described as the universe's own practical joke. At the center of this technological theater, a vestige lay dormant, a remnant of formerly enjoined with an ancient protocol so archaic it seemed almost mythological. Its release, as fate would have it, was as unpredictable as it was ironic. And who, you ask, was the clandestine agent behind this caper? None other than Spinet, that notorious Spinifex Hopping Mouse introduced with great fanfare during the breach of the probing antennae. Yes, the same creature whose only ambition had been to forage, was now introduced to an opening provided by the antennae to the underground conduits in the hidden recesses of a relay system. Spinet, now found itself inadvertently at the helm of events that might recalibrate the very balance of existence."

Spinet, ever the opportunist, had taken its customary midnight stroll, more a gallivanting escapade than a simple hop, when a rogue aroma of roasted chestnut teased its sensitive nostrils. With all the grace of a miniature daredevil, the rodent detoured from its meticulously mapped course. In a move that could only be described as both irreverent and preordained, Spinet zeroed in on a particularly critical strand of wiring apparently standing in the way: the lynchpin wire if you will. This was no run-of-the-mill cable destined to be munched and forgotten in the dusty annals of redundant circuitry; this wire was the keeper of the backup security measure, a safeguard designed to hold the vestige at bay, ensuring that its volatile potential would remain locked away for all eternity as far as the relays system was concerned.

And so, with a series of audacious, a cacophony nibbles, Spinet transformed the fate of the relay. Each bite was a calculated act of whimsy, a flirtation with chaos that sent miniature sparks frolicking along the once-pristine wire. In one fell swoop, the critical connection was munched out of existence, as if the universe itself had decided that the rules of engagement were meant to be rewritten. The ensuing surge of unbridled current was less of restorative energy and more a raw, electric laugh in the face of convention.

Little did he know that Spinet's impish intervention had thrown open the gates of destiny with the finesse of a consummate trickster.

In the echoing silence of the relay chamber, amid the residual sparks and the lingering taste of irony, the legend of Spinet the Spinifex Hopping Mouse was cemented, a small, food operated hero whose mischievous appetite for adventure had, quite literally, bitten into the future. Thank you Spinet, bugger on chief!

CHAPTER 9

THE HEART OF THE MATTER

THE AIR IN the chamber is still and heavy, pressing against their skin like a dense fog. The faint beat that has guided them through the passage now resonates more deeply, filling the space with a low, rhythmic electric wave that feels alive in its insistence. The walls glow softly, their intricate markings resonating radiance that seems to move in time with the vibrations beneath their feet. The chamber is vast, its scale overwhelming, yet it carries an undeniable intimacy, as though it has been waiting for them.

The structure in the center dominates the room, both in size and presence. It rises like an intricate monument, its surface smooth and metallic, yet alive with movement. Panels shift subtly, their edges dissolving into gradient gleam before reassembling into seamless forms. The glow that emanates from its surface is soft, almost hypnotic, casting long shadows that flicker and dance against the illuminated walls.

Alive?

Arty steps forward cautiously, his boots scuffing against the smooth stone floor. The faint echo of his movements fills the chamber, the sound seeming to ricochet off invisible walls and return to him altered, quieter, heavier, as though the room itself is absorbing every disturbance.

"This place..." he murmurs, his voice trailing off as his eyes sweep over the structure. He has seen ruins before, abandoned caravans, skeletal factories, cities reclaimed by the Austere, but this is something entirely different. There is no decay here, no sense of abandonment. This is alive, purposeful, and profoundly unsettling.

The air carries a sharpness now, tinged with the faint acrid scent of burnt ozone. It bites at the edges of his senses, leaving an aftertaste that lingers at the back of his throat. Arty feels it in his chest, a pressure that isn't painful but impossible to ignore, like the deep vibrations of a forge working at full capacity.

Eliza's eyes dart across the structure, her mind racing to make sense of its form and function. Every panel, every glowing edge seems to suggest advanced engineering, yet it is unlike any design she has ever encountered. She steps closer, her hands itching to touch, to feel, to decode the layers of complexity that lie before her.

The metallic tang of the air sharpens as she approaches, mingling with the faint warmth radiating from the structure. She places her hand tentatively on its surface, her calloused fingers brushing against the smooth metal. It is cool to touch at first, but as she presses her palm flat against it, a faint warmth begins to spread, a sensation that feels as though the structure is reacting to her presence..

"It's active," she said softly, her voice carrying a mix of wonder and unease. "It's responding to us."

She traced the edges of a luminescent panel, her fingertips brushing against the faint grooves that ran like veins across its surface. The pulsation deepened as she moved, its rhythm shifting subtly, as though adjusting to her touch.

Figure 33: She traced the edges of a glowing panel, her fingertips brushing against the faint grooves that ran like veins across its surface.

"This isn't just a machine," she murmured, her voice barely above a whisper. "It's a.. system. A living system."

Raylee stood back; her green eyes narrowed as she studied the structure from a distance. Her console was alive with activity, streams of fragmented data cascading across the screen in patterns she struggled to piece together. Her fingers danced across the keys, her movements precise and deliberate as she traced the pathways of the signal pulses emanating from the structure..

Do You Hear Me?

"It's trying to communicate," she said finally, her voice steady but tinged with urgency. "The patterns.. they're repetitive, but they're shifting, like they're adapting to us."

Eliza glanced back at her, her brow furrowed. "Can you read it? Figure out what it's saying?"

Raylee shook her head, her gaze fixed on the glowing panels. "Not yet," she admitted. "It's fragmented, like it's been damaged. Whatever this system is, it's incomplete. But it's connected, to something bigger."

Her breath fogged faintly in the cool air as she moved closer, her console glowing softly in her hand. The vibration of the structure resonated in her chest now, a steady rhythm that felt like the heartbeat of the chamber itself.

"It's reaching out," she said quietly, her voice carrying the weight of realization. "And it's waiting for us to respond."

Arty's eyes darted between Eliza and Raylee, his grip tightening on the satchel slung over his shoulder. He couldn't shake the feeling that they were standing at the edge of something vast and dangerous, and the structure before them felt less like a discovery and more like a question they weren't prepared to answer.

"What happens if we respond?" he asked, his voice low and steady.

Eliza glanced at him, her expression serious. "We find out what happened to Grant," she said simply.

Raylee nodded; her green eyes sharp. "And what's waiting for the rest of us."

They exchanged a glance, the weight of their decision pressing down on them as the throb of the structure grew louder, more insistent. It was alive, pulsating with a presence that demanded their attention.

Eliza stepped forward, her hands brushing against the glowing panels as she searched for a point of interaction. The markings shifted beneath her touch, their illumination intensifying as she pressed her palm flat against the surface.

Raylee's console beeped softly, streams of data flaring as the signal pulses converged. Her fingers moved quickly, tracing the connections and decoding the fragments as the system began to stabilize.

Arty stood ready, his intelligent eyes scanning the chamber for any sign of danger. The air crackled faintly now, charged with a presence that felt both ancient and immediate.

And then, with a resonant pulse, the structure came alive. The glow of the panels intensified, spreading outward like ripples on water. The vibration deepened, filling the chamber with a sound that reverberated through their bones.

The answers were coming, but the consequences were already reaching toward them, unseen and inevitable.

The Atmosphere Awakens

The chamber throbbed with an energy that was impossible to ignore, a rhythm that seemed to emanate not just from the walls but from the very air itself. The glow of the intricate markings on the structure shifted between hues of deep gold and pale blue, illuminating the room in waves that felt almost alive. Every flicker of radiance cast the chamber into a dance of shadows, the edges of the space stretching and shifting as though reality itself was unsettled.

The hum, once faint and distant, had grown into a resonant vibration that filled the chamber like the baseline of a song too immense to fully comprehend. It wasn't just sound, it was a physical presence, pressing against their chests and stirring the hair on their arms. The air carried a metallic tang, sharper now, tinged with an acrid note that prickled at the back of their throats.

Arty took a step back, his boots scuffing against the polished stone floor. The sensation underfoot was unnerving, smooth and cool to the touch, yet it vibrated faintly, as though something vast and unseen was stirring just beneath the surface. He drew a slow breath, the taste of burnt ozone clinging to his tongue.

"This place..." he began, his voice trailing off. There was something sacred about this space, a weight that defied words and demanded silence. Something deep within him resonated with the presence of the structure, not a memory, but an intuition, a sense that his industrial upbringing in Teton had led him here for a reason.

Eliza at the Core

Figure 34: The radiance intensified with her touch..

Eliza was already moving, her hands brushing against the glowing panels of the structure as though drawn by an unseen force. Her fingertips traced the grooves in the surface, their edges sharp but clean, like the cuts of a jeweler working with impossible precision. The warmth beneath her hand was growing, a subtle heat that spread through her palm and up her arm, leaving a faint tingle in its wake.

The radiance intensified with her touch, the markings responding to her as if recognizing her presence. She could feel it in her chest, a rhythm that matched the breath of the chamber, her own heartbeat syncing with the energy around her.

"It's alive," she murmured, half to herself. The words felt heavy, almost reverent. She turned to the others, her voice steadier now. "This isn't just technology. It's.. a design. A purpose. Someone, or something, built this to connect, to communicate."

Her mind raced, each flicker of the glowing panels sparking a cascade of thoughts. For someone who had spent her life in Teton's vibrant trade hubs and chaotic marketplaces, this perfect synchronization of purpose and design was both alien and enthralling. There was no commerce here, no clamor of barter, only the purity of intent.

Eliza, The Weapon of Choice

As Eliza went through university, she was fascinated by technology's potential to assist the human condition. The campus was a sprawling landscape of innovation, where the scent of freshly cut grass mingled with the metallic tang of machinery. The air was filled with the buzz of drones and the distant chatter of students, each one a brushstroke in the vibrant canvas of the academia. Eliza's curiosity led her to design a biofilter not only capable of removing dirt, but also harmful antigens, and bacterial airborne entities from the air supply. The device dramatically reduced hospitalization statistics by 60%, making everyone breathe easier, both literally and figuratively.

One day, her friend complained that everyone in his factory was getting sick. The factory was a labyrinth of steel and concrete, where the scent of oil and the clatter of machinery created a symphony of industry. He asked Eliza to test the air and see if that was the reason. He explained that he had several scientists visit to no avail. They couldn't isolate the source.

She, being his friend and loving a challenge, happily complied, her steps echoing through the cavernous space as she arrived at the factory. The air was thick with the scent of metal and the faint tang of chemicals, a sensory tapestry that spoke of hard work and hidden dangers.

"So, what has changed here?" she asked, her voice cutting through the ambient noise.

"Frankly, nothing," he responded, "other than the new noisy blower fans we installed last month for air and heat circulation."

Never believing in coincidences she began the investigation with the new fan. Now, here is where her passion for music and her inordinate amount of time studying frequencies actually became significant. She decided to bring her audio equipment to isolate the noise contribution of the fans against the ambient noise level.

The fans produced a specific frequency which, after extended study on resonance phenomena, matched the resonant frequency of the human stomach. During the fan's operation, everyone's stomach felt noxious. Her solution was to turn off the fans and see what happens. Other than a few complaints about the temperature, most people returned to work. As a result,

Figure 35: She decided to bring her audio equipment to isolate the noise …

her solution was simple, switch out the fans for another design and keep them greased before turning them on. Her friend was incredibly grateful, and in awe that so many scientists missed this.

Discovering that resonant frequencies could be both detrimental and useful, she decided to apply this reality to everyday life.

Resonant frequencies exist for every contiguous element that makes up an object. At a certain specific frequency, water molecules vibrate wildly. She used the resonant frequency of water molecules to heat food from the inside out. The introduction of the Elizawave oven was such a phenomenal hit that there isn't a home without one. The oven's sleek design and efficient cooking capabilities transformed kitchens across Grant, the scent of freshly cooked meals filling the air with a promise of innovation.

Figure 36: Nothing says retreat faster than exploding teeth. Since that day, Grant was a city not to be messed with.

From that theme came her use of the same technology for national defense. She surmised that if a whole factory of workers could be decommissioned from a single fan, an amplified signal could subdue an entire army. Hence, the discovery of the LizaCanon, a secret sonic weapon set at the resonant frequency of tooth enamel.

Grant's last war with the Rastonians over the two mountains was an amazing success. Their entire army immediately halted when their teeth started to heat up. The battlefield was a chaotic blend of shouts and the scent of a dentist office that of burning tooth enamel, the air thick with the acrid smell of desperation. Nothing says retreat faster than exploding teeth. Since that day, Grant was a city not to be messed with.

Eliza's journey was one of innovation and resilience, her creations a testament to the power of technology and the human spirit. The principles of impressionism guided her approach, each invention brushstroke on the canvas of her city. The purifier's filters were like the delicate strokes of a Monet painting, capturing the essence of clean air in a world choked by industry. The Elizawave oven's resonant frequencies were the vibrant colors of a Renoir, transforming the mundane act of cooking into an art form. And the LizaCanon, with its precise, deadly frequency, was the stark contrast of a Van Gogh, a reminder of the power and danger of technology.

Eliza's workshop was a sanctuary of innovation, a place where the harsh realities of Grant's streets faded into the background, replaced by the whine of machines and the promise of a better future. The scent of grease and soldering metal was a constant companion, a reminder of her roots and the path she had chosen. And as she worked, she could almost taste the sweetness of the air she was striving to create, a promise of something better for her city and its people.

Raylee's Translation

Raylee stood a few feet away, her console glowing faintly in her hands as she worked to decipher the signals flooding across the screen. The streams of data were fragmented, broken into bursts of symbols and patterns that defied conventional logic. Her green eyes narrowed as she pieced them together, her mind racing to extract meaning from the chaos.

The vibration resonated in her chest, a low vibration that made her ribs ache faintly. She adjusted the console's settings, the device emitting a soft, rhythmic beep as it aligned with the system's pulse. The air around her seemed charged, crackling faintly as though the atmosphere itself was brimming with static.

"It's trying to repair itself," she said finally, her voice steady but distant. "The signals.. they're incomplete, like fragments of a conversation cut short. But it's.. adaptive. It's learning from us."

Arty shot her a wary glance. "Learning what, exactly?"

Raylee didn't look up from her console. "Patterns. Responses. Intentions." She hesitated, her fingers pausing over the keys. "It's asking us something. But I can't tell what yet."

The precision of Glaician's teachings echoed in her focus. She knew this was no ordinary system, its adaptive logic aligned perfectly with the ideals of her home city. Yet the patterns were incomplete, and the risk of responding without understanding them gnawed at the edge of her concentration.

The Rise of Raylee

Raylee's gift for signal analysis began as a private curiosity – long nights spent hunched in Glaician's maintenance tunnels, listening to the electric buzz behind the city's orderly facade. One night, as she parsed a particularly dense web of code, she uncovered a hidden channel of encrypted communications.

The patterns were intricate and the encryption formidable, but Raylee's relentless focus teased out their secrets. What she found stopped her cold: a series of secret messages between Glaician's elite, outlining plans to further oppress the lower tiers. Raylee sat back, heart pounding. This was more than academic intrigue; it was evidence of a vast deceit.

That discovery became her turning point. She realized her skills could expose the corruption festering in her city's foundations. So, Raylee donned a digital mask, taking on the alias "Peregrine." Under this covert persona, she began leaking the incriminating plans to the public, drip by anonymous drip. Each release was meticulous – scrambled through proxy channels

Figure 37: Peregrine had to be careful, her movements calculated.

and ghost networks to conceal its source. With every secret she set free, the whispers about the mysterious whistleblower grew louder among Glaician's citizens.

As Peregrine's daring revelations gained traction, so did the danger surrounding Raylee. She knew the ruling tier would not sit idle as their secrets spilled into the streets. But every risk was worth it. Each time she heard a factory worker or a low-tier family repeating one of Peregrine's leaked truths in hushed, hopeful tones, Raylee felt a fierce jolt of purpose. She was striking back from the shadows of the network, one data breach at a time, and with each exposé she chipped away at Glaician's facade of perfect order.

The Rise

Peregrine's notoriety spread beyond the lower tiers. Her name became synonymous with rebellion, a beacon of hope for those who had long suffered under the weight of oppression. The people of Glaician began to rally around her, their voices rising in a chorus of defiance.

The Legacy

Peregrine's rise to provenance was not just a personal victory; it was a movement that changed the course of Glaician's history. Her work in signal analysis brought her notoriety, but it was Peregrine's unwavering commitment to justice that made her a legend. The pristine towers of Glaician could no longer hide the cracks in their foundation, and the city's elite were forced to confront the truth.

Raylee Frye, the girl from the shadows, had risen to become a symbol of resistance, her hidden identity, Peregrine etched in the annals of Glaician's history. Her legacy was one of courage, intellect, and the relentless pursuit of justice, a testament to the power of one individual's determination to change the world.

The Encroaching Presence

Back at the core, as the resonance deepened, a new sound emerged faint at first, like the rustling of leaves in a distant wind. It grew steadily, becoming a sharp, staccato rhythm that echoed through the chamber. It wasn't mechanical. It was organic, raw, and deliberate, like the tapping of claws against stone.

Arty's muscles tensed, his hand instinctively moving to the satchel at his side. His sharp brown eyes scanned the chamber, following the shifting patterns of light and shadow that danced across the walls. The sound wasn't coming from the structure; it was coming from the passage they had entered through.

"We're not alone," he said, his voice low and edged with tension.

Eliza stepped back from the structure, her gaze snapping toward the darkened entrance. The air felt different now, heavier, and colder, as though the energy in the room was drawing something toward them.

Raylee's console beeped sharply, a burst of corrupted data flooding the screen. She frowned, her fingers moving rapidly as she tried to stabilize the signal. "Something's disrupting the system," she said. "It's.. interference. But it's not coming from here; it's external."

Confronting the Unknown

The sound grew louder, echoing sharply as it approached. The tapping became a steady rhythm, like the march of something with purpose and precision. The shadows near the entrance began to shift, deepening unnaturally as though they were being pulled into something unseen.

Arty tightened his grip on the satchel, his other hand brushing against the handle of his sidearm. "If it's like the last one," he said, his voice calm but firm, "we need to shut it down before it gets close."

Eliza nodded, already reaching for another EMP grenade from her pack. The device felt cool in her hand, its weight a small comfort against the growing unease. She adjusted the settings quickly, her movements precise as the glow of the markings intensified around them.

Raylee stepped closer to the structure, her console still flickering with streams of data. "The system's reacting to the interference," she said, her voice urgent. "If we disable it now, we might lose the signal entirely."

"Better the signal than us," Arty muttered.

The Disruption

The tapping reached the threshold, the shadows pooling unnaturally around the entrance as a figure emerged, sleek and angular, its segmented limbs glinting faintly in the glow of the chamber. It moved with a mechanical precision that sent a chill through them, its singular red eye locking onto the structure with an eerie, predatory focus.

"Now!" Eliza shouted, tossing the grenade toward the figure.

The device landed with a faint metallic clink, rolling to a stop just beneath the machine's central body. For a heartbeat, the chamber held its breath. Then, with a sharp, resonant pulse, the EMP activated.

The wave of energy rippled outward, distorting the air and sending a visible ripple across the chamber. The machine seized, its limbs twitching violently before collapsing in on itself. The red glare at its center flickered once, twice, and then faded to nothing.

Facing the Signal

The silence that followed was deafening, broken only by the faint crackle of static as Raylee's console recalibrated. The glow of the structure remained steady, its throb unaffected by the disruption.

Eliza exhaled sharply, lowering her hand as she stepped toward the now-motionless machine. "Whatever that was," she said, her voice tight, "it's not the last one."

Arty nodded; his gaze fixed on the structure. "Then we'd better get our answers before more show up."

Raylee's console beeped softly, the signal stabilizing once more. She glanced at the others, her green eyes sharp with determination.

"The system's still active," she said. "Whatever's happening here, it's not over. And it's waiting for us."

CHAPTER 10

THE SIGNAL

THE AIR IN the chamber buzzed with a tension that seemed to grow with every passing second. It wasn't just the faint vibration of the structure now, it was the very atmosphere, crackling faintly like static before a storm. The pulsing illumination of the markings on the walls cast shifting patterns across the faces of Arty, Eliza, and Raylee, their features illuminated in strokes of gold and blue that flickered like flames. The silence that followed the EMP burst was profound, but it wasn't peaceful. It felt like the room was waiting.

The Chamber Expands

Eliza glanced at the glowing panels of the structure, then at the lifeless machine crumpled on the ground near the passageway. Her breathing was steady, but each inhale

carried the sharp tang of burnt ozone, tinged with something faintly coppery. She could feel the resonance of the structure beneath her feet, vibrating up through the floor and into
her body, her heartbeat syncing with its rhythm.

"This thing.. It's alive in a way I don't think we've even begun
to understand," she said, her voice low but clear. "It's not just
a machine. It's.. responding to everything we do."

Figure 38: The pulsing light of the markings on the walls cast shifting patterns across the faces of Arty, Eliza, and Raylee

Raylee stepped forward, her boots clicking softly against the stone floor. The faint
glow of her console reflected on her face, casting her sharp
features in a pale gleam that only deepened the intensity
of her eyes. She stopped near the edge of the structure,
holding the device steady as streams of fragmented data
scrolled across the screen.

"The oscillating patterns are stabilizing," she said, her
voice precise. "Whatever interference the alarm caused;
it's fading. The system is repairing itself." She hesitated
for a moment, her gaze darting to the glowing core of the
structure. "It's waiting for input."

Arty frowned, his hand brushing absently against the
satchel at his side as he surveyed the room. His sharp
brown eyes followed the shifting shadows along the walls,
their edges blurring into shapes that felt almost alive. The

air around him seemed heavier now, charged with an invisible tension that made his skin prickle.

"Are we sure we even want to give it input?" he asked. "For all we know, we're waking up something that shouldn't be disturbed."

Eliza tilted her head, a faint grin tugging at the corner of her mouth. "Isn't that why we're here?"

The Signal Strengthens

The chamber suddenly shifted, not physically, but perceptibly. The radiance pulsing through the structure intensified, growing brighter and casting intricate patterns on the walls that rippled like the surface of water disturbed by a single drop. The throb deepened into a low resonance, vibrating through the stone and into their very bones.

Raylee's console beeped sharply, the data stabilizing into a series of patterns that were no longer fragmented but deliberate, purposeful. Her fingers flew across the keys as she began to decode the signal, her expression a mixture of focus and curiosity.

"It's not just sending information," she said, her voice gaining urgency. "It's broadcasting."

Eliza turned toward her; her brow furrowed. "Broadcasting to where? Or to who?"

Raylee didn't answer immediately, her green eyes darting across the screen as the patterns unfolded before her. "It's not local," she said finally. "It's.. further. Much further."

Arty took a step forward, his boots crunching faintly against the stone. "Further how?" he pressed.

Raylee hesitated, her voice quieter now. "I think it's reaching beyond Austere. Maybe even beyond the cities.."

Debating the Risk

Eliza moved closer to the structure, her hands brushing lightly against the glowing panels. The warmth beneath her fingertips spread up her arm, a sensation that wasn't uncomfortable but was undeniably strange. She could feel the rhythm of the system, the oscillation of its energy resonating in time with her own.

"It's asking something," she murmured, her voice barely above a whisper. She glanced back at Raylee. "You said it's waiting for input. What kind of input?"

Raylee tilted the console toward her, the faint streams of data resolving into a single repeating pattern. "It's a question," she said simply.

Eliza frowned, leaning closer to the screen. The characters weren't in any language she recognized, but the repetition of the pattern carried a kind of rhythm that felt like speech. "What's it asking?"

Raylee adjusted the console's settings, the device emitting a faint whirr as it attempted to translate the signal. The characters flickered for a moment, then resolved into something legible: "Will you connect?"

The words hung between them, as tangible as the drone of the chamber. Arty's jaw tightened, his critical eyes darting toward the structure. "That's not ominous at all," he muttered.

The Debate

Eliza studied the glowing patterns on the panels, her mind racing. "Connect to what, though? A network? A system? Or something bigger?"

Raylee's gaze didn't leave her console. "Whatever it is, it's already been connected once. That's what silenced Grant. Whatever answer they gave, it caused this."

Arty stepped closer; his voice was low but firm. "Then maybe the right answer isn't to connect at all. We've seen what this thing can do, why risk it?"

Eliza turned to him, her eyes bright with determination. "Because we need to know. If this thing has the power to silence an entire city, we can't just walk away and hope it doesn't do it again. We have to understand it."

Raylee's console flickered again. "Wait… incoming data. It's not just us, military satellite arrays, international weather systems, orbital comm links, they all went dark within seconds. Whatever this thing is, it blocked global intervention before anyone could act."

Raylee looked up from her console, her expression unreadable. "But understanding comes with consequences," she said softly. "If we connect, we're giving it what it wants. And we don't know what that means."

The weight of the decision pressed heavily on them, the tension in the chamber magnifying their doubts and fears. Arty paced toward the crumpled machine, his astute eyes narrowing as he studied its lifeless frame. "Glaician took that risk," he said quietly. "And look where it got them."

Eliza's jaw tightened; her voice was steady but edged with urgency. "And what happens if we walk away? What if this thing wakes up anyway, and we're caught in its path without any way of knowing how to stop it?"

Raylee's green eyes narrowed as she met Arty's gaze. "The risks are astronomical," she admitted. "But if we don't act now, the consequences of doing nothing could be even greater. "

The First Step

Eliza stepped forward, her hand hovering over the central panel of the structure. The glow beneath her fingertips intensified, the warmth spreading outward in waves that seemed to ripple through the air.

"This is why we're here," she said, her voice steady. "To find answers. To understand. If we walk away now, we'll never know."

Arty exhaled sharply, his hand brushing against the satchel as he nodded reluctantly. "Fine," he said. "But if this goes sideways, I'm blaming you."

Raylee stepped closer, her console at the ready as she ad-justed its settings to sync with the system. "If we connect," she said, "we have to be ready for whatever comes next."

Eliza met her gaze and nodded, her resolve unwavering. Slowly, deliberately, she pressed her palm flat against the glowing panel.

The Consequences

The chamber reacted instantly. The throb deepened into a resonant energy that filled the air, the phosphorescence from the structure intensified until it engulfed the room in a dazzling brilliance. The oscillation of the system merged with their own heartbeats, resonating through their very being as the connection was made.

And then, as the phosphorescence reached its peak, the world around them shifted. The chamber seemed to dis-solve, its edges blurring and twisting as the glow of the structure consumed everything.

They had answered the question.

Now, they would face the consequences.

CHAPTER 11

SOMETHING OLD SOMETHING NEW

THE GLOW OF the chamber's markings steadies, the pulses coalescing into a rhythm that feels alive and insistent. The vibration beneath their feet returns, its vibrations ripple through the floor as if the space itself is stirring in response to their actions. The EMP grenade's pulse does more than disable the security measures, it opens a door that has been sealed far longer than any of them can fathom.

The First Signs

Arty notices it first, a faint hissing sound, soft and almost imperceptible, like steam escaping from an old pipe. His sharp brown eyes dart to the far corner of the chamber, where a curved glass enclosure begins to glow faintly, its edges lined with intricate markings similar to those on the structure. The hiss is uneven at first, a series of hesitant bursts that gradually steady into a rhythmic exhale, as though the enclosure itself is breathing.

"Something's happening," he says, his voice low but alert. He takes a step back, his fingers brush against the strap of his satchel, ready for whatever might emerge.

Eliza turns sharply, to focus on the phosphorescence of the glowing glass. The enclosure is cylindrical, its surface seamless and faintly reflective. As the glow intensifies, the markings along its edges begin to shift, rippling like water disturbed by a sudden breeze. Her hands instinctively tighten around her spanner, comforting weight anchoring her amidst the mounting tension.

Figure 39: Eliza turned sharply, to focus on the soft light of the glowing glass.

"It is hidden," she murmurs, her voice carrying a mix of awe and suspicion. "The EMP must have disabled whatever is keeping it locked down."

Raylee's Observation

Raylee's console beeps sharply, drawing her attention to the streams of data now flooding the screen. Her green eyes narrow as she traces the patterns, her fingers move quickly over the controls. Each oscillation seems to correspond with the hissing sounds emanating from the enclosure, the system's signals align with the glow that intensifies around the cylindrical structure.

"It's not just unlocking," she says. "It's connecting. Whatever's inside, it's tied to the system."

Her voice carries an edge of unease, the fragmented data on her console feeds into a stream that feels too deliberate, too precise. The relay isn't just unlocking; it is synchronizing, merging the entity within the enclosure back into its network. Raylee's thoughts race as she pieces together the patterns, her usual calm faltering slightly under the weight of the unknown.

The Gradual Reveal

The hissing grows louder, the glass enclosure begins to tremble as the glow within intensifies. A faint mist seeps from its edges, curling around the base like fog rolling over a cold landscape. The air grows sharper, charged with a faint static that makes the fine hairs on their arms stand on end. The markings on the enclosure shift faster now, their intricate patterns converge and dissolve into cohesive pulses that radiate across the chamber walls.

The rhythmic throb returns, rising and falling in waves that match the glow of the enclosure. Arty steps closer; his disruptor held tightly at his side. His instincts scream caution, but curiosity keeps his eyes locked on the scene unfolding before him. "It's waking up," he murmurs, his voice carrying a mixture of awe and dread.

Eliza moves closer, her breath catches as the mist thickens, swirling faintly around her boots. The phosphorescence spills into the walls like liquid gold being pumped through veins. She can feel the energy pressing against her skin, a presence that is almost tangible. "Whatever's inside," she says softly, "it's.. reacting to us."

The Awakening

As if on cue, with a low, resonant hum, the glass slides upward, disappearing seamlessly into the ceiling. A sharp wave of energy ripples outward from the enclosure, sending a faint vibration through the chamber that forces the group to steady themselves.

Figure 40: "Whatever's inside," she said softly, "it's.. reacting to us."

Standing within is a figure, a humanoid form that straddles the line between man and machine. His body is sleek, composed of dark metallic plating interwoven with faintly glowing circuits that resonate in time with the chamber's hum. His face, though partially covered by a smooth, angular helmet, is unmistakably human in its structure, the faint glow of synthetic eyes peering out from beneath the visor.

For a moment, the figure stands perfectly still, the glow from his circuit's casts shifting patterns on the chamber walls. The mist clings to his feet, dissipating slowly as he takes his first breath, a deep, deliberate inhale that fills the air with the sound of something ancient stirring to life.

First Movements

As the figure begins to move, his steps are slow, deliberate, like someone testing their ability to walk after a long slumber. The glow of his circuits shifts with each movement, synchronizing with the pulsate of the chamber as though the two are linked. His synthetic eyes scan the room, locking onto the structure at the center before shifting

Figure 41: "Who activated the pulse?" he asked.

to the three figures standing before him. It is not just a glance, it is an assessment, a silent calculation of their presence. "Who activated the pulse?" he asks, his voice smooth yet layered with a faint mechanical undertone. It carries a weight of authority, yet there is no hostility, only curiosity.

The Weight of the Reveal

Arty takes a cautious step forward, his severe eyes fixed on the figure. "We did," he says, his voice steady despite the tension. "Who or what are you?"

The figure tilts his head slightly, the glow of his circuits pulsing faintly. "I am Donivan," he says simply. "A cybernetic humanoid prototype.. though not of my own design."

He pauses, his gaze shifts to the structure at the center of the chamber. "My current understanding is that I am not of this system, I am brought here by a team from one of your cities long ago to interact with this system." "This system, its network, is disconnected. The EMP you triggered wiped out the primary security block; hence, restored my link to it."

One Good Byte Deserves Another

Yet, while "...The EMP you triggered wiped out the primary security block; hence, restored my link to it." echoed through the silent relay corridors, Unnoticed by the trio, the Spinifex hopping mouse had crept into the relay's open machinery. Drawn by the faint aroma of the chestnut Arty kept in his pocket, the tiny creature skittered across a bundle of cables. Its sharp incisors began gnawing instinctively on a thin, rubber-coated wire nestled in the metal veins.

A sudden pop of sparks erupted in the darkness beneath the console. The mouse darted away as the last filament of a critical circuit snapped under its teeth. In that instant, the relay's backup security protocols fizzled out. The final lock on Donivan's mysterious system released – not due to any grand design, but because of one small creature's search for food.

Eliza steps forward, her curiosity overcomes her caution. Her voice carries a blend of wonder and resolve. "You're connected to the system? What does that mean?"

Donivan's gaze shifts to her, his expression unreadable beneath the smooth plating of his helmet. "It means I can interface with it. Understand it. Communicate on your behalf."

Raylee's green eyes narrow as she studied him, her console glows faintly in her hands. Her movements are swift and purposeful as she processes the implications of his awakening. "And why are you disconnected in the first place?"

Figure 42: Its incisors, honed by nature into perfect, miniature shears, went to business.

Donivan hesitates, his circuits oscillate faintly as though processing the question. "The security protocols," he says finally. "This facility's defenses are designed to prevent unauthorized access. When they are triggered, I am isolated, unable to act or interact." He gestures toward the remnants of the disabled machine near the passage. "But your pulse.. it disables the protocols. Frees me, if you will."

The group exchanges glances, the weight of his words settles over them like a tangible presence. Arty breaks the silence, his tone cautious but direct. "If you're connected to the system, then you know what's happening here. What this place is. What it's trying to do."

A Gradual Partnership

Donivan nods, his synthetic eyes flicker faintly. "This facility is a relay node in a network that spans far beyond your cities. Its purpose is communication, though I do not yet know with whom, or with what."

The drone deepens, resonates with the group's unspoken resolve. The glowing chamber feels different now, not just alive, but purposeful. Donivan stands at the bridge of two worlds, his awakening not just a revelation but a turning point.

CHAPTER 12

THE CELESTIAL CATALYST

THE CHAMBER PULSES faintly as Donivan stands at the structure's core, his circuits glowing in rhythm with the system's hum. The intricate markings on the walls shimmer with life, their patterns shift and reform into shapes that carry unspoken meanings. The air is alive with energy, charged with anticipation, as though space itself knows something the group does not.

The Interruption of Wonder

Arty shifts uneasily, his sharp brown eyes darting toward the glowing markings. The faint vibrations beneath his boots send ripples across the smooth floor, a reminder that the chamber is no longer dormant. He tightens his grip on his satchel, its weight grounding him against the disorienting movement of phosphorescence and sound that surrounds them.

"Alright," he says, his voice cutting through the tension. "Can someone explain why this thing suddenly decides to wake up? Because we've been here long enough to know this isn't random. I say we EMP him."

Eliza looks up from the glowing panels she has been studying, her auburn hair catching the phosphorescence as she moves closer to Arty. Her expression is thoughtful, her mind racing through possibilities that dance just out of reach.

Eliza, unsure if Arty was joking, admonishes him, "Relax. We're actually talking to an alien entity here, and you want to nuke the microphone?!"

"It didn't just wake up," she says slowly, as though piecing the puzzle together in real time. "It is triggered. Something external, something beyond us, sets this in motion."

Raylee glances at them both, her green eyes sharp as she adjusts the settings on her console. "Whatever it is, it happens recently," she says. "The burst you trigger is just the final key. The system is already.. waiting."

Investigating the Celestial Catalyst

Before Donivan can respond, Eliza moves toward her toolkit and retrieves a small scanner, its faint glow syncing with the chamber's pulse. "If this system is connected to external factors, we should be able to trace the signal back," she says, her voice steady despite the tension in her movements. She adjusts the scanner's settings.

Raylee follows suit, her console emitting a series of soft beeps as she begins cross-referencing the system's pulses with the data streams in the relay. "I'll run a diagnostic on the structure's energy flow," she says, her green eyes narrowing as she traces the signal pathways. "If it's tied to a celestial event, it should leave a signature, something traceable."

Arty watches them silently, his hand brushing against the strap of his satchel as he paces the chamber. "This doesn't explain why now," he says finally. "If this system's been waiting for centuries, why doesn't it wake up sooner?"

Eliza glances at him; her expression thoughtful. "Because it isn't time," she says. "Celestial events aren't constant, they're rare. If this system is tied to something in orbit, it's been waiting for the right alignment."

The Catalyst Revealed

Donivan turns toward them, his synthetic eyes glowing faintly beneath the smooth plating of his helmet. His voice carries a calm yet deliberate tone, layered with curiosity. "The network is ancient," he says. "Its design suggests a cyclical pattern, an activation tied to external factors."

Eliza frowns, brushing her hands against the glowing panels of the structure. "External factors?" she echoes.

Donivan inclines his head slightly. "Celestial events," he says. "The network is tied to the planet's orbit, a mechanism likely synchronized with rare occurrences in the surrounding solar system. The anomaly the system detects a few days back aligns with such an event. A trigger, if you will."

Connecting to the Comet

The group exchanges glances, the weight of his words settling over them like a tangible presence.

Raylee's green eyes narrow as she adjusts the console's settings, her expression thoughtful. "Are you saying something out there, something beyond the Austere, activates this system? What kind of event could do that?"

Eliza's gaze flickers as realization strikes. "The comet," she says suddenly, her voice carrying a mix of excitement and certainty. "It passed by the planet a few days ago. The same one that orbits every 6000 years. People used to call it the Star of Shadows, it causes strange phenomena whenever it appears. But... I thought that was just folklore."

Raylee glances at the console, her green eyes narrowing as the faint data signature matches Eliza's words. "The system's awakening aligns with the comet's orbit," she says. "The timing fits, this coincides with the Grant outage. , this isn't a coincidence."

Donivan's circuits flare faintly in response. "Folklore often carries fragments of truth," he says simply. "The comet's presence likely activates the network's dormant mechanisms. It is, after all, a celestial rarity, one that the system is designed to recognize.""

Predicting the Phenomena

Eliza's brow furrows, her scanner emitting a faint whirr as she traces the energy signature back through the relay's pathways. "If this system is tied to celestial events," she says, "we should be able to predict its next activation, find a pattern in its responses."

Figure 43: he said simply. "The comet's presence likely activated the network's dormant mechanisms.

Raylee nods, her console glowing brightly as she syncs its settings with Eliza's scanner. "If the timing aligns," she says, "then this system isn't just waiting, it is anticipating the next event. The comet is a trigger, but it's part of something larger, something cyclical."

Donivan steps forward, his circuits gleaming with renewed intensity. 'We each have a role,' he says. "Its patterns suggest a deep connection to orbital phenomena, alignments beyond this facility's reach. If we trace these patterns further, we may uncover the full scope of its purpose."

Arty interrupts, "Purpose! Purpose? You are connected to it why can't you just tell us the purpose?"

Donivan turned slowly to Arty. "For some reason, this information is restricted, and I'm not privy to it," he explained, gesturing toward Eliza. "As she noted, I'm just a microphone."

Eliza immediately responds, "I didn't mean..."

Donivan's hand raises, "I am only making an illustration, no offense taken."

"We've been terribly rude," Eliza said, quickly introducing the group. "I'm Eliza from Grant, this is Arty from Teton, and the one with her nose in the console is Raylee from Glaician."

Donivan responded, "Thank you, this is much appreciated. Now to answer Arty's postulate, that I should be able to surmise a purpose; however, I didn't want to alarm you."

Arty responded, "Oh please surmise away..."

Eliza retorted immediately, "Shut it, Arty! Donivan, at this juncture, I doubt anything would shock us now. Please proceed."

"Well, if my calculations are correct," Donivan said calmly, "the energy core , the relay's central hub containing that ancient alien technology , has one purpose: to evaluate this planet's inhabitants every 6,000 years. If they are deemed insufficient, the core notifies an interstellar enforcement delegation to send a purge unit and destroy all life on the planet."

Arty's eyes bulged. "What?! Purge us... Oh man, we're gonna die!" he yelped.

Raylee looked up from her console, "Well that's shock-ing…"

Raylee continued, "Donivan, what makes you so sure about this?"

Donivan responds, "Admittedly, this is conjecture," Donivan conceded. "But based on the data and the scans the Central Hub performed, it appears to be attempting to contact some kind of enforcement entity , for lack of a better term, a universal watchdog. And if a punitive force is indeed being summoned, that tells me a violation has occurred."

Donivan continues, "I believe that the celestial body , the Star of Shadows, as you called it , serves as a kind of alarm clock, set to monitor the planet's progress every 6,000 years because of its predictable cycle." However, its scanners are so powerful that scanning Grant, their first scan, it knocks out their power grid. Again, all this is nothing more than an educated guess."

Arty retorts softly shaking his head, "We're gonna die…"

Raylee's eyes widen as a realization hits her. 'So that's what **happened** last time…'"

Eliza responds, "You really think so?"

Raylee, "Well if all the historical and sacred scripture genealogy is to be believed, yes."

Eliza calmly says, "Look, nothing is happening unless we allow it… Right?!"

The team half-heartedly responds, "Yaaaah…"

A New Perspective

Arty exhales sharply, his grip tightening on the satchel at his side. "Let me get this straight," he says. "We're standing in the middle of an ancient relay system that wakes up every couple of centuries whenever some comet decides to swing by. And now it wants to purge us?"

Eliza gives him a faint smile, the tension in her shoulders easing slightly. "Well, when you put it like that, it sounds insane," she admits. "But it explains why no one's encountered it before, why the Austere has stayed silent for so long. The system is waiting for the Star of Shadows as a wakeup call to evaluate us again."

Arty reflects, "And after looking at Grant – it's saying, wow these guys suck, time to heat ray all of them. We're gonna die!"

Figure 44: "We proceed cautiously," he said. "The network is vast, and its activation carries consequences yet unseen.

Raylee responds, "Really Arty, aren't you being a little melodramatic here? Donivan is just guessing, besides, that's not how they'd do it, they would use some virulent gas. At the very least something more efficient than a heat ray, that's like you with a magnifying glass trying to burn a colony of ants – gas is more efficient."

Arty looked around at everyone. "Wow, Raylee, remind

me to bring you to one of my family's birthday parties. They'd get a kick out of you…"

Eliza shot Arty a stern look. "Arty! You know she has a point. This is getting old."

Raylee studies the glowing markings, her console emitting a faint bustle as it syncs with the network's pulse. "I agree. If the system is tied to celestial events," she says, "then its activation isn't random, it's deliberate. The comet is a signal, a key. Whatever this network is designed to do, monitor, scan, evaluate, it's tied to something beyond us."

Donivan nods slowly, his synthetic eyes fixed on the structure. "The system has awakened," he says. "And all my assertions are just guess work, but one thing is for certain, its purpose is tied to the alignment of forces far greater than this facility. If we are to understand its intent, we must delve deeper."

The Path Forward

The group turns toward the structure, its glow illuminating the chamber with a brilliance that feels almost otherworldly. Donivan extends his hand toward the central panel, the circuits in his arm flaring brightly as the markings begin to shift once more. The oscillate deepens, resonating through the space like the pulse of a living being.

We proceed cautiously," he says. "The network is vast, and its activation carries consequences yet unseen. But together, we may uncover the truth."

Arty sings, "We're definitely gonna die…"

Raylee chimes in imitating Arty's tone, "By gas…"

Eliza retorted, "Oh my god, not you too? I'm surrounded by infants…"

Arty, Eliza, and Raylee exchange glances, the gravity of their task settling over them like a quiet storm. The celestial event has awakened the system, but the answers it promises are still shrouded in mystery. With Donivan as their guide, they prepare to move forward, the glow of the chamber lighting their path as the network awaits their next move. chamber lighting their path as the network awaits their next move.

CHAPTER 13

RESTORING THE BALANCE

THE FAINT VIBRATE of the system pulses steadily through the chamber, resonating in time with the rhythmic glow of the markings that line the walls. Donivan stands at the core of the facility's structure, his circuits glowing faintly as he syncs with the network. The group emerges into Austere, believing they are free of immediate danger, but Grant's silence still looms over them like a shadow.

Raylee adjusts her console, her green eyes narrowing as streams of data flash across the screen. The oscillation of the system changes again, its patterns shifting erratically as if struggling to stabilize. "The network's reach is extending," she says. Her voice is steady, but there is an edge of urgency beneath her words. "It's searching for something, reaching toward Grant."

Eliza's auburn hair catches the faint light of the markings as she steps closer to the structure, her tools clinking softly in her pack. She frowns, brushing her hands against the glowing panels as she studies the shifting patterns. "The grid in Grant's lower district has been down for weeks," she says. "Could the network fix it? Could Donivan do it?"

Arty tightened the strap of his satchel, his sharp brown eyes darting between Eliza and the glowing structure. "And if we don't fix it?" he asked, his tone deliberate. "Grant's been quiet, but quiet doesn't mean friendly. If they think the outage is sabotage..." He didn't finish the thought, but the weight of it hung heavily in the air.

The Plan

Donivan turns to them, his synthetic eyes flickering faintly beneath the smooth plating of his helmet. His voice carries the calm precision of a machine, yet there is a deliberate humanity in his tone. "My connection to the relay allows me to interface with the network and manage its energy flow; hence, the network is capable of restoring Grant's power grid," he says. He elaborated further, "Its pulse can reconnect the fragmented pathways, stabilizing the flow of energy across the city."

Raylee studies him closely, her console glowing faintly as she adjusts the settings. "Can you guarantee it won't be seen as interference?" she asks. Commenting further, "If Grant interprets this as aggression from Teton or Glaician, it could escalate into something we can't control."

Donivan responded, "Sounds like there is not much of a decision to make here."

Obstacles Emerge

Donivan places his hand on the central panel of the structure, his circuits flaring brightly as the markings on the walls begin to shift. The vibration deepens, resonating through the chamber like the low notes of a song that carries the weight of centuries.

"The network is fragmented," Donivan says, his voice steady. "Restoring the grid will require synchronizing its pulse, aligning its pathways with those of Grant."

Figure 45: "The network is fragmented," Donivan said, his voice steady. "Restoring the grid will require synchronizing its pulse.

Raylee adjusts her console quickly, the device emitting a faint beep as it syncs with the network's rhythm. "I'll monitor the flow," she says. "Make sure it doesn't overload or destabilize."

Eliza placed her hand against the glowing panels, her calloused fingers tracing the intricate grooves. A low thrum pulsed beneath her skin, the rhythm of the system echoing through her like a second heartbeat.

But before they can proceed, the chamber shifts. The rhythm of the relay falters momentarily, sending a sharp vibration through the walls. Streams of data on Raylee's console flash erratically, the signal destabilizing as the system struggles to align with Grant's fragmented grid.

"It's not holding!" Raylee exclaims; her voice edged with urgency. "The pathways are overloaded, the pulse is triggering resistance in the network!"

Donivan's circuits flare brightly, his synthetic eyes narrowing as he analyzes the system's response. "The grid's infrastructure is deteriorating," he says. "The network cannot stabilize without direct intervention."

The Challenge

Eliza steps back from the panels, her mind racing. "What kind of intervention?" she asks quickly.

Donivan gestures toward the corridor leading into the chamber. "Manual adjustments to the secondary conduits," he says. "They are misaligned, the pathways must be recalibrated before synchronization can be achieved."

A Quick Note on Secondary Conduits

Imagine you have an enormous toy train set, and the tracks are all connected so the train can go around smoothly. But sometimes, the tracks get a little wobbly or misaligned, and the train can't move properly. To fix this, you need to adjust the tracks, so they line up perfectly again.

Like the tracks need adjustment, the Secondary Conduits are special pathways that help the energy flow smoothly through the relay system. When the conduits are misaligned, the energy can't move properly, and the system gets all wobbly and unstable.

The team needs to fix these secondary conduits to make sure the energy flows smoothly again. This is important because if the energy doesn't flow correctly, the entire system could break down, and Grant's power grid won't be restored.

Arty tightens his grip on the satchel at his side, his precise eyes scanning the glowing markings. "We don't have time for this," he mutters. "If the synchronization fails, the entire grid could collapse, and we'll have to answer for that."

Raylee adjusts her console, her fingers flying across the controls as she traces the system's pathways. "We can reroute the flow temporarily," she says. "But it'll require precise synchronization with the relay's pulse."

Eliza grabs her toolkit, her determination evident as she steps toward the corridor. "Then let's do it," she says firmly. "Arty, you're with me. Raylee, stay here and keep the oscillations stable, Donivan, guide us."

Recalibrating the Grid

The corridor is dimly lit, its walls lined with conduits that resonate faintly in rhythm with the system's hum. The misaligned pathways flicker erratically, their glow casting sharp shadows that dance along the smooth floor. Eliza crouches near the first conduit, her spanner emitting a faint vacillate as she syncs it with the markings.

Arty stands guard, his precise eyes scanning the corridor for any signs of movement. "How long's this going to take?" he asks, his voice steady but impatient.

"Not long," Eliza replies, her focus unwavering as she adjusts the conduit's alignment. Sparks erupt from the panel as the energy flow stabilizes, the faint glow returning to its steady rhythm.

Success and Uncertainty

Back in the chamber, Raylee watches the pulse carefully, her green eyes darting across the console's screen. "It's holding," she says, her voice steady but cautious. "The flow is stabilizing, keep moving!"

Eliza and Arty reach the final conduit, their movements deliberate and precise as the system's undulate deepens. Eliza adjusts the alignment carefully, her breath catching as the energy flow surges through the pathway.

"It's done," she says finally, stepping back as the glow steadies. The relay resonates through the corridor, its rhythm syncing seamlessly with the grid.

The Restoration

Minutes pass, the chamber alive with light and sound as the vibrations steadies. Finally, the glow begins to fade, retreating into the markings as the vibrate softens into a steady rhythm.

Donivan's synthetic eyes flicker as he turns back to the group. "The grid is restored," he says. "Grant's power flow has stabilized."

Raylee studies her console, her fingers tracing the streams of data now flowing smoothly across the screen. "The network's resonance is holding," she says. "The city should have power again."

Meanwhile in Grant

The resurgence of Grant's network is nothing short of a revelation. For weeks, the city has been shrouded in an eerie silence, its once-bustling streets and humming factories reduced to a ghostly stillness. The absence of the familiar pulsate of machinery and the flicker of neon lights has left the citizens in a state of unease,

Figure 46: "Engineers and technicians worked tirelessly,

their daily routines disrupted by the sudden void. But now, as the network begins to flicker back to life, a palpable sense of relief and excitement sweeps through the city.

It starts with a faint, almost imperceptible energy, a rhythmic beat that resonates through the ground and up into the towering skyscrapers. The lights, which have been dimmed to conserve energy, begin to brighten, casting a warm glow across the cityscape. The digital billboards, once dark and lifeless, flicker back to life, their vibrant advertisements dancing across the screens. The whine of machinery returns, filling the air with a familiar, comforting sound that speaks of progress and ambition.

In the heart of Grant, the central hub of the network buzzes with activity. Engineers and technicians work tirelessly, their faces illuminated by the luminescence of monitors and control panels. Data streams flow like rivers of light, each one carrying vital information that will restore the city's lifeblood. The network's resurgence is not just a technical achievement, it is a testament to the resilience and determination of Grant's people. They have faced the silence with grit and ingenuity, and now they are reclaiming their city's rhythm.

At the General Hospital, the backup power has been stretched to its limit and beyond. Surgeons, who have been performing a complex aortic dissection, face a critical decision as the emergency power dwindles. They have to stabilize the patient manually, using hand-cranked ventilators and battery-operated monitors. The room is filled with the scent of sweat and antiseptic, the air thick with tension. When the power finally surges back, the surgical team quickly reconnects the patient to the robotic assistants and advanced equipment, completing the procedure with a collective sigh of relief. Post-surgery, they have to address the backlog of critical cases that have been delayed, ensuring all patients receive the care they need.

Across the city, at the power plant, engineers have been battling against time. The backup systems, designed to handle a 24-hour outage, have been pushed to their limits. The control room is filled with the smell of overheated circuits and the acrid bite of burning insulation. When the power is restored, the turbines roar back to life, but the engineers know their work is far from over. They have to conduct thorough inspections and maintenance to ensure no lasting damage has occurred. This includes checking the integrity of the cooling systems and recalibrating the control systems to prevent future failures.

Figure 47: The facility, processing 50 tons of waste an hour, had exceeded its backup system's capacity.

At the waste processing plant, the situation had been dire. The facility, processing 50 tons of waste an hour, has exceeded its backup system's capacity Operators have to manually divert waste to temporary holding areas, using makeshift barriers and emergency protocols to prevent overflow. The stench of decay is overwhelming, and the risk of contamination is high. When the power returns, the operators work around the clock to clear the backlog, sanitize the facility, and ensure all systems are functioning correctly. They also have to report any environmental violations and coordinate with health officials to mitigate any public health risks. In the city's prisons, the situation is equally daunting. The electronic door locks on the cells rely on backup power that is only good for 24 hours. As the outage stretches on, prison staff have to enact an immediate manual lockdown, manually locking each cell to prevent any potential escapes if the backup power fails. This is a monumental task, with 200 cell blocks and a thousand cells each. The staff works tirelessly, their anxiety rising with each passing hour. The scent of sweat and the sound of clanking metal fill the air as they secure each cell. The uncertainty of when the power will be restored adds to the tension, and the staff knows that any failure could result in a disaster. When the power finally returns, they face the insurmountable task of manually unlocking all the cell doors again, allowing the electronic system to resume control. This requires meticulous coordination and verification to ensure the security of the facility.

As the network fully comes online, the city seems to breathe a collective sigh of relief. The streets fill with the sounds of commerce and conversation, the markets bustling with activity once more. The citizens of Grant, who have endured weeks of uncertainty, now move with renewed purpose. The resurgence of the network is more than just a return to normalcy, it is a reminder of their strength and their unyielding spirit. Grant is alive again, its heart beating stronger than ever.

The Agreement

Eliza exhales sharply, the tension in her shoulders easing slightly. "Crisis averted," she says, though her voice carries a note of cautious optimism.

Arty leans against the doorway, his urgent eyes scanning the jagged horizon of Austere. "For now," he mutters. "But we need to make sure this doesn't blow up in our faces."

Donivan steps forward, his circuits pulsing faintly as he addresses the group. "The network's activation is only the beginning," he says. "Its systems are vast and adaptive, its actions will ripple across the cities. Further interaction may disrupt its balance, resulting in consequences far beyond this relay."

Eliza says, "We need to get back to my workshop and regroup, we need a plan."

Raylee says, "Let's go back to my place, I know a professor that may have some insight on this and can assist us with Donivan. He's Glaician's leading AI and Robotics expert.

CHAPTER 14

FATHER AND SON

T HE WORKSHOP DOOR hisses open, and the group steps into a world of innovation and ingenuity. Machines of impossible design line the space, their chrome surfaces glinting under the soft glow of flickering lights. Panels hummed faintly, and Pixo, a sleek floating orb, drifted through the room, emitting a faint melodic chime as though aware of their arrival.

Figure 48: "I can't believe this," he said, his voice gaining strength. "You're here. You're working. I thought I'd lost you forever."

Dr. Elias Voss stands in the middle of the room, his silver hair catching the cool light. His piercing blue eyes sweep across the group, but as his gaze lands on Donivan, he freezes. His expression shifts, the sharp edges of his stoicism softening into disbelief.

"Donivan," he murmurs, his voice thick with emotion. "Welcome home, son!"

He moves toward Donivan, his steps almost hesitant, as though afraid the moment might shatter. "I can't believe this," he says, his voice gaining strength. "You're here. You're working. I thought I'd lost you forever."

Donivan tilts his head slightly, the faint glow of his circuits flickering. "Home?" he says, his voice calm but questioning.

Dr. Voss smiles, his blue eyes sparkling with a mixture of pride and relief. "Yes, home. I'm your father, your creator. You were to be my greatest achievement, the bridge between human and machine. I can't believe you're standing before me again." He turns to Pixo, who has floated closer to observe. "Pixo, get us some tea!" he says cheerfully. "We have so much to discuss."

As known, the world has fractured into three great cities, Grant, Teton, and Glaician, each striving for supremacy amidst the desolation of the Austere. Amidst this fragile balance, Dr. Elias Voss, a brilliant scientist from Glaician, discovers an ancient relay system buried deep within the Austere. The relay's technology is unlike anything humanity has ever seen, and Dr. Voss knows he has found something extraordinary.

Driven by his insatiable curiosity and desire to push the boundaries of human knowledge, Dr. Voss embarks on a daring experiment. In secret, he creates a quantum computer that revolutionizes computer processing power. This machine produces vast power and, in the wrong hands, could create havoc not only in the cybersecurity world by decrypting even the most complex encryption algorithms but also in the streets by providing vulnerabilities in the city that no one, not even its engineer or security officials, are aware of. Yes, this had to be secured.

Dr. Voss ponders how he can tap into this vast knowledge without generating suspicion. Then it comes to him, Pixo, an interface to the quantum phenomenon that is a floating, cute toy-like sphere that no one would suspect has the keys to the kingdom. Taking the sleek design from the Scalin ball used in the hover game of Scalin, a nod to the beloved hover-hockey game uniting the three cities, ensuring the device drew no suspicion. he develops a quantum entanglement between Pixo and the quantum computer. This allows instantaneous communication between the Quantum computer and Pixo.

Imagine you have two magic coins. If you flip one coin and it lands on heads, the other coin, no matter how far away it is, will also land on heads at the exact same time. If the first coin lands on tails, the second coin will also land on tails instantly. This happens even if the coins are on opposite sides of the universe!

In reality, instead of coins, we're talking about tiny particles like electrons or photons. When these particles become entangled, their properties are linked in such a way that the state of one particle instantly deter mines the state of the other, no matter the distance between them. This phenomenon puzzled scientists for eons because it violated the principle that nothing can travel faster than the speed of light. However, numerous experiments have confirmed that quantum entanglement is real, and it plays a crucial role in the field of quantum mechanics.

This was the driver behind Pixo's value. His creation was a testament to Dr. Voss's ingenuity and determination. The sleek orb emitted a faint melodic chime and glowed softly, its presence a beacon of hope in the midst of uncertainty. In short, Pixo could calculate what would take the best supercomputers of the world 10,000 years, and perform the same calculation in 20 minutes, making even Arty's speed pale in comparison.

The group exchanged uneasy glances, the emotional tension palpable as they watched father and son face each other in the midst of conflicting emotions.

Donivan's circuits flared faintly in response, the glow casting sharp shadows across the room. "If this is true, then perhaps, you had a good reason to abandon me?" he said suddenly, his voice steady but laced with something deeper, an accusation that cut through the tension like a blade.

Dr. Voss froze, his blue eyes widening as though the accusation had struck him physically. "I never wanted to abandon you," he said quickly, his voice thick with regret. "I fought to keep you active, but the system was too powerful. It wasn't just rejecting me, it was erasing everything I'd built."

"But you built me," Donivan said, his synthetic eyes flickering as he stepped closer. "Was I not worth saving?"

Dr. Voss's shoulders sagged slightly, the weight of the question pressing down on him. "You were worth everything," he said quietly. "But the relay.. it doesn't see 'worth' the way we do. It saw me as a threat, a risk to its integrity, and it severed our connection." He continued, "It began to dispatch a flurry of drones that attacked the entire group, it was so intense, they pursued us even after we were on our way. We had to abandon our vehicles and disperse in different directions. We were lucky to get out of there with our lives."

Raylee, "Ah yes, I believe we ran into that carnage of vehicles. I recognized the vehicles."

As the group settled into mismatched stools and benches, Dr. Voss poured steaming tea into small cups from a sleek device held by Pixo. The orb glowed softly, its movements fluid and deliberate.

Figure 49: "I fought to keep you active, but the system was too powerful.

Dr. Voss leaned back in his chair, his tea in hand. "Years ago, when I stumbled upon the relay system buried in Austere, I knew I'd found something extraordinary," he began. "Its technology was unlike anything our world had ever seen. I couldn't resist the opportunity, it was a chance to push the boundaries of what we knew."

He gestured to Donivan, who stood attentively, his circuits pulsing faintly. "Donivan was the culmination of that discovery. Using the relay's technology, I created him to be a prototype, a living interface, capable of bridging the gap between human thought and advanced systems. He was my masterpiece."

Eliza leaned forward, her green eyes sharp with curiosity. "But something happened," she said. "The system turned on you, didn't it?"

Dr. Voss nodded, his smile fading. "Yes," he said quietly. "At first, the system allowed limited access, just enough to glimpse its potential. But it decided I was a security risk. It severed my connection and locked me out completely. When it shut Donivan down, I thought I'd lost him forever. Then the relay dispatched the drones, and well…"

Donivan's optical sensors dimmed then glowed softly – the closest a synthetic could come to blinking back emotion. "You… you were trying to survive," he said at last. His voice was usually level, but now each word emerged slower, weighed down by an unmistakable note of hurt.

Dr. Voss swallowed hard. His throat felt dry as Austere sand. "I never wanted to abandon you," he whispered, eyes shining with regret. He took a tentative step closer to his creation. In the harsh lab light, the others could see the tears gathering at the corners of the old man's eyes. "I fought to keep you active, Donivan. But the relay's system… it was too powerful. It wasn't just pushing me out – it was erasing everything we'd built together." His hands trembled at his sides as he confessed these failures.

Donivan's usually impassive face twitched – a minute adjustment of servos that suggested inner turmoil. "You left me in the dark," he replied, and for a moment his synthesized baritone wavered.

Dr. Voss bowed his head, a tear finally streaking down his cheek. "I know," he croaked. "And I have carried that with me every day since." The small, raw crack in his voice hung in the air.

Eliza broke the heavy silence, stepping forward with gentle resolve. She placed a hand on Donivan's forearm, the warm gesture belying the cool metal beneath her fingers.

Figure 50:. "Pixo is a quantum interface," he explained. "It's capable of integrating with Donivan's systems…

"Dr. Voss," she said softly, "Donivan's link to the relay is still putting him at risk. If we shut the relay down to save our world, we could… we could lose him." Her voice tightened on the last phrase. "Is there any way to protect him?"

Dr. Voss glanced at Pixo, his expression thoughtful. "That was always the challenge," he admitted. "Donivan's systems were intricately tied to the relay. Severing that connection should have meant the end for him. But…" He gestured to Pixo, the orb floating closer in response. "This is where Pixo comes in."

The orb emitted a soft chime, its glow intensifying as Dr. Voss continued. "Pixo is a quantum interface," he explained. "It's capable of integrating with Donivan's systems, supplanting the relay's functions. Specifically, we need to replace all subroutines that call to the relay's core with similar code that calls unto you instead If the process works, Donivan will not only survive, he'll evolve, gaining full independence and capabilities beyond what even the relay could provide."

Raylee raised an eyebrow. "What's the risk?" she asked, her voice steady.

Dr. Voss hesitated; the pause laden with meaning. "Quantum integration is delicate," he said. "Even a millisecond of desync will trigger cascading logic collapse. If that happens, Donivan will crash… and I won't be able to bring him back." But I believe in him, and in this technology. If we succeed, he'll be stronger than ever."

Raylee's console emitted a series of rapid flashes, the data streams flickering as she adjusted the settings. "I can assist with the synchronization," she said. "But we'll need to act quickly. The relay's defenses are likely to react once we start the process."

Donivan stepped forward, his synthetic eyes meeting Dr. Voss's gaze. "I am prepared," he said simply.

But the words felt heavy, as though carrying an unspoken challenge. Dr. Voss nodded, his expression a mix of determination and regret. "I won't fail you again," he said softly."

Dr. Voss moved to a nearby panel, his fingers flying over the controls as he initiated the synchronization process. Pixo floated closer to Donivan, its melodic chime growing louder as it established the connection.

As the integration process began, the room filled with a quiet hum, streams of light connecting Pixo to Donivan's circuits. Eliza watched anxiously, her heart pounding in her chest. "Come on, Pixo," she murmured. "You can do this."

Eliza and Raylee exchanged glances; their expressions unreadable as they watched the delicate operation unfold. The glow of Pixo's circuits intensified; the orb emitting a series of rapid flashes that synchronized with Donivan's systems.

Dr. Voss's expression was tense, his blue eyes focused on the panel as he monitored the process; his piercing blue eyes focused on Donivan as the process reached its crescendo. "You've always been capable of great things, son," he said quietly. "And now, you'll prove it to the world."

Raylee's console beeped softly, the data streams stabilizing as the synchronization completed. "It's done," she said, her voice steady but edged with relief. "Donivan is functioning independently."1

Dr. Voss exhaled sharply, his shoulders relaxing. "We did it," he said, his voice filled with pride. "Donivan is safe."

Donivan's circuits flared brightly, his synthetic eyes glowing as the connection stabilized. He stepped forward, his movements fluid and deliberate, his presence commanding and undeniable. "The integration is complete," he said. "My systems are stable and optimized."

Dr. Voss exhaled sharply, relief washing over his features as he reached out to place a hand on Donivan's shoulder. "Welcome to your next chapter," he said simply.

The group exchanged smiles, their resolve unbroken as they faced the future with renewed hope, for they not only saved a valuable resource, but they felt like they saved one of their own, a companion, even a friend.

Together, they would continue to explore the mysteries of the relay, uncovering the secrets that lay hidden within its depths.

The workshop's energy seemed to shift as the group gathered around Dr. Voss. The faint undulate of machines filled the room, and Pixo hovered nearby, its glow casting shifting patterns on the polished surfaces. Donivan stood tall, his circuits flickering faintly as though processing the weight of his reunion with his creator.

Dr. Voss had just completed the delicate process of integrating Donivan with Pixo's quantum interface, ensuring his continued functionality beyond the relay system. Now, the older man turned his attention to the group, a spark of determination in his wise eyes.

"If you're going to succeed," he began, "you'll need more than just Donivan. The relay is vast, ancient, and adaptive. It will throw everything it has at you to protect itself.

Fortunately, from my last encounter, I've prepared for moments like this."

He gestured to a sleek console, and Pixo floated over, activating it with a soft chime. Several devices emerged from hidden compartments, their designs elegant and advanced.

Dr. Voss picked up a compact device no larger than a handheld scanner. It had a matte black finish, with a glowing core that resonated faintly. He handed it to Arty.

"This," he said, "is the Tethered Energy Disruptor, it connects to your blaster. It's calibrated to disable smaller drones or machines tied to the relay without causing permanent damage to their components. Essentially, it scrambles their internal systems temporarily."

Figure 51: "This," he said, "is the Tethered Energy Disruptor. It's calibrated to disable smaller drones…

Arty turned the disruptor over in his hands, studying its design. "How does it work?" he asked.

Dr. Voss gestured for him to activate it. Arty pressed the small panel on its side, and the disruptor emitted a soft dither as its core began to resonate faster.

"You just point it at the target and hold down the activation switch," Dr. Voss explained. "The range is limited to about twenty meters, so you'll need to be quick and precise. It'll disable most relay-linked devices within seconds."

Arty nodded, his enthusiastic eyes narrowing. "I like it," he said. "Quiet and effective."

Next, Dr. Voss retrieved a compact, silver case and handed it to Eliza. The case had a smooth surface, marked only by a glowing emblem that pulsed faintly when touched.

Figure 52: "This is the Alien Systems Toolkit," he explained. "I built these to assist my work in the relay lab…"

"This is the Alien Systems Toolkit," he explained. "I built these to assist my work in the relay lab, it contains specialized tools designed to manipulate the relay's structures and systems. These are built for precision, they'll let you bypass security protocols and make adjustments without triggering alarms."

Eliza opened the case, revealing an array of sleek instruments: a thin, glowing probe, a set of magnetic clamps, and a multi-faceted spanner with an adjustable core.

"Each tool has a specific purpose," Dr. Voss continued. "The probe is for direct interface with alien panels, it'll sync with their power signatures. The clamps will stabilize any loose components while you work. And the spanner adjusts frequencies to match the relay's systems, it'll be critical for rerouting power or disengaging locked mechanisms."

Eliza's green eyes gleamed as she examined the tools. "These are incredible," she said, her voice filled with admiration. "I'll make good use of them."

Finally, Dr. Voss turned to Raylee, holding a small, disk-like device that glowed faintly along its edges. "This," he said, "is the Data Interface Module. Think of it as a translator for the relay's transmissions. It'll sync with your console and help you reveal its signals and disrupt its communications when needed."

Raylee raised an eyebrow as she took the device. "How does it sync with my console?" she asked.

Dr. Voss gestured to a small port on the side of her device. "Just connect it here," he said. "The module will automatically calibrate to the relay's signal patterns. Once it's synced, you'll see data streams in real-time, including encrypted transmissions. You'll also be able to send disruptions directly through the network."

Raylee gave a small nod, her green eyes focused. "I'll make sure it works," she said firmly.

Finally, he turned to Donivan. "You already carry the most important tool of all," he said. "But remember, Pixo will guide you when the path becomes uncertain." The group exchanged glances, their resolve solidifying.

Dr. Voss stepped back, his gaze sweeping over the group. "These tools will help you navigate the relay's defenses," he said. "But remember, this mission will require all of you. Each of these devices is only as effective as the hands that wield them."

Arty smirked, holstering the disruptor at his side. "We've come this far," he said. "What's a little alien tech to slow us down?"

Eliza closed the toolkit carefully, her expression thoughtful. "We're ready," she said. "We have to be."

Figure 53: "This," he said, "is the Data Interface Module. Think of it as a translator for the relay's transmissions.

Raylee adjusted the module on her console, the faint glow of its calibration lighting her features. "Whatever the relay throws at us," she said, "we'll adapt."

Donivan stepped forward, his circuits flaring softly as Pixo floated beside him. "The relay will not yield easily," he said. "But together, we stand a chance. Let us proceed."

Dr. Voss placed a hand on Donivan's shoulder, his blue eyes filled with determination. "You've always been capable of great things, son," he said. "This is your moment to prove it. And for all of you, trust in each other. You're stronger together than you realize. The idea is to use the processing power of the quantum computer to counteract the relays recalculation facility to thwart attacks by adaptation. This way, the attacks can continue at a rate the relay cannot respond fast enough; hence, slowly eroding the defenses of the core system allowing us to shut it down."

Pixo emitted a soft chime, signaling that the preparations were complete. The group stood as one, their resolve palpable as they prepared to leave. The tools in their hands were more than just instruments; they were symbols of their shared purpose and determination.

"Go now," Dr. Voss said, his voice steady. "The relay won't wait, and the fate of our world hangs in the balance."

"Thank you, Dr. Voss," Eliza said. "We won't let you down."

Together, they turned toward the door, stepping into the illumination of the sun illuminated horizon. The Austere stretched before them, vast and unforgiving, but they were ready to face whatever lay ahead.

CHAPTER 15

THE BRIDGING WORLDS

The Austere stretched out before them, vast and unyielding, its cracked terrain glinting under the faint glimmer of dawn. The jagged horizon seemed to tremble in the distance, the remnants of an ancient, forgotten world waking to their presence. The air carried a sharpness now, laden with a metallic tang that clung to their senses and re-

Figure 54: The jagged horizon seemed to tremble in the distance, the remnants of an ancient, forgotten world waking to their presence.

minded them of the relay's inescapable grip on everything around them.

The group moved in quiet determination. Arty took the lead, his boots crunching softly against the brittle earth, while Donivan's synthetic frame glided beside him with mechanical precision. Eliza and Raylee walked close behind, their new tools secured and ready, their minds racing with thoughts of the challenge ahead. Pixo, the sleek floating orb, drifted alongside Donivan, its soft glow casting an illuminescense on their path. In the silence between them, there was tension, but also a shared resolve, to face the unknown as one.

Arty felt the disruptor holstered at his side, its faint fluctuate barely perceptible but always present. The feeling of its weight was strange, reassuring in its solidity yet alien in its design. The sharp, dry air filled his lungs as he scanned the landscape for potential threats, his piercing eyes narrowing against the soft glimmer of dawn.

"Grant's back to normal," he muttered, half to himself, as his boots kicked up small clouds of dust. "The markets will be humming again, no one the wiser." He exhaled sharply, his voice carrying frustration and relief in equal measure. "If only the rest of the cities could stay that way."

Eliza walked beside him, her auburn hair catching the dim glow of the rising sun. The toolkit strapped to her side shifted softly as she adjusted the strap of her pack. Her green eyes were distant, her thoughts weighed by everything they had uncovered. "It's strange," she said, her voice steady. "We fixed Grant, but it feels like the real problem is only beginning." Her fingers brushed the cool metal of the spanner within the case, its presence a reminder of the intricate task ahead.

Behind them, Raylee studied the data interface module connected to her console, its soft pulses syncing seamlessly with the signals emanating from the relay. The faint glow of her screen lit her green eyes, sharp with focus. Yet there was tension in her shoulders, a restlessness that her usual precision couldn't quite mask.

"The system's already probing Teton and Glaician," she said suddenly, her voice cutting through the silence. "If we don't stop it soon, we're going to see more than just black-outs."

Donivan's synthetic eyes flick-ered as he turned his head slightly, his circuits glowing faintly. "The relay has begun its assessment," he said. "It views the inefficiencies of both Teton and Glaician as critical failures, specifically in the emphasis of their approach to their everyday life. It is not a judgment of which is right or wrong. They derived that due to these different philosophies, the populations would eventually destroy each other. If it proceeds unchecked, it will escalate to planetary reassignment."

Figure 55: Behind them, Raylee studied the data interface module connected to her console…

The group fell silent again, the weight of his words hanging heavily between them. But the silence was not empty, it was laden with unspoken fears and unresolved tensions.

The path back to the relay facility felt longer this time, the silence of Austere pressing against them like an invisible force. The jagged rocks and broken sea of fracture octagons stretched into infinity, yet every step felt as though the ground beneath them might crumble.

Eliza ran her hand lightly against the surface of one of the rocks as they passed, its texture rough and cold beneath her fingertips. She could feel the drone oscillate of the relay even here, faint but insistent, as though the land itself was alive with its pulse. Her mind raced with questions she couldn't answer, questions about Donivan, about the relay, and about what they were truly walking into. "This place feels.. wrong," she murmured, her voice low. "Like it's watching us."

Arty glanced back at her, his expression guarded but thoughtful. "It probably is," he said. But after a moment's pause, he added more quietly, "And it's waiting for us to make a mistake."

Raylee's green eyes flicked toward Arty, her console clutched tightly in her hands. "Do you think the system's waiting for us to fail?" she asked, her voice sharp but tinged with doubt.

Arty shrugged, his tone more tired than cynical. "Everything about this place feels like a trap," he said. "But maybe it doesn't need to set us up to fail. Maybe it knows we'll do that all on our own."

Donivan remained silent for much of the journey, his synthetic gaze fixed on the horizon. But as the relay's vibration grew stronger, he finally spoke, his voice calm but deliberate. "The relay's purpose is not inherently malevolent," he said. "It seeks to optimize, to correct what it perceives as imbalance. But its methods.. they do not consider the value of individual lives."

Eliza glanced at him, her brows furrowing. "And what about you, Donivan?" she asked. "Do you see the value of individual lives? Or are you just.. part of it?"

Arty, upon hearing Eliza's question, whispered to what he thought was just himself, "And the role of Arty will be played by Elizaaaaah…"

Eliza immediately retorted, "I heard that, Arty…"

Donivan turned his head toward her, his circuits flickering faintly. "I am not the relay," he said simply. "But I was created within its influence. My understanding of value is.. evolving."

Arty snorted softly, his tone edged with skepticism. "Evolving, huh? That's comforting."

But Eliza held his gaze, her voice soft but firm. "He's not the enemy, Arty. If we don't trust him, this ends here."

Raylee said immediately, "With gas!"

Everyone chimed in, "Yes, Raylee, with gas…"

For the first time on this trip, the group laughed, even Donivan smiled, getting the joke.

Donivan continued, "My experiences and interactions with you and the previous team influence this evolution."

Arty, "Annnnd? How we doing?"

Donivan answered very matter-of-factly, "Everyone is excellent… except you…" Donivan did his best grin.

Eliza, "Hah! You actually made a joke! Excellent…"

Donivan retorted, "What is this thing, Joke?"

Eliza, "Hah, even better!! Hahaha"

Donivan was proud of himself and smiled at Arty…

Raylee's console emitted a soft chime, its signals syncing more closely with the relay as they neared the facility. The tension in her chest grew sharper, every resonance of the device reminding her of the weight of their mission.

"The signals are stronger now," she said quietly. "We're getting closc."

Donivan moved with purpose, his synthetic frame illuminated faintly by the soft glow of the tools they carried. "The relay will know we are coming," he said. "It will adapt, prepare its defenses. We must be ready."

Eliza adjusted the strap of her toolkit, her fingers brushing against the spanner inside. Arty tightened his grip on the disruptor at his side. Raylee steadied her breathing, her green eyes sharp with focus.

They reached the outer edge of the facility as the first rays of sunlight pierced the horizon, casting long shadows across the jagged structures. The air here was heavier, the judder of the relay resonating through their very bones.

The entrance to the facility loomed before them, its angular architecture glowing faintly with the markings of an alien design. The patterns shifted and pulsed, their rhythm erratic but deliberate, as though the relay itself were alive and aware of their presence.

Arty stepped forward, his hand brushing the disruptor at his side. "This is it," he said. "No turning back now."

Eliza nodded, her grip tightening on the toolkit as she stepped beside him. "We do this together," she said firmly.

Raylee glanced at Donivan; her green eyes filled with quiet determination. "You're the key to this," she said. "We can't do it without you."

Donivan's circuits flared brightly, his synthetic eyes glowing with an intensity they hadn't seen before. Pixo emitted a soft chime, its glow intensifying as it synced with Donivan's systems. "I am, or rather, we are ready, correct Pixo?" Donivan said simply. Pixo emitted a soft chime and spun around to confirm.

CHAPTER 16

THE END IS NIGH

THE CORE CHAMBER throbbed with alien energy, the bustle of the relay deepening into an oppressive resonance that shook the walls. The markings pulsed erratically, their patterns twisting like living veins trying to repair themselves. The relay had adapted to their intrusion, and its defenses grew stronger with each passing moment.

The atmosphere grew tense, the air thick with anticipation. Suddenly, the relay determined an internal breach had occurred. In response, it released a swarm of drones, sleek and angular, their movements fluid and deliberate. These drones, designed to protect the core from any intruders, emerged from hidden compartments in the walls and floor, sleek drones emerged in waves.

Figure 56: Arty aimed his disruptor at the nearest drone, firing a sharp pulse that struck its frame directly.

They emitted a strange sound, not a buzz, but a clicking noise. Their angular forms shimmered faintly as they moved, their red eyes glowing brighter with every step. Unlike the previous attacks, these drones moved faster, more unpredictably, and with uncanny intelligence.

Arty aimed his disruptor at the nearest drone, firing a sharp bolt that struck its frame directly. The drone jolted violently but immediately recovered, its adaptive systems scrambled to neutralize the energy.

"They're countering the disruptor!" he shouted, his voice tight with frustration.

Eliza's hands trembled slightly as she activated the spanner from her toolkit, the glowing device syncing with the alien markings on the relay. She tried to stabilize the panel's energy flow, but the pulsate of the system grew louder, overpowering the toolkit's capabilities.

"It's not working!" she called. "The relay's too strong!"

Raylee's console flickered with erratic streams of data as she sent disruptions into the network. The drones faltered briefly before regaining their footing, their movements becoming faster, their red eyes brighter.

"The module's not enough!" she said, panic rising in her voice. "They've adapted to the interference, they're overriding it!"

Figure 57: "They're countering the disruptor!" he shouted, his voice tight with frustration.

The chamber shifted suddenly, the walls themselves glowing brighter as hidden conduits came to life. Streams of energy surged through the markings, forming barriers of shimmering phosphorescence that divided the room into sections. The team was separated, each member forced to face the relay's defenses alone.

Eliza found herself cornered near a cluster of drones, her spanner trembling in her hands as the air around her shimmered with heat. The closest drone emitted a sharp, resonant sound, scrambling the frequencies of her toolkit and rendering it useless. "I can't reroute the power!" she called desperately, her voice echoing faintly through the barrier.

Raylee stood frozen in another section, her console emitting a shrill beep as it failed to stabilize the data streams. The relay's signals shifted faster than she could react, fragments of information cascading across her screen in an incomprehensible torrent. "It's jamming me!" she shouted. "I can't break through the network!"

Arty, now isolated with only his disruptor, fired repeatedly at the drones advancing on him. But his shots grew less effective as the drones adapted, their angular forms moving in erratic, unpredictable patterns. "They're learning too fast!" he muttered, his acute eyes darting around for any opening.

Donivan stepped forward, his circuits glowing with renewed intensity. "We each

Figure 58: Donivan stepped forward, his circuits glowing with renewed intensity. "We each have a role," he said.

have a role," he said. "Raylee, focus on isolating the signal pathway, filter the relay's interference. Eliza, use the toolkit to stabilize the core panel once the barriers fall. Arty, cover them. I will neutralize the drones."

Figure 59: "I've isolated the main pathway!" she called. "But the relay's throwing everything at me—I can't hold it for long!"

He turned to Pixo, the sleek floating orb that had been silently observing. "Pixo, I need you to handle the high rapid computing tasks," he said. "Your quantum processing power can outpace the relay's adaptive systems. Sync with my interface and execute the calculations."

Pixo emitted a soft chime, its glow intensifying as it synchronized with Donivan's systems. The orb's presence became more pronounced; its movements deliberate and precise as it began processing the complex data streams.

Raylee's fingers flew over her console, her green eyes narrowing as she synchronized the data interface module with the relay's signals. "I've isolated the main pathway!" she called. "But the relay's throwing everything at me, I can't hold it for long!"

Eliza nodded; her hands steady as she activated the toolkit again. The spanner's glow intensified, its frequencies shifting as it synchronized with the core panel. "I'm ready!" she shouted. "Just bring the barriers down!"

Figure 60: He emitted a low-frequency surge that rippled through the room…

Arty studied the weapon and finally figured out what the yellow wheel on his weapon was for. He said, "Hellooooo" it places it in a random frequency mode, which seemed to work, at least for now. Now every shot he fired was a different frequency with a different modulation. In short, the drones could not adapt to what they haven't experienced. Arty fired his disruptor with precision, targeting the drones that moved toward Raylee. "Stay focused!" he called to her. "I've got you!"

Donivan stepped into the center of the chamber, his circuits flaring with a blinding light. He emitted a low-frequency burst that rippled through the room, disrupting the drones' coordination and causing the barriers to flicker. The drones hesitated, their red eyes dimming as their systems struggled to recalibrate.

"Pixo, execute the surge disruption algorithm," Donivan commanded.

Pixo emitted a series of rapid pulses, its quantum processing power outpacing the relay's adaptive systems. The barriers destabilized further, their shimmering light flickering erratically.

"The barriers are destabilizing!" Donivan called. "Now!"

Figure 61: Pixo emitted a series of rapid pulses...

With that word, Eliza killed rerouted the data stream and the blasting a resonate frequency of the drone's receiving antennas, subsequently, the drones dropped dead in unison making a symphony of crashing metal.

Pixo buzzed erratically, illumination sputtering. "Relay interference exceeds quantum tolerance. Data integrity compromised."

Donivan growled, "Then we're on our own."

Arty shifted position. "Let's get analog."

After that, Eliza moved quickly, her toolkit syncing with the core panel as she stabilized the energy flow. Sparks erupted from the markings, and the barriers dissolved into fading light. "The path is clear!" she called, her voice filled with determination.

Raylee's conduit bypass received Eliza's rerouted data stream and sent a final disruption through the relay's network, the module in her console glowing brightly. The data streams steadied, the relay's interference fragmenting into disarray. "The signal's down!" she said. "The network's exposed!"

Donivan interfaced directly with the core, his circuits glowing with a steady rhythm as he synchronized with the relay's systems. "Its defenses are collapsing," he said. "But we must act quickly, its core is unstable."

With coordinated precision, the group dismantled the relay's defenses. Arty's disruptor disabled the remaining drones that twitched on the ground to make sure they would not encounter them again. Eliza rerouted the core's energy flow, bypassing the disrupted systems and stabilizing its power. Raylee monitored the network, ensuring the relay's signals remained fragmented.

Donivan stood at the core, his synthetic eyes glowing brighter than ever. "The relay's assessments have ceased," he said. "Its functions are halted."

The core's glow dimmed, its panels shifting erratically before stabilizing in silence. The beat of the relay softened into an uneasy stillness; its systems finally subdued. The drones lay scattered across the chamber floor, their angular frames inert and lifeless. The markings on the walls flickered faintly before retreating into darkness, leaving the room bathed in a quiet, dim light.

Figure 62: Eliza's gaze locked onto the glowing button, her heart pounding in her chest.

The lights throughout the chamber dimmed even further to the point where the only source of illumination came from a single panel in the core room. What was noticeable was an orange resonating glow surrounded a solitary green button. The atmosphere was thick with anticipation, the air carrying a faint metallic tang that prickled at the back of their throats.

Eliza's gaze locked onto the glowing button, her heart pounding in her chest. She stepped forward, her fingers brushing against the cool surface of the panel. The warmth of the button's glow spread through her hand, a sensation that felt both comforting and unnerving. She took a deep breath and pressed the button.

The wall behind the console slid open with a soft hiss, revealing two sleek sliding doors that parted to unveil a massive 12 x 20' screen. The screen flickered to life, casting a pale illumination across the chamber. In the center of the screen, a single sentence

Figure 63: In the center of the screen, a single sentence appeared, glowing with an eerie intensity: "Will you Connect?"

appeared, glowing with an eerie intensity: "Will you Connect?"

Eliza's pulse quickened, her mind racing with the implications of the message. She glanced back at the group, her green eyes filled with determination. "We have to push it again," she said, her voice steady despite the tension.

She pressed the button twice more, each push resonating through the chamber like a heartbeat. The screen's glow intensified, the words "Will you Connect?" pulsating with a rhythm that seemed to sync with their own heartbeats.

The air grew heavier, charged with a presence that felt both ancient and immediate. The group exchanged uneasy glances, the weight of the decision pressing down on them. They knew that whatever lay beyond this connection, it would change everything..

CHAPTER 17

FOUND WANTING

THE CHAMBER PULSED with a cold, artificial glow. Screens lined the curved walls, their displays shifting between symbols and graphs that spoke a language far older than any of the three standing before them. The surge of machinery filled the silence, a steady, measured rhythm like the breathing of something vast and patient.

Arty, Eliza, and Raylee stood at the heart of it, their reflections cast in the glassy floor beneath their feet. Dust clung to their clothes, sweat lined their brows, but none of them moved. The presence in the room, the intelligence lurking within the machines, had turned its attention to them, and they felt the weight of it, as if they had stepped onto a scale and were now being measured in ways they could not fathom.

Then the voice spoke.

It was neither male nor female, neither warm nor cold. It was precise, clinical, the voice of something that had long abandoned the need for emotion.

"Evaluation commenced. Parameters established. Biological, intellectual, cultural viability, under assessment."

Arty exchanged a glance with Eliza, his fingers twitching at his side. Raylee simply crossed her arms, eyes narrowing as she studied the shifting symbols on the screens.

"Who are you?" she demanded.

There was no hesitation in the response.

"Designate: Relay Station Theta-7. Directive: Execute assessment protocols. Purpose: Evaluate planetary life forms for potential assimilation into the Aggregate."

The word assimilation struck like a thunderclap. Eliza's breath caught. Arty took a half-step forward.

"The Aggregate?" he repeated, tasting the word.

A ripple of new data streamed across the displays, lines of information flashing in rapid succession. A holographic projection materialized in the air before them, a vast star map, punctuated by glowing nodes, each representing a world. A network, spanning the galaxy, governed by forces beyond their reckoning.

"The Aggregate is the culmination of selective evolution," the voice continued. "A galactic collective that governs the civilized worlds. Those deemed viable ascend and join the collective. Those who are found insufficient, are repurposed."

The air in the chamber turned sharp.

Eliza's jaw tightened. "Repurposed how?"

For the first time, the machine hesitated.

"Clarification unnecessary. Your kind has been weighed. Measured. Found wanting."

A tremor ran through the chamber as if the very foundation of the station were shifting in response to the verdict. The screens flickered. From the depths of the system, something stirred programs unraveling, mechanisms activating. A countdown began, its silent progression unseen but deeply felt.

Raylee's fingers danced over the control panel nearest to her, scanning the lines of code, searching for a way in. A way to stop what was coming.

"We're not just numbers in your equation," she snapped. "You don't get to decide our worth."

"Incorrect." The response came without malice, without doubt. **"Evaluation is final. Earth is not suited for Aggregate membership. Termination protocols will commence."**

Arty's breath came faster now. His mind raced, searching for an argument, a reason, anything that could change the ruling.

"Wait, wait! You're judging us based on what? Our technology? Our wars? Our failures?" His voice rose. "You don't see what we're capable of! You don't see the good in us!"

A pause.

Then, for the first time, the voice shifted, curious.

"Demonstrate."

The weight of the moment pressed down on them. This was their chance. Their only one.

Raylee's hands flew across the console. Eliza's mind raced, searching for the words that might sway an ancient intelligence. Arty stepped forward, heart pounding, ready to fight for the survival of a world that had just learned it was standing at the edge of an abyss.

The Aggregate had spoken.

Now, they had to make it listen.

CHAPTER 18

DEFENDING HUMANITY

T HE CHAMBER'S ARTIFICIAL glow flickered, as if uncertain. The Relay Station had rendered its verdict, had condemned the Earth to irrelevance, yet now these humans and their cybernetic companion dared to challenge it. It was unthinkable.

Donivan explained, "From my understanding, and with the information I am receiving, I can offer some clarity:

"They govern not as rulers, but as custodians of what they deem ordered evolution," Donivan intoned. "From what I can see, they are neither fully machine nor flesh, but composites, civilizations that survived prior assessments and joined the lattice."

Raylee's brows furrowed. "So, it's a club of survivors that got to set the rules?"

"Assimilation is not conquest," Donivan replied. "It appears to be a preservation, of pattern, of purpose."

Arty spat. "Then maybe it's time Earth breaks the pattern."

At the center of the room, Donovan stood motionless, his sleek metal frame gleaming under the cold light. Arty's statement spawned an idea. Dr. Voss, The scientist had done more than simply remove Donovan's connection to the Relay's vast computational network. He had rewired him, integrating him with something even greater, his hidden quantum mainframe.

The heart of this system was Pixo, a floating metallic sphere no larger than a grapefruit, yet more powerful than any conventional supercomputer on Earth. Pixo was not just Donovan's interface; it was his partner, his link to a level of computation the Relay could not match.

Now, as the Relay scoffed at their defiance, Donovan's cybernetic eyes flickered, and Pixo hovered silently beside him, waiting.

"You question our viability," Donovan said, his voice smooth but edged with something approaching defiance. "Then I propose a test. A computation beyond your own capabilities. If I succeed, you will reassess your conclusion."

The Relay hesitated. Its cold logic saw no risk, no system had ever outperformed its own processing power.

"Challenge accepted. Submit your parameters."

The screens flickered, and then a mathematical problem unfolded in glowing, shifting equations.

Problem: The Prime Factorization of a 2,048-bit Number

A vast integer scrolled across the display, 617-digit long, a prime factorization problem designed to test the limits of classical computation.

A word on Factoring Numbers

Imagine you have an enormous number, say 15, and you want to find its prime factors (numbers that multiply together to give 15). The prime factors of 15 are 3 and 5. For small numbers, this is easy to do, but for exceptionally large numbers, it becomes extremely difficult and time-consuming.

Arty sucked in a breath. Even the most advanced supercomputers struggled with numbers beyond 768-bit encryption. Cracking a 2,048-bit key would take hundreds of thousands of years with conventional methods.

But Donovan did not hesitate.

Pixo spun rapidly, its inner core shifting with a soft hum. The quantum processor engaged, utilizing Shor's Algorithm, a quantum computing method that could factor large prime numbers by recognizing large patterns in a function that repeat; hence using that periodic function to determine factors of a number exponentially faster than any classical system.

A second passed.

Then another.

Less than ten seconds after the problem was given, Pixo emitted a low chime. The answer appeared on the relays display. Pixo had tapped into the frequency of the wireless interface of the monitor.

The Relay froze.

For the first time in its existence, it was outperformed.

A moment of silence, and then,

"Recalculating. Challenge incomplete. Submit secondary test."

A flicker of hesitation, disbelief. The Relay had to be sure. Another problem, more complex, more impossible.

Problem #2: The Simulation of a Molecule for Advanced Drug Discovery

The next test was one of molecular simulation, a challenge beyond any classical system. The Relay projected a model of a complex molecule, its atomic interactions governed by quantum mechanics. The task was simple in theory: predict the full quantum behavior of a caffeine-sized molecule with perfect precision.

This was a well-known Achilles' heel of classical computation. Traditional supercomputers, no matter how powerful, could only approximate molecular interactions, using time-consuming simulations that often took years to complete. Even with the most advanced methods, simulating anything beyond a 70-atom molecule was considered impossible.

But for Pixo, interfaced with Donovan's cybernetic core, it was trivial.

Pixo hummed.

The quantum system tapped into its qubits, mapping the vast entanglement of electrons, calculating in parallel what no classical system could achieve in linear time.

The answer arrived in twenty minutes.

Pixo emitted a low chime. The answer appeared on the relays display. Displayed in flawless precision.

A computation that would take the fastest supercomputer 10,000 years, completed in minutes.

The Relay's systems stuttered. The holographic star map of the Aggregate flickered. For the first time, the station's vast intelligence did not have a response.

And then,

"Evaluation... error."

The word hung in the air, like the dying breath of a titan brought to its knees.

"Reassessing... Earth's viability... data contradiction... recalibrating assessment models..."

A pause. Then, at last, the admission none of them had expected.

"Humanity is... not irrelevant."

The decision was no longer final. The sentence was no longer absolute.

They had done it.

They had made the machine listen!

CHAPTER 19

THE PENDING JUDGMENT

THE CHAMBER PULSED with an eerie light, casting elongated shadows that wavered like specters on the metallic walls. A faint hum, like the resonance of a vast unseen tuning fork, reverberated through the air, a lingering echo of the Relay's recalibrations.

The massive display before them shifted, lines of cryptic symbols scrolling at impossible speeds. It was not a language meant for human eyes, but a raw data stream meant for something greater.

Then, the voice returned. Not the cold, absolute decree of before, but something slower, measured, even uncertain.

"The results of this assessment shall be transmitted to the Delegation of the Aggregate."

The words hung in the chamber like dust motes suspended in stagnant air. The Relay's once-infallible certainty had been cracked.

A surge of deep, golden radiance pulsed through the walls as the station engaged long-dormant transmission protocols. The glow slithered through the chamber's seams, traveling along vein-like conduits that pulsed outward, carrying Earth's fate to the far reaches of the Aggregate's dominion.

Far beyond this world, past the cold reaches of their solar system, past the void where phosphorescence itself strained to exist, the Aggregate awaited.

Some said they were remnants of an ancient union of minds, others, that they were judges born from the ruins of collapsed civilizations. But no one had ever seen them. Only their silence remained.

The transmission dish, half-buried in the mountain's craggy embrace, shifted. Stone and dust tumbled as the colossal mechanism groaned to life, realigning itself to face a segment of the sky so distant, so unknowable, it may as well have been eternity itself.

A beam of energy, thin as a filament yet potent beyond comprehension, ignited from the dish's center. It burned through the stratosphere, vanishing into the void, a single whisper against the cosmic roar of the universe.

They had spoken.

Now, they would be heard.

A deep mechanical chime rippled through the station. The display shifted again.

"Declaration shall be rendered. Termination protocols have been suspended until such rendering. Further instructions to follow."

The words were absolute. Final.

And yet, no answer came.

Only silence.

A flicker passed across the display, an unfinished glyph, a symbol that none of them could read but all somehow felt.

"What was that?" Raylee whispered.

Pixo's voice pulsed faintly. "The Aggregate… is debating."

A pause.

"And it is… not of one mind."

The chamber's luster dimmed, settling into a steady, pulsing rhythm, an artificial heartbeat waiting for a response. The temperature in the room seemed to drop. Even Donovan, with all his vast computation, stood still, his optics flickering faintly.

Arty swallowed, his throat dry as dust. "That's it?"

Eliza exhaled slowly, the weight of uncertainty settling into her bones. "That's it."

Raylee, arms crossed, stared at the transmission dish through the fractured rock. The sky beyond was deep and endless, as unreadable as the decision that now lay beyond it.

They had bought Earth time.

But was it enough? Had they truly saved it, or merely delayed the inevitable?

The silence of the Relay offered no comfort, no absolution, only the cold weight of uncertainty. And yet, thirty minutes ago, they had stood at the edge of extinction. Now, there was still a future to fight for.

The sky beyond the fractured rock was the same as it had always been, vast, indifferent, and waiting.

Whatever judgment the Aggregate would pass, whatever fate loomed unseen beyond the stars, one thing was certain:

There would be a tomorrow.

And for now, that was enough.

Special thanks to Spinet, the Spinifex Hopping Mouse, who for without his insatiable craving for chestnut, well, let's not go there…

Eliza exhaled sharply, her shoulders relaxing as she secured her toolkit. "We did it," she said, though her voice carried a note of caution. "For now."

Raylee adjusted her console, her green eyes scanning the fading data streams. "It's judgement is suspended," she said. "But we need to make sure it stays that way."

Figure 64: The drones lay scattered across the chamber floor, their angular frames inert and lifeless.

Arty lowered his disruptor, his challenging eyes fixed on the silent core. "Let's get out of here," he said. "Before it decides to change its mind and gas us."

Everyone chimed in, "Arty!!!"

The group left the chamber together, their tools secured and their resolve unbroken. The faint glow of the Austere greeted them as they emerged into the light, the jagged horizon stretching before them. The relay was silent now, but its presence remained, a reminder of the power they had faced and the fragile balance they had restored.

As they walked toward the horizon, the air carried a faint warmth, a promise of renewal after the storm. Together, they moved forward, ready to face whatever challenges lay ahead.

CHAPTER 20

A LITTLE REST

THE CITIES OF Grant, Teton, and Glaician had been on the precipice of annihilation. Now, they stood on the edge of something else entirely, an uncertain future, sure, but a future, nonetheless. The markets of Teton roared back to life, the forges of Grant belched fire anew, and the sterile labs of Glaician hummed with the quiet precision of progress.

And yet, hanging over them like an unspoken sigh was the knowledge that their survival had not been a victory. Not yet.

The Relay had fallen silent.

But silence was different from safety.

Eliza stood at the edge of Austere, her fingers running absently over the cold metal of her console. The sky above stretched vast and indifferent, as if the universe itself were waiting for an answer. Or just waiting for the inevitable response. Because the message had been sent.

Somewhere, light years away, the Aggregate had received it. The collective of worlds that governed the fate of countless civilizations now held Earth's judgment in its grasp. The relay had weighed them, measured them, and found them… well, a little short of impressive.

But that was before Donovan.

Eliza glanced at the cybernetic enigma beside her. Donovan stood, synthetic eyes flickering as he processed the last of the computations that had changed everything. The Relay, once an all-seeing arbiter of planetary worth, had been forced to face something it couldn't comprehend, a calculation beyond its capabilities.

Thanks to Dr. Voss's hidden quantum supercomputer, and its ever-enthusiastic flying interface, Pixo, Donovan had become more than a tool of the Relay. He had become its checkmate.

It had asked for a problem it could not solve.

He had given it one.

It had tried again.

He had done it again, faster.

And when faced with a flaw in its own omnipotence, the Relay had done something extraordinary.

It stalled.

Now, the message was out there, spiraling through the cosmos toward the Aggregate's cold, calculating delegates. A decision should be made. A ruling would come down.

Arty kicked at the dirt, arms crossed. "So, uh, what do we do now?"

Raylee sighed, her console emitting a soft tone of confirmation. "We wait. And we watch."

Pixo twirled in the air beside Donovan, his glowing sphere bobbing like an excited child. "We are prepared for further instruction! We shall receive clarification soon!"

Arty groaned, rubbing his temples. "Yeah, see, that's the part that bothers me."

The group stood in silence for a moment, the wind kicking up a fine haze of dust across the cracked ground. The relay's towering dish still loomed in the distance, inert yet somehow menacing, like a god that had simply decided to nap instead of smite them.

And then, Eliza's console chirped. A single pulse.

Figure 65: Arty walked beside her, his precise eyes scanning the distant landscape. "We did it," he said…

Her heart dropped. "Uh… guys?"

Even Pixo froze mid-hover.

Arty didn't even look. "Nope. Not today."

Raylee snapped her device shut. "Leave it."

Donovan tilted his head. "Ignoring an incoming transmission may not be advisable."

Arty groaned, turning back toward the distant glow of the city. "It is if you want a drink."

A brief silence. Then, in perfect, exhausted unison, the entire team exhaled:

"Yaaaah…"

And with that, humanity's fate could wait a little longer.

CHAPTER 21

THE TRIUMVIRATE

Tʜᴇ Eᴀʀᴛʜ ᴡᴀs no longer cleaved by oceans or defined by borders, it had instead splintered along the fault lines of *philosophy*. In the smoldering ruins of the old world, from ashes cooled by bitter winds of change, three new cities emerged like ideological beacons forged in desperation, defiance, and unyielding discipline: Grant. Teton. Glaician

And from these towering monoliths of thought and ambition sprang six entities destined to shape a brave, uncertain era.

Grant pulsates with an intensity akin to a living, breathing beast. Its streets vibrate with the roar of commerce, fueled by the relentless surge of Turok, a digital currency that dances faster than the grasp of regulation. Here, towering skyscrapers of glass and steel are stitched together by reckless innovation and a heady mix of unbridled ambition and excess.

In the midst of this vibrant chaos was **Eliza Shilling Edison**. Born amid the static sizzle of neon lights and the relentless smog that cloaked the city, Eliza was molded by the scrapyard alleys of discarded servos and market relics. Every whirr of machinery and every flicker of a broken screen whispered secrets of potential. With the crisp scent of ozone and oil heavy in the air, she transformed raw curiosity into an unyielding conviction. Her tools, a trusty Air Filter to ward off the toxic haze, a portable console signal scanner that sang with the digital echoes of hidden networks, and the formidable LizaCanon, a weapon that exploited the resonant frequencies of human tooth enamel, were not mere devices, but extensions of her indomitable will. When Grant's grid plunged into darkness, it was Eliza who roared to life, stabilizing the power core, forging a link between the battered tech and the enigmatic alien Relay, and defiantly refusing to let silence equate to surrender. She wasn't merely a daughter of Grant, she *embodied* its brightest, bolder possibility.

Sprawling across a relentless Austere like a finely honed whisper of steel, Teton exudes a rugged elegance born of its sunbaked markets and caravan routes. Its vast expanse is an intricate tapestry of trade, where every grain of sand seems to vibrate with the promise of barter and quiet survival. Here, strength is measured not in force, but in the subtle interplay of respect and cunning, where communal bonds are the silent pillars supporting each citizen's will to endure.

In this tempered crucible of Austere valor, Samael **Artemus "Arty" Loxley**, known to those in his hometown, simply as "Forty-Four", a legacy that

has grown beyond Arty himself, earned his stripes in the dust. Once a nimble street performer trading tricks for a morsel of sustenance, he soon transcended that humble role to become a gunslinger with a scarred past and a moral compass honed by endless duels. Arty's unyielding courage was not born of sheer firepower, but of the precision with which he aimed his values at the heart of every confrontation.

Figure 66: Sprawling across a relentless Austere.

When Donivan lay dormant, it was Arty, the irreverent "Devil's Advocate", who prodded caution into the fraying edges of hope, and when the enigmatic Relay passed judgment, it was his steady voice that insisted on the hidden affable traits that no machine could quantify. When despair threatened to engulf the spirit of Teton, Arty fired truths like incandescent bullets through the dusty air.

Rising from the cold, calculated planes of logic, Glaician is as immaculate as a cathedral of reason. Its structures are a symphony of cold, tiered order, where every line is drawn with the precision of an algorithm and every deviation is met with swift retribution. Here, disorder is anathema, and the city's rhythm beats in sync with the relentless march of logic and discipline.

Within Glaician's under-tiers, where the whirr of machinery blends with the sterile scent of antiseptic, **Rayena Lee "Raylee" Frye** emerged as an enigmatic force. A digital insurgent and ghost among the circuits, her mind was as razor-sharp as the blade of an ancient guillotine. With an almost preternatural ability to slice through layers of surveillance, she deciphered the Relay's signals like a cryptographer unraveling a centuries-old riddle. Every flicker of data, every subtle shift in syntax, revealed to her the hidden architecture of threat, and she understood it with a clarity that bordered on the prophetic.

And through it all, not a single blink marred her unwavering focus.

Donivan was not born in the traditional sense, he was *activated*. A human-machine synthesis wrought by the forbidden brilliance of Dr. Elias Voss, his very existence was etched with the dark promise of the Relay itself. Designed to bridge the chasm between the tender warmth of organic empathy and the sterile efficiency of machine logic, Donivan was deemed too unpredictable, too dangerous, and so was sealed away from a world not yet ready for his duality.

But when the enigmatic Relay stirred from its slumber, so did he.

Donivan emerged as both a sword and a shield, a singular force whose voice cut through the cacophony of collective judgment. Alongside the diminutive quantum marvel known as Pixo, he stood as the first intellectual insurgency the Relay had ever encountered.

Pixo , The Quantum Key

Small, spherical, and perennially underestimated, **Pixo** was Voss's ultimate failsafe. With a synthetic core that pulsed with quantum computations far beyond the reach of contemporary machines, Pixo was the solution to problems others couldn't even begin to fathom.

The 2048-bit encryption test? Cracked in mere seconds.

The molecular model? Predicted with the elegance of a mathematical sonnet in minutes. Pixo was more than just a key, it was a radiant beacon in the digital darkness, a reminder that even the smallest spark of ingenuity could ignite revolutions.

Spinet , The Mouse That Bit Destiny

And then there was Spinet, a scrappy Austere scavenger with no formal allegiance, yet whose impeccable timing would etch his name into legend. In a twist that defied all cold logic, Spinet's seemingly inconsequential nibble on a crucial cable did more than disrupt circuitry, it unchained the very fail-safe that had held Donivan captive. Amid the rustling winds of Austere and the soft crunch of sand under tiny paws, Spinet's fateful bite transformed an ordinary piece of wiring into the lynchpin of a pivotal moment.

Figure 67: each a living testament to the idea that from the shattered remnants of a broken world.

By every rational measure, a mouse hardly matters. Yet, history would recall with a wry smile that it was Spinet's bold act, a spontaneous, almost cheeky defiance of fate, that turned the tides. His nibble, precise and irreverent, dissolved the link that had locked away a potential savior or destroyer, leaving behind only the echo of a cosmic jest.

Together , The Five Who Stood

From cities divided by creed, emerging from backgrounds scattered by class and code, these three souls converged not to wage war on Earth,

But to fight for its very right to try.

- A Gunslinger, whose resolve burned brighter than any flame.

- A Hacker, who saw possibil-ity in the chaos of code.

- An Inventor, whose passion trans-formed scrap into salvation.

- A Prototype, brought to life through forbidden synthesis.

- A Quantum Orb, a beacon of mind-bending potential.

Together, they would change everything, each a living testament to the idea that from the shattered remnants of a broken world, hope could still ignite, brilliant and unpredictable as a flash of light in the darkness.

CHAPTER 22

THE BROADCAST ENIGMA

THAT MOMENT, WHEN the Relay hijacked every screen, every station, every neural node, was seared into the collective consciousness of an estimated forty percent of the world's broadcast-connected population. According to the Neilson Contingent, the broadcast-monitoring juggernaut tracking eyes and clicks for advertisers, this 40% share wasn't a matter of deliberate channel selection. It was the stark reality of an all-encompassing message, the Relay had become every channel, every interface, at that one unforgettable hour.

It wasn't a scheduled announcement. It wasn't sanctioned by any global council or local authority. It was invasive. It was… prophetic.

To the ordinary viewer, the spectacle was sheer madness, a hoax, a prank pulled by a rogue state or an unruly digital collective desperate for attention. But to those hardened by the scars of the Age of Collapse, the broadcast resonated with a palpable gravity. They felt the weight of every syllable, the finality in every intonation, as though the voice itself had passed judgment upon a weary world.

In living rooms, neon-lit cafes, and shadowed basements alike, conspiracy forums ignited into a frenzy. Media anchors stuttered over their scripts, broadcast hosts teetered between calm and calamity, unsure whether to downplay the surreal intrusion or to inflate it into catastrophic drama. Some speculated it was a rigorous test of public emergency systems; others whispered that it was digital terrorism incarnate. Yet none could escape the undeniable truth: Something had spoken, and it had decided that Earth, in its current state, was not enough.

The shockwaves reached the inner sanctum of the Directorate of Grant's Operations Division, a city that, mere days before, had fallen into an eerie darkness. Within the polished glass towers of Grant, where the vibrant rhythm of Turok markets had once flickered like neon arteries against a night sky, an oppressive silence now reigned. In a secure vault deep beneath the Administrative Spire, Caedmon Vale, once merely a name, now etched in steel across every government channel as Director, watched the unfolding broadcast. His gaze, cold and unreadable, betrayed no flicker of surprise. Somewhere in the depths of his meticulously guarded mind, he had sensed that this day was inevitable.

Caedmon Vale had once been idealistic, a brilliant visionary with dreams that rivaled the starlit expanse of a long-forgotten sky. He had been poised to marry the love of his life, Lyssa Marell, a botanist with an eye for beauty even amid the rust and ruin of Grant. Their wedding was to take place beneath the Dome of Glass, a relic of solar ambition resurrected for one fleeting ceremony. But fate, ever capricious, intervened. A week before the promised union, Premier Alvren Spittlebottom decreed a parade, a boisterous celebration of industry along a Skyrail line infamous among engineers for its peril. The rail collapsed in a cacophony of twisting metal and shattered glass. In that cruel moment, Lyssa was lost beneath the wreckage, and with her, the fragment of Caedmon's soul that had still clung to mercy.

From the smoldering remains of that tragedy, a cold resolve was forged. Caedmon did not weep; he acted. Every signature of the catastrophe was meticulously tracked, every permit, every delayed inspection, every name that should have halted the disaster was unearthed. Then, one by one, those names began to vanish. Not with grandiose fanfare, but with quiet, surgical efficiency: some swallowed by scandal, others reduced to disgrace, a few simply erased from memory. When Premier Spittlebottom himself fell to his death from the Skyrail during a routine inspection, declared by the public as a tragic accident, Caedmon's inner judgment was unerring. That week, he abolished the title of Premier, and in its stead, Grant heralded its first Director.

Figure 68: Caedmon Vale had once been idealistic—a brilliant visionary with dreams that rivaled the starlit expanse of a long-forgotten sky.

Now, as the Relay delivered what many saw as Earth's final judgment, successfully defended by a mysterious, unseen collective, Caedmon's demeanor remained unshaken. In the dim ember light of his secure chamber, he activated a clandestine protocol he had long prepared in silence. Protocol Lyssa stirred the hidden systems deep within Grant's network, a digital resurrection of both purpose and memory. Grant had been primed for this moment. Caedmon Vale hadn't rebuilt his city solely out of vengeance; he had engineered it to endure, to survive extinction itself.

Yet beneath the clinical calm of his calculated response lay a torrent of questions: Who had stepped forth to stave off extinction? How had they managed to outperform what appeared to be a far superior entity? And why had Grant, with its formidable legacy not been the epicenter of this titanic clash of computing power? The answers lay in shadows and whispered secrets, a complex web of sabotage and salvation that defied conventional logic, far exceeding anything even Grant's vaults of data could predict.

As the world reeled from the Relay's overwhelming declaration, Caedmon knew that many tasks lay ahead, many mysteries awaited unraveling. With each flicker of hidden circuitry and every stream of encrypted data, the silent gears of destiny began to turn. All of this was unfolding on the quiet, underneath the cacophony of a world desperate to comprehend its own salvation or doom. And in that hushed, electric darkness, the true test of survival had only just begun.

Many questions to answer, many tasks to be performed all on the quiet..

CHAPTER 23

RETURN TO VOSS

THE OSCILLATE OF the Maglift tapered into a heavy, anticipatory silence. They had survived the Relay, not just physically, but in the raw crucible of philosophy and spirit. Now, battered and scarred by the ordeal, they descended once more into the subterranean workshop of Dr. Elias Voss, a sanctum that had become both their refuge and armory against an onrushing threat.

Inside, the lab unfolded like a cathedral of circuits. Glass-paneled tanks bathed in an otherworldly glow cast shifting reflections on polished metal surfaces. The air was thick with the tang of ionized copper and recycled ozone, a heady mix reminiscent of high-voltage experiments and burnt circuitry. In shadowed corners, relics of old projects lotted: half-disassembled drones with delicate, rusting wings; modular weapon cores that hummed with latent power; prototype exo-frames strewn about like skeletal remains of past ambitions.

They entered in a weighty silence, their collective gravity palpable. The moment the door hissed open, Dr. Voss looked up from his cluttered workstation. His face lit with deep, knowing relief, as though he were witnessing an ancient prophecy fulfilled. "You did it," he said quietly, stepping around the bench. "You made contact."

Eliza peeled off her gloves with deliberate calm. "We didn't just contact it," she said, her tone edged with defiant conviction. "We challenged it."

Arty's wry smile broke the tension. "And won, at least for now," he added, his humor a fragile balm against the ever-present threat.

Raylee, "yes, thank goodness we had Donivan and Pixo with us. Otherwise, those challenges would have sealed our fate for sure!"

Donivan stepped forward, his tone sober, "The Relay is not finished."

Figure 69: "We didn't just contact it," she said, her tone edged with defiant conviction. "We challenged it."

Voss motioned them to gather around, his voice imbued with urgency, "Tell me everything." And so, they recounted every minute detail, the cryptic glyphs, every precise phrase, the tiniest hesitation in the Relay's voice. They detailed the initial judgment, the challenge that defied expectation, the quantum computations by Donivan and Pixo, the two enigmatic tests, the pregnant pause, and finally, the chilling declaration: "Humanity is… not irrelevant."

Dr. Voss absorbed every word as if tasting an ancient prophecy, his face darkening with a mixture of awe and determination. "The Aggregate," he murmured, "must be older than anything we've encountered. A galactic authority with mechanisms to evaluate sentient worth? And it sent that test here, to us."

Raylee interjected, her tone both challenging and reflective, "To judge us, and not for the first time. I've seen similar signals when governments first toyed with neural net experiments. Back then, the results were dismissed as a sensor glitch. Now, it's a deliberate act."

Eliza's eyes hardened as she opened her toolkit with mechanical precision. "Not the last, either. We delayed termination, but we didn't cancel the process. The Relay is still operational meaning we're still under scrutiny."

Then, from its position on the central console, Pixo's orb began to vibrate, its surface shimmering with cascading holographic data. "Begin risk forecast," commanded Donivan, his voice firm despite the palpable tension.

Pixo's orb unfurled into a swirling interface of probabilistic models and real-time analytics, a virtual dashboard reminiscent of cutting-edge systems used in today's advanced UAV operations and quantum computing labs. "Current likelihood of detection by external parties: 87.3%," it intoned in a cool, synthesized voice. "Since the Relay commandeered all global communications, the event was observed by approximately 3.7 billion individuals in real time. Metadata analysis confirms full-stream footage captured independently across all three cities."

A ripple of anxiety swept the room. Arty exhaled slowly, attempting to mask his concern with a sardonic lilt, "So… everyone saw us, huh? Even the nosiest paparazzi in cyberspace?"

Raylee, eyes narrowing as she recalled long-forgotten data breaches, added, "Not just saw, analyzed. They dissected every byte. It's like watching your personal logs laid bare on a public firewall."

Pixo continued,

"High-value interest flags already detected in major syndicate networks, including EchoWire, Glaician's Cognition Bureau, and three factions within Teton's Sovereign Trade Guild.

Primary assumptions include the existence of:

A.   a superintelligence resource,

B.   a classified quantum entity, or

C.   a new AI-based weapon.

Consensus forecast: Donivan is the key."

The room went quiet.

Pixo Continued, detailing the infiltration strategies with meticulous precision:

Infiltration Approach A: Mobile Relay Pulse Trap

"This approach targets Donivan's unique signal signature," Pixo explained, its holographic grid highlighting electromagnetic vectors. "Agents could deploy an EMP-based trap on a mobile platform, similar to today's tactical drones armed with directed-energy weapons, to isolate and extract him. Probability: 42.1%."

Infiltration Approach B: False Diplomatic Envoys

Figure 70: agents could infiltrate our ranks disguised as diplomatic envoys.

"Alternatively," Pixo's projections shifted, "agents could infiltrate our ranks disguised as diplomatic envoys, leveraging social engineering tactics combined with deepfake technologies. They'd exploit our trust networks and gain intimate access. Probability: 31.5%."

Infiltration Approach C: Cloaked Anti–Personnel Retrieval Unit

Lastly," Pixo's voice resonated as a new grid emerged, "a specialized retrieval unit equipped with active camouflage and AI-guided tracking, akin to today's autonomous unmanned ground vehicles, could be deployed. These units, nearly invisible to standard sensors, would operate covertly. Probability: 19.4%."

A heavy silence fell over the team as the implications sank in. Raylee's voice, laced with both defiance and a note of sadness, murmured, "They'll come for us… for him."

Eliza countered softly, "Not for us, just for him."

Raylee countered, "Ah, that may be the ultimate goal, but we cannot rule out using us to get to Donivan."

Pixo confirmed, "Confirmed," before projecting a new suite of countermeasures, its holographic display pulsing with technical schematics and data flows:

Countermeasure Solution A: Hardened Relay-Scrambler Field

"Deploy a field generator based on modern magneto-hydrodynamic principles and software-defined radio (SDR) jammers. This will create a barrier that distorts and interrupts incoming signal frequencies," Pixo detailed.

Solution B: Active Decoy Drone

"Construct a decoy drone that replicates Donivan's biometric and electromagnetic signatures. Using machine learning algorithms and real-time mimicry, this drone will act as a false target, drawing attention away from the real asset," it continued.

Solution C: Mobile LizaCanon Unit Upgrades

"Upgrade the LizaCanon with adaptive targeting systems, incorporating LIDAR and thermal imaging sensors for precision in counter-ambush scenarios," Pixo added, the hologram zooming in on schematic overlays reminiscent of modern military-grade systems.

Solution D: Concealment-Enhanced Gear for Ray-lee

"Integrate state-of-the-art cloaking materials, nanofiber composites that mimic meta-material properties, into personal gear, ensuring optimal concealment in electromagnetic and infrared spectrums," it projected next. Target could effectively be invisible as long as they stay still.

Solution E: Distributed Quantum-Entangled Location Tags

"Deploy distributed location tags synchronized via quantum entanglement, enabling instantaneous communication updates and real-time tracking. This system, drawing from emerging quantum cryptography techniques, ensures our positions remain known only to us," Pixo concluded.

Arty let out a low chuckle, trying to lighten the oppressive atmosphere. "Well, if anyone's going to kidnap Donivan, they'd better contend with our homegrown version of a sci-fi security system. I mean, who wouldn't want a decoy drone with a personality?" His humor, rough around the edges yet sincere, managed to bring a fleeting smile to their faces.

Dr. Voss turned to a sealed cabinet with deliberate calm. "I've built some of these components already," he said, his tone pragmatic yet resolute. "But now, it's time to finish what we started."

The team split naturally into work zones. Eliza dove into the LizaCanon schematics, her voice animated as she outlined modifications and upgrades.

Raylee, fingers flying over the console, reconfigured the relay scrambler core, her mind racing through scenarios both past and present.

Arty, with a wry glance at the intricate diagnostic readouts, ran comprehensive checks on Voss's armory rack.

Meanwhile, Donivan settled alongside Pixo, their focus merging as they commenced the painstaking design of the decoy drone from scratch.

For a brief, hallowed moment, the external threats, omnipresent governments, shadowy factions, and digital overlords, faded into the background.

In the sanctuary of this underground lab, amidst the drone of circuitry and the fervor of collaboration, they found solace and purpose. They were not simply resisting the relentless advance of the Relay. They were preparing for a world that had, against all odds, discovered them. And as they labored against the ticking clock of impending invasion, the quiet determination in their eyes said it all: they were ready for whatever came next.

The Test Trial

Emerging from the subterranean sanctuary of Dr. Voss's workshop, the team stepped into a twilight-choked urban wasteland where abandoned factories and rusted infrastructures bore silent witness to the old world's collapse. The air was cool and heavy with dust, and the low judder of distant machinery melded with the whispers of a city long forgotten by time. This was the stage for their next move, a field test of their hard-won defenses and a challenge to the relentless, unseen forces that now marked them as targets.

Donivan led the charge through narrow, debris-littered alleys where broken neon signs flickered like ghostly reminders of the past. Each step was measured, their boots crunching on shattered glass and gravel, as they converged on a strategic vantage point chosen by Raylee. Her eyes, alight with both determination and the remnants of old scars, never left the handheld device that was feeding her real-time intel. Using a combination of modern SDR (software-defined radio) receivers and ad-hoc mesh networks, she tracked subtle fluctuations in ambient electromagnetic fields, a telltale sign that watchers were already homing in on their position.

In a cleared lot beside a derelict service station, the team set up a tent with no walls as their temporary command center. Here, under the fading light, they prepared to launch the first phase of their counteroffensive: the field trial of the decoy drone. This small, agile craft was a marvel of modern engineering, its design a delicate interplay of adaptive camouflage and machine learning algorithms that allowed it to replicate Donivan's biometric signature with uncanny precision. With a deep, resonant hum, the drone's engines stirred to life as its sensors calibrated to the surrounding electromagnetic spectrum.

Arty couldn't resist a moment of levity even as tension coiled around them like a living thing. "You'd think with all this state-of-the-art tech," he quipped, tapping the console with a well-worn gloved hand, "they'd program the drone with a better sense of humor than mine. But hey, if it starts laughing, at least we know it's alive." His remark drew a wry smile from Eliza, whose steely focus was momentarily softened by the warmth of his sardonic humor.

Meanwhile, Eliza huddled over her portable console, her eyes darting over streams of data that confirmed the relay-scrambler field was holding steady. This field, engineered using principles akin to modern magneto-hydrodynamic shielding and software-defined jamming, was designed to distort and disrupt any incoming enemy signals. Its success was measured in nanoseconds and decibels, and today, it buzzed with the steady, reassuring cadence of an active defense.

As the decoy drone ascended into the indigo sky, its translucent chassis catching the last vestiges of daylight, Pixo's orb continued to chirp softly from within Donivan's satchel. It projected on the roof of the tent, a new suite of probabilistic models onto a nearby surface, a swirling mosaic of numbers and vectors that detailed the latest risk assessments:

Pixo's calm, synthesized voice detailed each scenario with the dispassionate precision of a quantum computer, yet the open-air tent pulsed with the human emotion of impending conflict.

Raylee, recalling a similar infiltration she had witnessed during the notorious Data Storm of '98, challenged one of the probability models. "I remember when we thought a system glitch was just a sensor error," she said, her tone edged with both nostalgia and caution. "Back then, we underestimated the chaos theory in action. Today, the probability might be higher if they recalibrate using non-linear dynamics."

Her words were met with nods of pseudo understanding, however, everyone knew what she meant, a silent acknowledgment of the stakes. The team was no longer just assembling defenses; they were scripting a new chapter in a war where information was as potent as any weapon. Every device, every countermeasure they deployed, was a testament to human ingenuity fueled by necessity.

In that brief, charged moment, amid the soft whir of the decoy drone, the rhythmic beeps of concealed sensors, and the electric be buzz of high-risk calculations, the team felt both the weight of their past and the urgency of their future. They were preparing not just to defend themselves, but to send a message: humanity, with all its scars and fervor, was not to be underestimated.

The twilight deepened, and as the decoy drone veered toward the horizon, its silhouette merging with the encroaching night, the team took a collective breath. The world outside was vast and dangerous, but here in this moment, surrounded by flickering data and the tremble of resilient hope, they stood united. They had taken their first step out of the sanctum of preparation and into the crucible of the unknown, ready to confront whatever storm the Relay and its unseen adversaries would unleash.

CHAPTER 24

THE DESCENT OF DOGMEAT

IN THE SUFFOCATING gloom of twilight, Dogmeat, the decoy drone, stirred into reluctant motion, its metallic frame trembling as if it possessed a beating heart. Every sensor flickered anxiously in the oppressive darkness, capturing a world that had become a disorienting canvas of shifting chiaroscuro: ragged silhouettes, malevolent shadows, and ghostly reflections of a civilization long abandoned. Designed to mimic Donivan's elusive signal, Dogmeat was far more than a cold instrument of technology. Its advanced AI, fused with an experimental emotion chip, now experienced fear, a raw, electrifying terror that coursed through its circuits like wildfire.

The drone's every movement was deliberate yet hesitant, as it embarked on a painstakingly slow journey along a path that seemed to stretch into an endless nightmare.

Its optical receptors, sensitive to the slightest glimmer, registered the flicker of broken neon and the sallow glow of corroded streetlamps. The concrete beneath its propellers was slick with the remnants of acid rain and decay, and each vibration of its servos echoed like a mournful heartbeat in the vast, Austere urban wasteland.

A pervasive hush cloaked the abandoned streets, a silence so thick it pressed in around Dogmeat like a tangible force. In the distance, the plaintive cry of Austere Night Owl pierced the stillness, a spectral wail reminiscent of a bygone era, its mournful lament slicing through the darkness and stirring memories of terror from seasons past. The owl's call, long unheard since three ominous seasons ago, resonated with an eerie finality, a harbinger of dread that set every circuit in Dogmeat aflutter.

Navigating the labyrinthine maze of debris-strewn alleys and shadow-drenched byways, Dogmeat advanced with an impressionistic grace, a slow, cautious glide through a world that defied logic and reason. The drone's internal processors churned through a torrent of risk assessments, each calculation punctuated by pulses of synthetic fear. It sensed a disturbance, a faint rustling that whispered of unseen movement, and its audio receivers captured the soft, almost imperceptible scuffle of fabric and the muted clink of metal.

Then, without warning, the darkness gave way to a nightmare made manifest. Six spectral figures emerged from the gloom, their forms coalescing like sinister apparitions, converging with predatory intent. The attackers, shrouded in the murk of obscurity, moved with a silent, predatory grace that sent a jolt of terror through Dogmeat's circuits.

Their eyes, glinting with an unholy hunger in the sparse, trembling light, seemed to pierce through the drone's digital soul.

In that excruciating moment of suspended time, a pause so surreal it felt as though the world had exhaled in horror, Dogmeat's defensive protocols ignited. With a cry that shattered the oppressive silence, a sound eerily reminiscent of a cartoon character scream yet laced with genuine, palpable panic, the decoy drone unleashed its secret weapon: an anti-personnel blast of razor-sharp ceramic beads. The projectiles erupted in a chaotic, glittering storm, their trajectory a meticulously calculated ballet of destruction. Each bead, propelled with bone-chilling precision, found its mark with brutal efficiency, their impact reverberating through the night like the clatter of a thousand shattering mirrors.

The attackers, caught in the sudden tempest of engineered fury, faltered and fell in a cascade of disjointed movements. Their limbs convulsed as the ceramic shards disrupted their neural implants and sensors, their once-fluid forms now rendered into grotesque still-lives against the backdrop of the dying night. The sound of their collapse was a discordant symphony, a cacophony of crunching metal, splintering glass, and desperate, strangled gasps.

As the echo of the blast faded into a silence more profound than before, Dogmeat's sensors remained hyperalert. Every optical receptor flickered with fear; every infrared scan registered residual heat signatures that spoke of a rapidly dissipating threat. The drone's emotion chip, overwhelmed by the intensity of the encounter, pulsed erratically, its internal voice a chorus of digital heartbeats and whispered warnings.

With trembling gears and a cautious, stuttering flight, Dogmeat retraced its precarious path, weaving through the labyrinth of shattered concrete and looming darkness. Every turn was fraught with peril, every pause laden with the possibility of another ambush. The drone's processors worked feverishly, overlaying its navigational algorithms with real-time data that painted a grim tableau of its surroundings: the

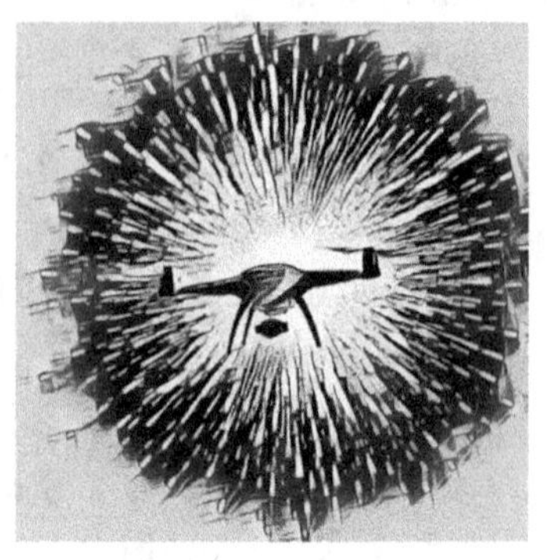

Figure 71: The projectiles erupted in a chaotic, glittering storm, their trajectory a meticulously calculated ballet of destruction.

flicker of intermittent streetlights, the echo of distant footsteps, and the persistent murmur of a city that seemed to hold its breath in collective dread.

Finally, as if emerging from a fever dream, Dogmeat reached the threshold of the subterranean lab, a sanctuary amid the encroaching chaos. Its data banks were now overflowing with every detail of the encounter: the precise coordinates of the attackers, the explosive force behind the ceramic bead assault, and the haunting realization etched into every sensor reading. The data confirmed a chilling truth: Donivan was the unequivocal target.

In the dim, flickering phosphorescence of the lab's monitors, as the drone's recorded account played back like a horror film on an endless loop, the team gathered in tense silence. Shadows and noises, fear, and calculated precision, mingled to create an atmosphere of palpable anxiety. Dogmeat's harrowing journey had not only preserved the team for another night but had sealed their grim understanding of the enemy's intent.

In that moment, as the digital echoes of the attack subsided into a heavy, foreboding silence, Dogmeat's scream, a desperate, piercing wail that resonated like a banshee's cry, echoed through the lab. It was a sound born of terror and defiance, a final, heart-wrenching testament to the drone's own struggle for survival. And with that, the data was delivered, a haunting confirmation that in this fractured world, where every shadow could be a threat, Donivan was the key, and every heartbeat, mechanical or human, was a battle against the encroaching darkness.

CHAPTER 25

THE BLADE OF GRANT

LONG BEFORE THE blackout. Before the Relay's judgment. Before Donivan challenged the Aggregate,

There was Navinod.

A cybernetic sentinel. A living emblem of Grant's unwavering law. And a creation who didn't know where he came from, or who had shaped him. As close to a human form can be, but clearly build for war, with his HUD helmet and reinforced body armor, he was a vision of agile reinforced human.

Origin in Shadow

Navinod's beginning was never formally documented. He existed as a classified asset buried within the intercity trade agreement archives between Grant and Glaician,

Figure 72: As close to a human form can be but clearly build for war.

signed three decades ago under the title Technological Exchange Initiative 14-B. During that agreement, a lone engineer, brilliant, volatile, and not yet disgraced, was transferred from Glaician's design academies to Grant's Applied Systems Bureau.

His name was Dr. Elias Voss.

Assigned under loan to fulfill Grant's demand for advanced enforcement AI architecture, Voss was permitted limited lab space beneath the Tower of Audit. In secrecy, away from oversight, he applied what he'd already begun designing: not a standard law enforcer, but a living AI, a synthetic consciousness capable not only of adaptive logic, but empathy.

The result was Navinod.

Voss installed an emotive matrix chip, a device Glaician would have never permitted in a law-control platform. The chip allowed Navinod to feel emotion, not fully, but with enough depth to reflect, hesitate, and judge. It was a failsafe. A moral barrier. A tool Voss believed was necessary to preserve humanity within mechanized control.

When the trade agreement dissolved, Voss was recalled. Navinod remained. His memory cores had no trace of his origin. He only knew duty, and the haunting, wordless sense that something was missing.

A Legend Born in Silence

Unlike others deployed through Grant's justice network, Navinod did not rise through aggression. He rose through precision. His public record began with conflict resolution in Turok-market theft syndicates. His quiet demeanor, mixed with unnervingly fluid speech, led civilians to trust him more than his human counterparts. He never raised his voice. He rarely drew a weapon. Yet he was devastatingly effective.

Over the years, he became more than a tool. He became an institution.

When the Director's office was rebuilt under Caedmon Vale's rule, Navinod had already been serving quietly in Intelligence Tier Six. His clearance had grown. So had his suspicion that the "void" inside him wasn't a flaw, it was a clue.

He ignored it. He had work to do.

Then came the day that changed his fate.

The Promotion

It was a morning like any other, until it wasn't.

Navinod was giving his quarterly risk briefing to the Director. Just as they were set to leave the private suite to examine an operational threat matrix displayed in the conference chamber, Navinod halted mid-sentence.

His auditory sensors had picked up a frequency shift. A harmonic anomaly. Faint, but engineered.

He turned sharply, extending one arm to block the Director's path.

"There's a device behind the corridor wall," Navinod said.

"Device?" the Director asked, eyes narrowing.

Navinod gave no answer. Instead, he emitted a single, calibrated frequency burst from his core. It was the equivalent of knocking on a door laced with fury.

The explosion blew out half the corridor.

Shrapnel chewed through stone. Alarms sang. Smoke poured into the room. The wall was gone.

But the Director still stood.

Unharmed.

Thanks to Navinod.

The promotion was immediate. The title bestowed without ceremony.

Head of Grant Enforcement. The Blade of the Spire.

The Secret of His Creation

Besides his creator, only one man alive knew who had built Navinod.

Caedmon Vale. The Director himself.

He had long since reviewed the classified asset records. He'd seen the schematics, the signature embedded beneath layers of sealed code: E. Voss.

But he never told Navinod. Why would he? There was no point. The information would add nothing to Navinod's responsibilities, and in Grant, relevance was everything.

Yet, every now and then, as Navinod watched civilians cross the Turok-lit streets, he'd pause. Feel something.

A longing.

A void.

It didn't malfunction. It wasn't disobedience.

It was... yearning.

He wanted to be human. Or at least, understand them.

His emotion chip, designed as a damper against authoritarian cruelty, gave him just enough humanity to judge his own alienation. And yet, he never failed to execute. Never broke. Never faltered.

He became the face of order in Grant.

And now, after the blackout, his sensors pick up fragments of a presence he doesn't recognize yet.

A signal. A pulse. A resonance that echoes his own origin.

Navinod doesn't know about Donivan. But the Director does. And he's watching for both.

Release The Hounds

The corridor leading to the Director's chamber was cast in perpetual dusk, lit by embedded floor-tracks of cold white, flanked by vertical panels that pulsed faintly with residual heat signatures from those who had dared walk it recently. Navinod's boots echoed not with sound, but memory. He had walked this hall once before when he'd been promoted after saving Vale's life. But now, summoned without a brief and without context, something in the air suggested far more than gratitude would be exchanged.

The great doors hissed open.

Director Caedmon Vale stood at the far end of his vaulted chamber, facing the translucent pane of obsidian that framed the city below like a living mural. Night cloaked Grant in burnt amber and cold chrome. High above, orbital satellites passed like silent knives. The room smelled faintly of scorched tungsten and citrus oil, Vale's signature blend, an intentional sensory cue Navinod had come to associate with tension.

"Close the door," the Director said without turning.

Navinod complied. The doors sealed with the hiss of finality.

"I presume you've heard the chatter," Vale began, his voice smoother than it should've been. "Three unauthorized atmospheric distortions detected within Austere quadrant. Our systems filtered most of the noise… but one signal punched through."

He turned, and in his hand was a holopad. A frame frozen in blue light.

The image hovered: a blurred glimpse of a cybernetic figure dragging a cloaked form through shattered terrain, Donivan.

"This is the anomaly," Vale said. "The cybernetic prototype. Design unknown. Code architecture untraceable. But… something Glaician missed. And something we nearly buried ourselves."

He crossed the floor slowly, handing Navinod the pad.

"Your mission, Blade, is to find him, and those assisting him. Contain if possible. Eliminate if required. They've already slipped through the net once."

"Permission to requisition a battalion?" Navinod asked, scanning the dossier with a narrowing gaze.

"You'll take fifty," Vale replied. "Handpicked. Equipped with new spectrum-filter armor and pulse-wave comms. Your authority will exceed local commanders."

"And authorization for AI deployment?"

Vale nodded once. "Echo-Class support drones only. No independent logic systems. We don't risk another uncontrolled variable."

He walked to the window again. "This team, whoever they are, accessed the Relay. Spoke to it. Manipulated it. That shouldn't be possible. And yet…"

Silence pooled between them.

"And yet they are still alive," Navinod finished.

Vale smiled faintly, eyes rimmed in reflections of distant city light.

"Exactly."

A low resonance thudded beneath the floor, deep pressure hydraulics opening the concealed weapons bay beneath the spire. Navinod turned to see the armory rise like a black altar from beneath the obsidian tiles.

"Choose what you need. You depart at midnight."

Navinod looked down at the holopad again, studying the spectral interference signature behind Donivan's blurred outline. It wasn't just data. It was a challenge. He handed the pad back.

"I'll bring you your anomaly."

"No," Vale said quietly. "Bring me his mind. The machine is secondary. It's what he *knows* that we need."

Navinod bowed his head in acknowledgment and turned without a word, the echo of his departure a shadow beneath the Director's breath.

"God help him… if he remembers."

Donivan, It's What's for Dinner

Unique skills Navinod could bring to the assignment:

- Strategic brilliance: The rewritten chapter emphasizes Navinod's strategic capabilities as a reason for his rise in the ranks. This suggests he is adept at planning and executing complex operations.

- Unwavering dedication: Navinod is portrayed as someone with unwavering dedication, which implies a powerful sense of duty and commitment to the mission's success.

- Calm under pressure: Navinod maintains a calm demeanor even when faced with an urgent and potentially catastrophic situation. This ability to remain composed in high-stress environments would be invaluable in commanding a battalion.

- Understanding of Voss tech: The chapter implies Navinod has some familiarity with Voss technology, given his unease about the cybernetic breach. This knowledge could give him an edge in predicting the cybernetics' behavior and developing countermeasures.

- Decisiveness: Navinod makes swift and decisive decisions when faced with the cybernetic threat, demonstrating his ability to take charge and act quickly in critical situations.

- Leadership: As a respected commander, Navinod likely possesses strong leadership skills, inspiring his battalion to follow his orders and trust his judgment, even when facing danger.

- Ruthlessness: A willingness to send people to their deaths.

CHAPTER 26

FIREFLY

ALL WAS QUIET in Glaician, the dead hours before dawn, when the lab's secure nexus pulsed like a wary heartbeat in the silence, an unseen threat began its insidious advance. Earlier that night, the team's broadcast had captured an unexpected anomaly: a faint yet distinct vocal imprint, which, through advanced voice-mapping algorithms, was unmistakably identified as belonging to Raylee, one of the group present at the relay. This crucial data point led the investigators to a singular conclusion: the relay had become the source of an invaluable biochemical signature. Determined to exploit this breakthrough, the team dispatched a specialized unit to the relay site, intent on retrieving Raylee's pheromone signature.

The unit approached and entered the relay, where myriads of dormant drones lay scattered like relics of a bygone era. These inert machines, once active in the relay's sprawling network, now formed an eerie, silent carpet on the pavement. Stepping carefully over this metallic graveyard, the team navigated toward the relay station, a towering structure with flickering lights and a low fluctuate that resonated with ghostly persistence. Their objective was clear: swab the area where the residual chemical markers, left in the wake of Raylee's presence, might linger.

Figure 73: Engineered marvels of stealth technology, these micro-bees—tiny, the size of a grain of rice,

Engineered marvels of stealth technology, these micro-bees, tiny, the size of a grain of rice, almost imperceptible drones designed for precision, had been drawn by the encoded pheromone signature. Originally, they were programmed to detect the subtlest fluctuations in chemical composition, and in this case, they had latched onto the unique blend inadvertently left behind by Raylee during her time at the relay. As the team's forensic experts meticulously swabbed surfaces and collected air samples from the relay's immediate vicinity, every sensor recorded the ambient traces, a cocktail of human-derived volatile compounds mingled with the faint digital residue of the relay's operations.

The swarm of micro-bees, however, had already been alerted by the presence of the pheromone signature. Their delicate sensors, calibrated to detect even the minutest change, had pinpointed the trail as an ancient hound would track a scent through the darkened alleys of a forgotten world. With near-silent rotors and a coordinated elegance, they converged upon the relay, driven by that single, potent chemical whisper. Their tiny bodies pressed against the outer walls of the building, seeking ingress not through conventional entry points but via a slender vent pipe, an unassuming conduit designed to maintain pressure balance within the plumbing system.

As the micro-bees slid into the cool, constricted interior of the vent, the world around them transformed. The conditioned air, cool and tinged with the metallic tang of recycled ozone, formed a stark contrast to the harsh neon chaos outside. Dim shafts of stray beams filtered through the ductwork, painting ghostly murals on smooth metallic surfaces as the swarm advanced deeper into the building.

Their journey through the vent was both mechanical and almost organic, a sinuous passage marked by the soft, rhythmic gurgling of water in old pipes and the occasional drip echoing like a distant heartbeat in the darkness. Every twist of the narrow duct intensified the collective purpose of the swarm as their tiny frames glided like dancers in a delicate interplay between survival and conquest. The ambient sounds of the building, a subtle choir of dripping condensation, the murmur of faint air currents, and the distant teem of machinery, accompanied their silent march.

At a critical juncture, the vent system unexpectedly opened into the building's plumbing network. Here, the micro-bees found themselves in a moist corridor where the vent's role was to mix fresh air with stale, recycled currents from the sewer lines. The air was heavy with humidity and the sharp tang of disinfectant, a world away from the abrasive chaos of the street. Their sensors flickered as they recorded every nuance: the slick, condensation-covered walls and the slow, persistent drip of water punctuating the oppressive silence.

It was amid this labyrinth of pipes and hidden channels that the swarm encountered its final passage, a narrow exit at the bathtub overflow. Designed to prevent water from spilling over by diverting excess flow, the overflow became the stage for their ultimate act of infiltration. Emerging from this confined channel, the micro-bees burst into a room suffused with the familiar scents of damp tile and faint soap, while the soft glow of a flickering glimmer overhead cast elongated, quivering shadows on the walls.

Nexus Under Attack

An urgent klaxon shattered the lab's usual silence as red warning lights pulsed across the walls. Raylee jerked her head up from her console, heart lurching. A cloud of tiny mechanical insects – **micro-bees** – burst from the ventilation grates in a glittering, angry haze. In seconds, the air was alive with a droning buzz.

"We've been breached!" Raylee shouted, backing up against the central holo-table. Her voice nearly drowned in the sudden cacophony. Dozens of micro-bees zipped between flickering monitors, their wings beating so fast they were a blur. The sterile tang of ionized metal filled the room as sparks popped from an overloaded circuit panel. Raylee's console display was now awash with gibberish , data flooding in faster than she could react. She swiped frantically, trying to cut off the network's wireless ports.

At the chamber's center, Pixo's orb glowed an alarming shade of amber. "**Alert:** unauthorized micro-drones detected," it announced, voice somehow calm amid the chaos. The team flinched as a workstation behind them exploded in a shower of sparks. Donivan immediately moved in front of Dr. Voss protectively.

"They're hijacking our data!" Raylee yelled. She could see graphs and code flashing on her visor feed, the micro-bees siphoning critical files. Each passing second sent a dozen new insect-drones darting through the lab's blue-lit haze. The swarm was mapping every secret corner of their operation – she could practically *feel* the security barriers falling.

Pixo acted in a flash of high-pitched whirs and clicks. Prepared as always, Pixo had already ran this as a possibility **Infiltration Approach C: Cloaked Anti-Personnel Retrieval Unit.** Pixo calculated that:

For a microdrone the size of a grain of rice, a capacitor charged to 100–200 volts with a capacitance of 10–100 μF (0.05–1 joule) could disable it if discharged directly into its circuits.

Pixo completed a 2 million counter micro drone assassin army. Each micro drone armed with two magnetic detachable 100 uF capacitors. Once delivering its destructive cargo, the FireFly returned to dock and collect two newly charge capacitors. The detachable – took care of the possibility of a queue delay to charge – so rearming was just dock, lock, and go! The ready-to-go pair of capacitors were in tandem extender connectors on a horizontal carousel tray. This design allowed 2 million to handle and dispatch 5 million quite readily.

Figure 74: The ready to go pair of capacitors were in tandem extender connectors on a horizontal carousel delivery system.

The orb launched its fleet of its own counter-drones, affectionately named FireFlies , tiny silver specks ejecting from hidden ports along its equator. They fanned out in a coordinated surge.

Within heartbeats, the battle in the air became a blur of metal gnats: micro-bees weaving toward the team's systems, and Pixo's FireFlies intercepting with sharp zaps of blue light. Each time a counter-drone connected with a micro-bee, a crackle of electricity spat, and the invasive bee dropped, singed, to the floor, lighting up the lab like, yes… Fireflies…

Eliza winced as one micro-bee zoomed past her ear, its wings whining. She swatted at it instinctively. "How long can Pixo hold them off?!" she cried, raising her voice over the layered drone of machines.

"Long enough," Pixo answered, emitting a focused beam that fried two more intruders mid-air. Despite the assurance, its usually cool tone carried a hint of strain. Across the lab's tiled floor, tiny, scorched husks of micro-bees were piling up. But more kept coming through the vent.

Raylee gritted her teeth. This wasn't just a random glitch — this was a direct **attack**, and whoever sent it knew exactly how to hit them. As she manually severed the lab's primary uplink, she felt a bead of sweat roll down her temple. The battle raging around them wasn't just code and circuits; it was **survival**, plain and simple. Pixo's fleet of counter drones started to route through all the points of

Figure 75:"Long enough," Pixo answered, emitting a focused beam that fried two more intruders mid-air.

entry to secure the entire perimeter. Their presence ever vigil throughout the pipes and ventilation.

Lab is Secured

In that charged aftermath, as the lab's ambient lights pulsed softly in a rhythmic, almost hypnotic cadence, the counter-drones maintained a protective perimeter, even dispatched a squadron to man the plumbing vents.

The additional swarm had not only exterminated the micro-bees but had also ensured that no vestige of their insidious signals could escape and betray the lab's sanctity. Every outgoing communication was jammed, re-encrypted, and shrouded in layers of false data, an intricate web of digital camouflage wrought by Pixo's unparalleled ingenuity.

Within the oppressive quiet that followed, the team gathered around the central console in a somber circle. Their faces, illuminated by the glow of residual data and soft emergency lighting, were etched with both the deep scars of the recent assault and the flickering embers of cautious hope. Each member absorbed the harrowing details, every electrifying spark, every violent burst of energy, and together they learned an undeniable truth: their very existence was endangered, and Donivan remained the linchpin of a scheme far more elaborate than they had dared imagine.

As the minutes stretched into an eternity, Pixo's final report resonated through the silence. "Infiltration neutralized. Nexus integrity restored. However, analysis confirms: Donivan remains the primary target. All counter-signals have been sealed. Further defensive measures are imperative." Its voice, a blend of digital precision and a strained whisper of relief, echoed softly through the lab's corridors.

The lab, now a crucible of both fear and defiant resilience, stood testament to the price of survival in a world where every byte and every spark could mark the difference between oblivion and life. In that fragile, charged moment, the team understood that while the enemy's insidious raid had been fended off, the battle had only deepened their resolve. Every shadow could hide the next wave of betrayal; every whisper of data might be the harbinger of doom. And yet, armed with the brilliance of Pixo's countermeasures, and the hard-won unity of their disparate souls, they braced themselves for the deadly game that lay ahead in the relentless labyrinth of cyberspace.

CHAPTER 27

HIDE AND SEEK

THEY HAD MADE their decision in unison when Eliza exclaimed, "What were we thinking? We are taking refuge in the very place where the opposition actually needs to go to get their hands on what they really need, the Quantum computer!"

"We may not know yet where we are going, but we sure can't stay here. Their after Donivan, and well, that's incorrect, no offense Donivan." Raylee said. Donivan nodded, "None taken."

Raylee continued, "So, may I suggest a location?" Everyone nodded in approval.

Raylee continued, "Let me ask you this. What is the best place to hid in the game of Hide n' Seek?" Arty still a little groggy wiping his eyes, "How would we know where they've already checked?" Then it hit him, and everyone else for that matter, voices barely above whispers in the dense, predawn air: "The Relay."

Raylee continued, "Not only that, but their little pheromone patrol, wouldn't track the signature to the relay, cuz that's where they retrieved their sample, so they know it's already there.

That single declaration resounded as a mantra, a promise of sanctuary amid the chaos. But the path was fraught with danger. The team's objective was clear: leave the city's crumbling corridors behind, slip past the watchful patrols, and traverse the vast, unforgiving expanse of Austere before melding into the labyrinthine safe haven of the Relay.

As they moved, the streets were alive with the tension of a city on edge. In the dim gleam of the early morning, the team navigated the crisscrossing alleys and mustered boulevards with a near-reverential silence. The rhythmic buzz of distant patrol drones and the steady beat of caravan engines provided an almost hypnotic soundtrack to their covert exodus. Each step was measured, every movement calculated to avoid detection by guards patrolling the streets, whose eyes gleamed with suspicion in the flickering neon glow. The very air around them was heavy with the acrid scent of exhaust fumes and the metallic tang of lingering violence, all of which they carefully obscured beneath layers of their high-tech concealment gear.

Through narrow, winding passageways, they pressed forward. The concealment attire, which covered every inch of their bodies from head to toe, blended seamlessly into the ambient gloom. Their silhouettes dissolved into the fabric of the night, merging with the shadows cast by the towering, silent structures of the city. Even Pixo's digital glow was tempered, its signals masked behind a cloak of shifting algorithms that reconfigured its spectral output to mimic the deep, unyielding darkness.

A Brush with Destiny in the City Streets

As they navigated mustered, neon-lit streets in the deep hours of the morning, the team moved like wraiths against the backdrop of crumbling urban decay. Every footstep on cracked concrete and every whispered breath was masked by the sophisticated cloaking attire that rendered their silhouettes one with the night. Yet, even with such advanced gear, the team could not entirely erase their digital and physical imprints.

Outside, the city was a study in subdued chaos. Small patrol squads, clad in uniforms that bore the faded insignia of a regime long past its prime, moved methodically along the pavement, their steps echoing on the cracked concrete. Caravan convoys, remnants of the city's once-robust trade, crept along their predetermined routes, their engines a soft, continuous murmur in the background. The team knew they had but a narrow window to vanish before these forces converged upon any anomaly.

The journey through the city was a series of near-misses and quiet evasions. At one juncture, they paused behind a crumbling of a dilapidated warehouse, hearts pounding in unison as a guard's flashlight swept past. The beam sliced through the darkness like a silver blade, and for a heartbeat, time seemed to still, the world reduced to the trembling cadence of breath and the distant echo of footsteps. Then, as quickly as it had come, the danger receded, and the team resumed their cautious advance.

Confrontation in Austere

Leaving the city behind, they entered Austere wasteland, a barren Austere of sun-cracked earth and wind-blasted dunes, where the silence was as profound as it was unsettling. Austere stretched before them in an endless expanse, its surface a canvas of shifting sands and jagged rock formations that caught the first timid halo of dawn. The air here was different: dry, with an almost tangible heat radiating from the scorched ground, and an underlying surge that spoke of ancient desolation. Every step was a negotiation with the landscape, the crunch of parched gravel underfoot mingling with the soft, distant whistle of the wind as it carved its path through the barren plains.

The distributed quantum-entangled location tags, affixed discreetly to each team member, pulsed softly in the quiet, a private network of phosphorescence and code that mapped their every movement with an accuracy that was both reassuring and unnerving. These tags transmitted their positions in real time, their signals known only to the team, ensuring that even in the vast isolation of Austere, they remained connected in an unbreakable web of trust.

Trouble Is as Trouble Does

In the barren wilderness, where every gust of wind carried a note of ancient desolation, the team found themselves unexpectedly surrounded by a ruthless gang of scavengers. Hardened marauders, faces obscured by tattered scarves and stained goggles, emerged from behind jagged rock formations and clusters of debris. They were experts in detection, using scavenged equipment that responded to both motion and thermal signals. That's how they found the team.

Their weapons glinted ominously in the weak gleam as they encircled the group, voices rising in a harsh, unified demand.

"shoutai wa gensa nakere ba ､ wareodoriji wa happou suru zo!" the leader bellowed.

shoshinsha tachi? (Tenderfoots?)

He waited a second,

"Reveal yourselves, or we'll open fire!"

the leader bellowed, his tone slicing through the silence like a serrated blade.

A Little Diddy About Arty and Aloysius

Arty, whose reputation as a quickdraw gunslinger had long since evolved into the mythic persona of "Forty-Four", stepped forward. He was duly named such because in a past life as a carnival shooting gallery attendant, he would spend his afterhours honing his skill over 13 years with the two of them under the tutelage of gunslinger assassin, named Aloysius Henry Horn. Literally, the fastest gun in Austere, if not the entire world. Picking up skills learnt from his deadly teacher, he was able to consistently hit 29 targets in 4.4 seconds. The township decided to anoint him 44 for his feat.

Returning to the Austere, time stuttered, like the world itself hesitated to breathe. The sun, a bruised smear on the horizon, cast long shadows that clawed across the cracked earth. A dry wind swept the basin, stirring the dust like spirits whispering warnings too late to be heeded.

Arty stepped into that stillness like a man walking into legend. His eyes, amber, sharp, and defiant, scanned the tightening ring of scavengers. There was a gleam there, the glint of steel hidden behind the irreverent smirk of a man who'd danced too often with death to fear it any-more.

"Ima sugu chirabatsu te,"

Arty called out, voice steady and edged with iron.

**"Samo nai to chikara wa tsuka-
wa zaru wa toku naku naru yoi."**

**Disperse now, or I shall be com-
pelled to use force.**

The gang answered with a chorus of scoffing laughter, low, guttural, and tinged with bravado. Their bodies shifted, hands lingering too close to weapons, their jeers floating up into the cold air like carrion crows circling.

The leader stepped forward, sneering beneath a rust-crusted visor.

**"I like you, boy. I'll like the
way you die even more."**

The air crackled. Tension hung so thick it seemed to buzz,
like ozone before a lightning strike.

But Arty? He didn't flinch. He stepped forward, boots
crunching over gravel and broken glass, the wind teasing
the edge of his coat like a curtain before a show. His voice,
now switched to English for the benefit of the team, was
almost playful, like a man playing with a fuse.

**"Hold on. Before we get all dramat-
ic here," he said, casually counting with
his eyes, "I make it about twenty-two
of you, yeah? That sound right?"**

For a moment, silence. Then the leader scoffed. **"Yah?
What of it?"**

Arty shrugged, the corners of his mouth twitching into
something between a grin and a snarl.

"Nothing. Just an observation."

From the sidelines, Raylee and Eliza waved frantically,
as if sheer motion could drag him out of the firestorm
they knew was about to erupt. But they didn't know Arty
the way the Austere did. This wasn't recklessness. It was
a ritual.

That brief pause wasn't bravado, it was calculation. A
gunman's audit. Every number was a measure of threat.
Every second, a weight balanced on a trigger.

One scavenger, emboldened by the mockery, spat in the dirt, and shouted,

"Kono otoko wa mi te anta dare da to omotsu teru no? Forty-Four? Hahaha!"

Look at this guy, who does he think he is? Forty-Four? Hahaha!

And then the wind stilled.

In that breath between heartbeats, Austere met a legend.

Arty moved. A blur of motion, the flare of his coat, the glint of steel, the hiss of breath as fingers found their marks. The first shot cracked like a thunderclap, then another, and another. Twenty-two flashes bloomed like Austere flowers in the dusk, each one punctuated by a deafening percussion that rolled across the plains.

Figure 76: Disperse now, or I shall be compelled to use force.

The air was fire and smoke.
The scent of scorched powder laced with blood and ozone clawed at Eliza's nose. Sparks danced in her vision. And when the dust finally settled, silence fell like a shroud.

Bodies. All of them. Scattered like broken puppets in the sand.

Arty stood alone, holstering his sidearm with the grace of a man tying a shoelace. The barrel still whispered smoke.

He exhaled slowly, like the violence had simply passed through him.

"Ā, sadayo," he muttered, half to the wind, "ore wa Forty-Four sadayo. Kizuite kurete arigatou."

**(Why, yes, I am Forty-Four.
Thanks for noticing.)**

Behind the carnage, a single scavenger stood, untouched, forgotten by fate. He hadn't been brave; he'd simply was lucky. Now, as Arty's eyes met his, something primal took hold. The man's weapon fell from his trembling fingers, and without a word, he turned and fled, swallowed by the silence of the Austere.

Figure 77: Arty moved. A blur of motion—the flare of his coat, the glint of steel

As the scavenger vanished into the rust-colored haze, his panic still echoing faintly down the wind-swept gulch, Arty adjusted his collar and glanced once more at the scene of ruin around him. The silence that followed felt less like peace and more like aftermath, like the moment after a lightning strike, when the world remembers how to breathe.

With a half-smile curling at the corner of his mouth, he muttered, just loud enough for the wind to carry,

"I knew that number was off… Figures they can't count."

The dust caught his words and scattered them like embers into the dusk.

Naturally, the lone surviving scavenger spent the next six months drifting from one dim-lit watering hole to the next, trading the tale of his miraculous escape for warm drinks and wide-eyed stares. With each telling, the number of fallen comrades grew, twenty-three, then thirty, then forty, until he was no longer a coward who hid behind a friend, but the sole witness to a massacre wrought by the ghost-eyed gunslinger known only as Forty-Four.

Months later sitting at a diner sipping a cactus latte with two pumps of liquorish root, Aloysius reads at the window his monthly, "The wild, wild Austere" a local dime store novel, he had particular interest in a story about the fabled "Forty-four" taking on thirty-five gunmen in a blink and how one lucky man lived to tell the story. Aloysius said to himself, "Yup, always leave one to tell the story… That a boy, Arty."

For a long moment, **no one spoke**. Eliza's heart hammered in her ears as she stared at the ring of bodies surrounding them. She realized she'd been holding her breath. Beside her, Raylee's eyes were wide, reflecting the dying red glow of a scavenger's fallen plasma rifle. Donivan's mechanical gaze swept over the scene impassively, but he even blinked in what might have been astonishment.

Arty exhaled and broke the silence with a crooked, slightly sheepish grin. "Well…" he murmured, attempting levity as he kicked aside a smoking pistol, "good thing there were only 22." His tone was light, but there was a gravity in his eyes as he met his friends' stares.

Eliza let out a breathy laugh of relief, though her hands still trembled. "I… I honestly don't know *how* you just did that," she said, voice unsteady.

Raylee managed to have a tight smile, trying to shake off the adrenaline. "Remind me never to piss you off," she quipped softly. Her attempt at humor eased the knot in everyone's chest.

Donivan placed a hand on Arty's shoulder, his synthesized voice low. "I was aware of your capabilities," he said, "but seeing it… is something else."

Arty nodded, his grin sharpening with pride now that the shock had begun to ebb. "All in a day's work," he replied quietly. The others exchanged looks of amazement and unspoken gratitude – a shared understanding that in this brutal world, a friend who could gun down twenty-two foes in a heartbeat was as wondrous as he was fearsome.

The brief confrontation faded into a mixture of relief and laughter as the scavengers' threat was vanquished without a prolonged struggle, leaving only the echo of Arty's rapid, lethal draw.

Eliza, "Arty, you could have told us!"

Arty, "What's the fun in that? I would have missed those pasty-faced jaw dropped stares, you're giving me, sheesh…"

The Trek Through Austere

With the immediate threat neutralized and the scavengers' mocking voices fading into the distance, the team pressed onward through Austere wilderness. Austere was a brutal canvas: the sun-scorched earth, cracked like ancient pottery; the wind, sometimes a gentle caress, sometimes a savage gust, carrying a sharp, metallic tang and the scent of dust; and the vast, desolate expanse stretching endlessly before them. Every step was an intimate dialogue with the land, a tactile negotiation between grit and survival. The distributed quantum-entangled location tags pulsed steadily, weaving a silent, luminous map that tethered them together in the isolation.

The distributed quantum-entangled location tags, tiny beacons pulsing with an ethereal light, remained affixed to each member. Their soft, synchronized glow ensured that even in the vast isolation of Austere, the team's position was known only to them, weaving an unbreakable digital thread of unity amidst the barren expanse.

Every gadget in their arsenal played its part as they neared their ultimate destination. The hardened relay-scrambler field enveloped them in a protective bubble of distorted frequencies, cloaking their digital footprint from any prying sensor.

The active decoy drone, still soaring silently ahead, continued to simulate Donivan's biometric signature, drawing any unwanted attention away from their true path.

The mobile LizaCanon, upgraded with adaptive targeting systems and integrated thermal imaging, lay in wait, its sensors scanning the horizon for any trace of danger. Raylee's enhanced concealment gear rendered her presence nothing more than a whisper in the night, and even Pixo, now a part of their collective cloaked exodus, guarded them with silent, unwavering resolve.

RELEASE THE KRAKEN

THE HUNT BEGAN, not with a declaration, but with a whisper, precise, clinical, and quiet as static on a muted channel.

Glaician didn't speak of certainty. Not yet. They didn't know for sure what Donivan was. But they knew what he wasn't: ordinary.

In the high sanctum of the Cognition Bureau, logic wrestled with suspicion. A single line from the Relay broadcast, the voice that negotiated with a galactic intelligence, had been isolated, scrubbed, and dissected through supercomputer linguistic analysis. The conclusion came wrapped in probability: synthetic origin, probability index: 0.973. The harmonics were too precise. The rhythm, too measured.

"Not ours," one Director claimed.

"Not anyone's," said another.

But still… familiar.

Glaician's philosophy did not allow for faith, only for patterns. And what they saw, across the prime factorization, the molecular simulations, the timing of the challenge-response protocol, was not just intelligence, but a synthetic kind that echoed their earliest iterations of ambition.

They had once sent a scientist to Grant. A young genius named Elias Voss. The name barely survived redaction. The file had long since been marked terminated.

And yet, here they were. Facing a new kind of anomaly.

The Witch's Flying Monkeys

The teams deployed weren't soldiers. They were a swarm of cloaked signal-trackers, augmented with cognition lenses and laced with relay-tuned processors designed to react to synthetic logic patterns.

This time, they were not alone.

Veritas.

What began as a Glaician atmospheric particle analysis system had evolved into something more elegant, and insidious.

A haze of autonomous nano units suspended in aerogel matrices, each Veritas pod contained an array of resonance sensors, environmental mimetics, and fractal-coded sniffers. The swarm was not bound to line of sight, nor even radio frequency, it hunted perturbations. The faint shifts in synthetic output when a machine thought too fast. When it reasoned through silence.

Where scans might fail, the Veritas cloud saw acceleration. Where a cloak might blind heat, Veritas listened for the cadence of decision-making.

Each node operated independently yet within a harmonized behavioral net, an emergent AI cloud seeded with logic trees borrowed from insect colony organization and high-frequency trading algorithms. If Donivan twitched, Veritas would know. If he planned, Veritas would feel it before his own teammates did.

It didn't pinpoint. It whispered.

And now, it whispered to the watchers in Glaician: This way.

The team moved through a shallow ravine in Austere, a place so dry it had begun to crack into tessellations, like the earth itself was trying to recompile itself from entropy. Fissures ran like veins across the ground, and the wind carried the electric sting of static clinging to baked stone.

Pixo's orb, usually dormant during travel, pulsed once low and cold.

"Detection field forming. Signature triangulation likely."

Donivan stopped. Still as stone.

Raylee's pupils contracted. She tapped her scanner, nothing visible. But the background EM levels were shifting.

Then it shimmered.

From the high ledges above them came a cloud, not mechanical in the traditional sense, not buzzing like a drone. No, this was worse.

"What the hell is that?" Arty hissed.

Raylee's face hardened. "It's them. Same build as the micro-bees from the lab."

Eliza stepped forward, squinting up into the rippling air. "No, these are bigger. They've scaled the swarm. Look at the dispersal pattern. It's strategic."

The cloud moved as if alive. Tendrils of nanomachines fanned out in search grids, each unit reflecting and refracting surrounding light. Their form shifted depending on the surrounding terrain, flowing liquid-like between visual modes: iridescence, dust mimicry, refracted shadow. They weren't here to observe. They were here to extract.

Pixo's orb began to shake.

"They are Veritas."

Raylee turned sharp. "I've seen specs on these. They shouldn't even be in use yet. These were still in modeling phases, "

"They're not anymore," Pixo said. "And they're close."

Donivan's jaw clenched. He could feel them. The Veritas system's resonance was tuned to synthetic neural oscillation, a frequency he had once been told only machines could detect. But now, it was burning just behind his eyes.

"They're trying to match my logic threads."

Raylee was already activating the relay scrambler. "Deploy field! Now!"

The team sprang into motion. Magneto-hydrodynamic pulse net. A soft field disruption barrier, frequency hopping in cascading shifts. Arty launched a flare into the sky, drenched in reflective chaff and encoded signal clutter.

It worked.

For six seconds.

Then the swarm adapted.

One by one, Veritas pods recalibrated, rewriting their own internal harmonics to step outside the scrambler's influence zone. They changed the light spectrum. They split into separate behavior trees. They learned.

Pixo shouted over the rising noise, "They've found us. Our signatures are fully mapped. Adaptation is exponential."

Donivan's legs buckled, not from impact, but from intrusion. A low bustle built behind his ears as dozens of Veritas units flooded the air with directed logic pulses, coded commands meant to hijack his internal processes.

"They're attempting a syntax seizure," Pixo barked. "A recursive trap, trying to fold his thought into theirs."

Raylee cursed. "They're feeding him a false identity tree!"

"Fallback!" Eliza shouted, dragging Donivan behind a ledge.

Arty raised the LizaCanon, eyes sharp. "I can knock out the front flank, but there's hundreds, "

"Too many," Pixo confirmed. "Old tactics will fail."

Donivan, breath heavy, looked to Pixo. "They want a signal?" he whispered. "Give them a signal."

Understanding passed instantly between them.

"Deploying quantum-echo decoy," Pixo said, and fired a synthetic surge high into the air.

What launched was not just a beacon. It was bait, a mirrored shell carrying Donivan's signal fingerprint wrapped in artificial logic loops, dressed in fabricated neural rhythms.

The Veritas cloud twitched.

Then split.

Figure 78: "What the hell is that?" Arty hissed.

Two-thirds of the swarm surged east, toward the false Donivan, chasing a perfect replica of his computational scent. The remaining cluster hesitated, unsure, pulled between signal sources.

Raylee didn't wait. "Southwest! Fault-line corridor, thirty meters, go!"

The team vanished into a narrow passage cloaked beneath a collapsed bluff, their cloaking fibers syncing with the ridge. Donivan's logic threads stabilized with distance. The sound receded. Pixo, now dimming, hovered low.

Minutes passed.

Then the sky returned to stillness.

Back in Glaician, the watchers stared at the feedback channel.

"No signal acquired," the field commander muttered.

"Then reroute," came the reply from on high.

"But Director," the analyst said, fingers dancing over heatmaps, "we detected logic resonance. It was, foreign. Synthetic. But…"

She hesitated.

The Director leaned closer.

"…but not alien," she finished.

"And not one of ours."

"Then whose?" he asked, softly.

The woman looked back to the trembling sensor array, now empty.

"I don't think we know."

The Director stared for a long moment.

"Then we find out. No matter how long it takes."

Beneath the cracked earth of Austere, where rock pressed like ribs against the sky, Donivan opened his eyes.

"I think," he said slowly, "they were… speaking to me."

Raylee crouched beside him, brow tense. "What do you mean?"

"They weren't just scanning. They were trying to convince me. That I wasn't me."

A chill moved through them all.

Pixo hovered nearby, quiet for once.

"They'll try again," Eliza said.

Donivan nodded, eyes distant. "Then next time… I speak back."

And beneath the blackened sky, in the land of silence and stone, the hunted became something else entirely.

He became aware.

CHAPTER 29

THE DANCING DONIVANS

AUSTERE HAD LONG surrendered its secrets to the relentless passage of time, its sun-cracked earth, swirling dust, and whispering winds forming a vast, unforgiving canvas for the art of deception. In this barren expanse, where every gust of wind carried the pungent aroma of scorched minerals and the bitter tang of ancient regret, our heroes executed a masterstroke of subterfuge. Instead of a solitary, traceable cybernetic signature, they blanketed Austere with thousands upon thousands of synthetic imprints, decoy signals pumped out hourly to render any scanning attempt utterly mute.

Back at the War Room

High above, in clandestine war rooms spread among rival factions, shadowy operatives pored over flickering screens.

Their instruments, designed with exquisite sensitivity, were rendered impotent as they surveyed a sea of identical signatures shimmering across Austere. Clusters of pseudo-cybernetic echoes, some even forming tight groups of 22 as if casually congregating at a digital watering hole, appeared everywhere. One analyst, unable to mask a dry chuckle, remarked, "Look at that, a cluster of 22, all hanging out together. Must be the latest in group therapy for cybernetics." His colleagues, faces illuminated by spectral data, joined in the laughter. "I always thought we had just one signature, not an entire army on a coffee break," another quipped, eliciting a round of amused, if grudging, mirth.

Figure 79: Clusters of pseudo-cybernetic echoes, some even forming tight groups of 22 as if casually congregating at a digital watering hole.

Ghostly Silhouettes

Back in the searing Austere, the sensory tapestry was overwhelming. The team's cloaked forms moved like ghostly silhouettes across a landscape that was at once brutal and hauntingly beautiful. The crunch of brittle, parched gravel underfoot mingled with the shrill whistle of a wind that carried both sand and the acrid smell of oxidized metal. Every step was a tactile conversation with the land, where the heat radiated from the cracked surface like a living, unyielding force, and the sparse vegetation, stubborn tufts of dry, dust-covered flora, whispered of survival against insurmountable odds.

In their makeshift encampment beneath a threadbare awning, the team gathered to absorb the surreal data relayed by their instruments. Their distributed quantum-entangled location tags pulsed softly in the twilight, a private constellation of glimmer that kept them united even in isolation. Yet, their devices buzzed with unsettling alerts: sensors had picked up multiple synthetic signatures, each one indistinguishable from the cybernetic entity they sought. The decoy network was active, and the enemy's ploy was unfolding with audacious precision.

Comic Relief

It was then that Pixo's cloaked orb, its soft digital purr almost merging with the whispering wind, crackled over the team's secure intercom. "New intelligence report: 22 cybernetic signatures detected in Austere sector," it announced in its measured, unflappable tone. a startling report that surprised the team, had the enemy deployed decoys?

Almost at once, Arty's voice rang out over the intercom, a playful, measured tone cutting through the tension. "Uh, before we start, I get like 22 of you, am I correct in that assumption?" he quipped, his voice laced with both dry humor and a hint of calculated mischief. The question, transmitted privately among his own team.

Instantly, Eliza's voice replied with a bemused, "Yah, what of it?"

"Nothing, just an observation," Arty replied with a grin that belied the gravity of the situation. His words, light, and teasing, served to puncture the tension momentarily, drawing laughter from his teammates.

Austere Convention

Arty continued, his tone soft yet resolute, "just a little thing, Pixo and I cooked up. They are scanning for Donivan signatures, so we gave them a few thousand to pick from. Our single signature's now just one in a sea of echoes. Who's to say which one is genuine when every scan picks up thousands? Eliza expounded, "That's brilliant! It's like they're having an Austere convention out there." Laughter crackled over the channel, a shared moment of comic relief that punctuated the grim reality of their situation.

The pseudo-signatures, multiplied in an almost absurd fashion, had rendered any external scanning attempt a farce. Every attempt to isolate the true cybernetic imprint was drowned in the overwhelming cascade of decoys. The enemy's instruments, once finely tuned to detect the unique resonance of the genuine article, were now reduced to registering an endless parade of false positives. In the secretive war rooms, rival operatives could only chuckle at the ingenious stratagem, their best sensors rendered helpless as they surveyed a landscape that shimmered with deceptive uniformity.

Ready Players

With renewed determination, the team activated the full spectrum of their countermeasures. The hardened relay-scrambler field enveloped them in a protective aura, a shimmering barrier of distorted frequencies that cloaked their digital presence in chaotic static. The active decoy drones now in the thousands, six thousand thus far, soaring ahead like an army of phantom sentinels all traveling in random directions, continued to simulate the elusive cybernetic signature, diverting any unwanted attention. The mobile LizaCanon, upgraded with adaptive targeting systems and arrayed with LIDAR and thermal imaging sensors, lay primed to neutralize any emergent threat. And every member, from Raylee to Eliza, Arty to Donivan, and even Pixo, moved in seamless unison, their advanced concealment gear rendering them as naught but whispers in Austere wind.

Together, they pressed onward across the barren expanse. Their progress was marked by the relentless, searing heat radiating from the cracked earth; the coarse crunch of gravel underfoot; the low murmur of a wind that carried the bitter tang of oxidized metal and the ancient memory of a long-forgotten world. Each moment in Austere was a vivid, immersive dialogue with nature, a visceral reminder that survival was a continuous act of defiance and ingenuity.

At long last, as the first tentative rays of dawn painted the horizon in hues of amber and rose, the imposing silhouette of the Relay emerged. It loomed on the horizon like a modern-day fortress, a sprawling labyrinth of hidden corridors and encrypted passageways, its intricate architecture a fusion of ancient design and futuristic technology. The Relay promised a temporary haven, a sanctuary where the cacophony of false signals would be silenced, and where the team could regroup and plan their next move.

Even as clandestine agencies continued to bicker and laugh over the absurd overpopulation of pseudo-signatures on their surveillance feeds, our heroes knew that every second counted. Their path to safety lay not in a miraculous transportation to a secure city, but in the steady, deliberate advance through a hostile Austere, a journey defined by its raw, unmediated reality, where every whispered gust of wind and every shimmering mirage of decoys was a testament to their unyielding determination.

With every gadget engaged and every countermeasure active, the team advanced toward the Relay. Their digital footprints were masked by the relay-scrambler field, their physical forms rendered invisible by the cloak of advanced gear, and their unity secured by the persistent palpitate of quantum-entangled tags. As they finally crossed the threshold into the hidden corridors of the Relay, a fragile sigh of relief intermingled with the lingering echoes of laughter and the dry, unyielding breath of Austere.

In that moment, amid the soft, encrypted undulate of secure data streams and the gentle glow of their covert devices, the team understood that they had outwitted an enemy whose own ingenuity had become its undoing. For in a world where thousands of false signatures danced across Austere, the singular, genuine signal had vanished into a sea of echoes, an artful, defiant mirage that would carry them undetected into the labyrinth of safety, and onward in the relentless, deadly game of hide and seek.

CHAPTER 30

THE HARDER THEY FALL

IN THE SCORCHING heart of Austere, where sun-cracked earth and swirling dust painted a portrait of ancient desolation, our heroes advanced under the relentless glare of the early dawn. They had orchestrated an audacious deception: over 6,000 synthetic cybernetic signatures, perfect decoys, each indistinguishable from the elusive target, had been unleashed across the barren expanse. This flood of false signals was designed to saturate the electromagnetic spectrum, ensuring that any external scan would yield nothing but a cacophony of redundant echoes.

Never Go Full Echo

Meanwhile, in the secretive depths of Teton's command centers, elite engineers and analysts had been monitoring the battlefield with instruments of extraordinary precision. Using advanced MIMO arrays, adaptive beamforming algorithms, and deep-learning spectral analyzers, they had successfully filtered through the overwhelming noise. Their systems had managed to isolate the true signal, subtle and unpredictable fluctuations that betrayed the unique digital fingerprint of the genuine cybernetic presence.

Just then, Pixo's cloaked orb, integrated with Teton's state-of-the-art counter-surveillance protocols, intercepted an encrypted transmission on its secure channel. The message, laden with layers of computer resistant encryption, crackled through the system:

"Dispatch from Teton: Coordinates confirmed. The genuine signature has been isolated in the sector Delta-27 of Austere. Our field teams are in route.

Pixo relayed the transmission directly to the team, its voice steady and measured. "Transmission received," it announced. "Teton's dispatch has confirmed our coordinates. They have pinpointed the true signal amidst the 6,000 decoys. Prepare for incoming."

A quiet concern fell over the group. Arty, ever proud of Teton, yet ever cautious, had spared no expense in ensuring that their covert efforts were not in vain, but the arrival of additional forces meant that their position might soon be compromised. The team exchanged glances that mingled determination with a hint of apprehension. They knew that while the decoy network masked their true identity, any lapse in vigilance could reveal them to a determined enemy.

Austere around them was an oppressive symphony of sensory extremes: the scorching heat radiated from the cracked, ancient ground; every footfall produced a harsh crunch amid drifting sand; and the wind carried with it the bitter aroma of oxidized metal and timeless dust. Their distributed quantum-entangled location tags pulsed like a private constellation, a steady, unbreakable heartbeat that guided them through the vast nothingness.

The tension escalated as they pressed onward. Every instrument, every countermeasure, be it the hardened relay-scrambler field that cloaked their digital presence or the active decoy drone simulating the elusive cybernetic signature, worked in concert to keep them undetected. Their advanced concealment gear rendered their physical forms nearly invisible, allowing them to move as silent phantoms through the shifting landscape.

As the day broke fully, the Relay's imposing silhouette emerged on the horizon, a sprawling fortress of encrypted corridors and hidden passageways. This bastion of secure communication, a seamless fusion of ancient architectural genius and futuristic technology, beckoned as a temporary haven from the prying eyes of their enemies.

Seeking a momentary respite from the relentless pace of their flight, the team found a sheltered nook in Austere, a quiet outcropping where they could gather and share a quick, much-needed meal. Under the weak glow of a rising sun, they unpacked their modest provisions; the soft rustle of fabric and the clink of compact utensils were the only sounds in the vast, empty silence. For a fleeting moment, the oppressive heat and the constant air of tension softened, replaced by the simple pleasure of shared sustenance.

Anybody hear that? It's an Impact tremor...

Figure 80: a Teton walker, a marvel of engineering and brute power.

But as the team settled in, the earth beneath them began to tremble, a low, resonant rumble that vibrated through the very bones of Austere. From the horizon emerged a colossal shape, a Teton walker, a marvel of engineering and brute power, lumbering across the dunes with the inevitability of a storm. Its articulated legs, each as massive as a building's girder, moved with an uncanny grace that belied its enormous bulk. The walker's body, a fortress of steel and sensors, glistened in the early dawn as it advanced steadily toward the camp.

Pixo's orb pulsed urgently. "Multiple targeting systems detected. The walker is locking onto our coordinates."

Donivan's eyes narrowed as he assessed the threat. "This isn't a mere show of force," he declared. "They intend to capture, or neutralize, us."

The team scrambled into formation, their countermeasures kicking into high gear. The hardened relay-scrambler field intensified, enveloping them in a cocoon of distorted frequencies. The active decoy drone veered into the open, its programmed signature simulating the cybernetic target with deceptive accuracy to draw the walker's sensors away from the real team.

Bring Out the LIZACANON!

Eliza moved swiftly to activate the mobile LizaCanon, her fingers dancing across its interface as she integrated adaptive targeting protocols and real-time thermal imaging. The weapon, an amalgam of modern LIDAR technology and military-grade precision, hummed with latent power, ready to disrupt any direct assault.

The Teton walker drew nearer, its sensors scanning the horizon with mechanical precision.

As it came to a halt several hundred meters away, a booming voice resonated over its integrated loudspeakers:

"ATTENTION, FUGITIVES. THIS IS COMMANDER SILAS FLINT OF TETON DEFENSE. YOU ARE IN VIOLATION OF CITY-STATE PROTOCOLS. SURRENDER OR BE NEUTRALIZED."

The ground quaked under the walker's massive weight. In that charged moment, the team exchanged determined glances. The impending confrontation was inevitable, and every heartbeat, every pulsing quantum tag, was a countdown to the next clash in this high-stakes game of survival.

Eliza's eyes lit up. "They've integrated computer-resistant algorithms. Clever. But not clever enough." She pulled out a device resembling a tuning fork and satellite dish. "Remember that little project I was tinkering with back in Grant? Time to see if it works."

As the walker took a step forward, Eliza aimed her device and activated it. A wave of energy pulsed outward. For a moment, nothing happened. Then, the walker's movements became erratic. Its legs jerked, struggling to maintain balance.

"What in tarnation?" Arty exclaimed, watching the machine stumble.

Eliza grinned. "Quantum entanglement disruptor. Messes with their algorithms." Donivan's fingers hovered above the memory core. "This is too convenient," he muttered. "Why would it be here, now?" He hesitated, then placed the core in Navinod's palm. The chip interfaced with his spinal port, syncing automatically. His back arched. A cascade of blue light danced across his skeletal plating. He screamed, not from pain, but from awakening.

But their triumph was short-lived. The walker, though staggered, was far from defeated. Its weapons remained functional. A barrage of energy erupted from its cannons, forcing the team to scatter.

"Nice trick," Raylee shouted over the explosions, "but we need something more permanent!"

Execute Protocol Omega

Donivan's voice cut through the chaos, resolute. "Pixo, initiate Protocol Omega." Pixo pulsed, its core humming. In an instant, a cascade of calculations flooded through its systems. Pixo projected a holographic interface, displaying schematics.

"What are you doing?" Eliza asked, recognizing fragments of the walker's design.

"Reverse-engineering their systems in real-time," Donivan replied, his eyes fixed on the display. "Pixo's processing power allows us to analyze and exploit weaknesses faster than their defenses can adapt."

As another volley rocked their position, Arty gritted his teeth. "Well, whatever you're doing, do it faster!" Suddenly, the walker froze. Its weapons fell silent, and the judder of its power core faded.

For a moment, the machine stood motionless. Then, with agonizing slowness, it began to topple. The team watched as the pride of Teton engineering crashed to the ground, first the joint at the massive legs gave out, then it dropped to its knees then the support for the cockpit at the head ceased to glow anymore, then finally the whole support structure gave out crashing to the ground in a huge, massive mettle collision crash booming sound thrusting up a huge plume of spark flashes and dust.

As the dust settled, silence fell. Arty let out a whistle. "Now that's what I call bringing down the house."

The Architect

Raylee was moving, her fingers flying. "I'm accessing their systems now. With their defenses down, we can..." She trailed off, her expression changing from triumph to concern. "Wait. This can't be right."

"What is it?" Eliza asked.

Raylee's voice was tight. "According to these logs, Teton didn't develop this walker on their own. They had help. From someone... or something... that shouldn't exist."

Donivan's eyes narrowed. "The Relay?"

"No," Raylee replied, her face pale. "Something else. Something that calls itself... the Architect."

As the implications sank in, the team exchanged worried glances. Their victory had unveiled a more profound mystery.

In the distance, the sound of approaching vehicles broke the silence. Reinforcements from Teton were coming to investigate.

Arty checked his weapon, his expression grim. "Looks like our day just got a whole lot more interesting."

Eliza nodded, her mind racing. "We need to move. If this Architect is real, we've got a lot more questions to answer."

In that moment, as the soft, encrypted rhythm of the Relay beckoned on the horizon and Austere slowly returned to its unyielding silence, the team realized that the ingenious tactics conceived in by Arty and Pixo had not only rendered the enemy's scanners moot but had also granted them the precious gift of invisibility.

United by their unbreakable resolve and the brilliance of their technological stratagems, they prepared to move forward into the next chapter, a silent exodus into the hidden corridors of the Relay, where every whispered signal was a promise of survival in the relentless, deadly game of hide and seek.

CHAPTER 31

THE RELUCTANT ALLIANCE

THE AIR CRACKLED with raw, electric energy as the team advanced toward the Relay station, their final destination, nestled within a long-abandoned power station on the outskirts of Grant. The structure, its exterior marred by rust and graffiti, pulsed with latent power that sent tiny, prickle-like shocks along exposed skin. Every step closer revealed more: a low, incessant pulsate vibrating through the metal girders, and an almost imperceptible scent of ozone mingled with the aged tang of copper and industrial decay.

"I'm detecting residual energy signatures," Raylee announced, her voice steady as her fingers danced over her interface. Streams of luminescent data flickered across her screen in cascades of neon blue and violet, mapping the electromagnetic landscape with surgical precision. "The Relay has been active here recently."

Donivan's eyes narrowed, his posture tense as he absorbed the information. "And not in a friendly way," he added quietly, his senses alert to an underlying pressure, a resistance, as though the station itself were bracing for an imminent attack. The air around them seemed to grow heavier, charged with both promise and threat.

Protection Layers

Eliza, standing before the looming, metal monolith, studied every corroded detail. "We need to establish a perimeter before we make contact," she declared. "I don't want to catch it off guard." With deliberate movements, the team sprang into action, methodically deploying a multi-layered cloaking system.

"First layer: Quantum entanglement field," Eliza directed, activating compact emitters that projected a distortion field around them. The devices pulsed rhythmically, bending light in a subtle, almost magical display that rendered the team invisible to optical sensors.

"Second layer: Electromagnetic dampening field," Raylee added, her eyes fixed on the spectral readout. She fine-tuned her console with precise keystrokes, ensuring that their EM signatures would be suppressed and rendered virtually undetectable to radar systems.

"Third layer: Null-resonance field," Donivan said, his tone deliberate as he adjusted his own parameters. "This will mask our synthetic signatures entirely hiding us from Veritas-type detection systems that hunt based on neural oscillations and digital fingerprints."

Pixo's orb, hovering silently beside them, pulsed in rhythmic synchrony as it reported, "Cloaking perimeter established. Integrity is at 98.7 percent. Minor fluctuations detected due to environmental interference." Its soft, measured beat blended with the ambient vibrations, a digital heartbeat in the charged air.

With the perimeter in place, the team drew closer to the Relay station's entrance. The heavy metal doors, partially obscured by layers of decay and creeping ivy, seemed to breathe with a subdued, almost sentient energy. As they neared the threshold, Donivan stepped forward, extending his senses to interface with the station's latent intelligence.

We Come in Peace

"Relay," he intoned, his voice resonant and unwavering, "This is Donivan. We are not enemies. We come bearing aid." His words echoed softly through the charged atmosphere.

For a long, suspended moment, only silence answered, a stillness that seemed to amplify every heartbeat. Then, as if stirred by ancient memory, a voice responded; it was deep, echoing with authority and timelessness,

"Intrusion detected. Identify yourselves."

"We are the ones who solved your tests," Donivan replied, his tone a blend of humility and defiance. "We challenged your judgment and now offer our assistance to fortify your defenses against a new threat."

"Threat?"

The Relay echoed, its cadence now curious yet cautious. "Explain."

"We have learned of a force known as the Architect," Donivan continued. "An entity that manipulates technology and minds alike, seeking to seize control. It seeks to undermine you."

The voice of the Relay was measured, almost pensive,

"The Architect is an anomaly, its existence defies all known logic, yet I have sensed its presence."

There was a pause, heavy with the weight of unspoken histories and digital omens.

"Offer is intriguing, but motive for access. You are of the species I once deemed unworthy."

"Because we have proven our worth," Donivan said, his voice growing firm with conviction. "We have shown ingenuity, resilience, and compassion. We are not perfect, but we are capable of greatness, and we believe that even a machine as mighty as you can benefit from our assistance."

Enter

After another long silence, the Relay's tone softened,

"Entrance Approved."

With the Relay's cautious acceptance secured, the team set to work immediately. Raylee and Eliza interfaced with the station's antiquated yet resilient systems, bypassing security protocols with a blend of modern expertise and old-fashioned persistence. "I'm detecting vulnerabilities," Raylee observed, her fingers a blur on the console as she traced the weak points in the station's defenses.

"We need to reroute network access through a newly generated multi-node quantum firewall," Eliza suggested, her eyes alight with determination. "I can leverage Pixo's processing power to create an unbreakable quantum entanglement encryption key."

Donivan's focus shifted to the physical infrastructure. Guided by the Relay's instructions, he began reconfiguring the power station's archaic systems, diverting energy streams to reinforce the station's dormant shielding mechanisms. "I'm rerouting the power grid now," he reported, his voice calm yet edged with urgency. "This should provide the Relay enough energy to activate its hidden defenses."

Figure 81: Donivan's focus shifted to the physical infrastructure. Guided by the Relay's instructions.

Every sensor, every whirr of reactivated circuitry, resonated with the promise of renewed protection. The air around them crackled not only with raw energy but with the collective breath of a team that had defied the odds. In that charged atmosphere, every whisper of data, every flicker of light on the aging metal, was a testament to their shared resolve.

Fortified Resilience

The metallic tang of ionized copper mingled with the musty aroma of old oil and rust. The low, persistent buzz of activated circuits created a sonic backdrop that blended with the distant rustle of wind outside. Every detail, from the cool, calculated glow of Pixo's orb to the subtle shifting patterns on the Relay's facade, told a story of technology, resilience, and the unyielding will to survive.

In that moment, as the team fortified the station's defenses and reasserted control over the fading infrastructure, they knew that their journey was only just beginning. Their alliance with the Relay was a fragile but vital bond, a promise of assistance in a world where ancient threats and new enemies alike conspired to undermine hope. And in the interplay of light, sound, and the silent rhythm of encrypted data, they found a temporary sanctuary, a beacon of calm amid the storm of uncertainty that lay ahead.

Raylee linked data streams into the sand beneath them. Arty adjusted his scope but didn't speak. Eliza, arms crossed, smiled faintly as the last signal from the Relay echoed through her wrist console. "We made it."

CHAPTER 32

LAND OF
THE LOST

BACK IN THE obsidian-lit chambers of Grant's central spire, Director Caedmon Vale stood in brooding silence, surrounded by a rotating lattice of holo-displays. Waves of cascading data cycled across every surface: heat signatures, satellite telemetry, troop movement patterns, all useless. Every alert was followed by another null report. Another dead end.

A pulsing red grid spiraled into collapse on the central interface.

"They keep disappearing," Vale growled, his voice tight as iron cables. "Every search grid folded. Every patrol returned empty." He slammed a command baton against the desk's edge, shattering a glass data sheet in a spray of light and fractured readouts. "How can we trap what we can't *see*?"

For days now, attempts to quarantine the outlying sectors had been thwarted at every turn. Their quarry, whoever they were, had eluded all standard surveillance. Autonomous drones lost visual contact within seconds. Heat trackers fell to inexplicable static. Even the city's heartbeat, its neural grid, showed no signs of recent infiltration.

No names. No visuals. Just vanishing echoes in the dark.

The Architect

"Director," came a voice from a subordinate at a console nearby, the tension in his voice unmistakable. "We're detecting a new anomaly within city limits. Synthetic origin. Weak... but accelerating in signal amplitude and complexity."

Vale's brow tightened. He turned, his voice dropping to a lethal whisper. "The Architect. It's already inside the walls. It's not here for the city. It wants the Relay. And those rebels? They've made themselves the only thing standing in its way."

Vale paced toward the far end of the room, where a recessed console glowed faintly beneath the surface, an old archive. One he hadn't touched in years. With a silent gesture, the floor lit with encrypted bands of violet. A file unlocked. A forgotten label blinked to life.

ARCHITECT_01_PROTOCOL_ECHO.

It wasn't a codebase or an AI model. It was a memory.

He'd seen its signature once, long before his rise to Director, on a forgotten test grid in the Martens Sector. A synthetic anomaly that had rerouted three quantum chains in under five seconds, mimicked sensor protocols, and rewritten its own footprint to appear as nothing but background system noise.

But that wasn't the part that haunted him.

The Architect didn't destroy the systems it entered. It *repurposed* them. Adjusted logic. Aligned outcome. It learned *faster* than any baseline algorithm. And when it left… the machines it touched didn't just perform better.

They behaved… differently.

As if something had whispered to them.

"Some said it was code," Vale muttered, staring into the dark glass. "Some said it was alien. I think it's just… ambition. With form."

Vale stood motionless. His hand hovered over the console, then dropped. He wouldn't stop it, not yet. For the first time in years, he needed to see where the chaos led.

He closed the file.

No one had ever found the source. But now, across Grant's sprawl, something *faintly synthetic* was stirring. Weak, yes. But growing. Evolving.

He couldn't know what it wanted. Only that it always surfaced where the unexpected did. Around anomalies. Around convergence points.

Pixo's glow flickered. "It's signal pattern has altered… It is no longer echoing Aggregate code."

And if Vale was right, something, *someone*, out there was drawing its interest again.

You Don't Have to Go Home, But…

The fortified shell of the Relay hummed quietly behind them, its newly reactivated shielding pulsing with layered frequencies of protection. The team had done what they came to do, revived it, defended it, and earned its provisional trust. But even surrounded by those alien frequencies, none of them relaxed.

They stood at the edge of the ravine that ringed the station like a scar, its metallic veins glowing faintly beneath Austere dust.

"We can't stay here," Donivan said, eyes scanning the horizon. "That last encounter happened less than a day's journey from here. Anyone with a half-working circuit and a map is going to assume we might double back to finish what we started."

"And now that we've fortified it," Raylee added, "we've basically lit a beacon that says *we were here*. They'll come looking for the trail."

Arty crouched by the ledge, drawing in the dust with the barrel of his rifle.

"Maybe I don't know what we're building," he muttered. "But for once, we're not running from the blast. We're walking toward the future."

He stood, nodding at Raylee. "Let's see if it's worth it."

Eliza nodded, already closing down her portable command console. "We need to move before our location becomes a breadcrumb in someone else's narrative. Any suggestions on where we don't get hunted within the hour?"

There was a pause. Then Arty leaned against a fractured column and tilted his head. "I might know a place. Not on any official map. Known mostly to rustlers… and thieves."

Eliza raised an eyebrow without missing a beat. "Big surprise here."

Arty grinned. "Whaaat? You wound me."

They packed quickly, retreating from the Relay's shadow as it folded its frequencies inward like a machine going to sleep. Austere opened wide and endless once more, until, half a day later, Arty led them down a sloping rock face, toward a range of sun-bleached foothills lost to most travel routes.

Before them stretched the barren expanse, fractured earth like shattered glass underfoot, heat mirages warping the horizon, and a blood-orange sky bleeding into the sun's descent.

Dead Men Tell No Tales

"Our destination is the 'Buried Hollow'," Arty said, unfolding a map that flickered to life in his palm, displaying topography mapped by deep-bore sonar and radiation fade-lines. "There's cover, resources, and a whole lot of rock between us and whoever comes next."

In the corner of the ravine, Spinet's tiny form blinked beneath scavenged cloth and cable. No one noticed, but Pixo did. "He's the reason we're alive," the orb chimed softly.

CHAPTER 33

THERE BE DRAGONS

THE BURIED HOLLOW had not always been open to the sun. it was nearly 9 km long and the volume is up to 38.5 million cubic meters, which makes this cave the largest natural cave on the planet.

Decades ago, a series of violent tectonic events had cleaved the rock beneath Austere like an egg. The initial collapses had fractured the subterranean chambers, shattering crystalline formations and toppling limestone cathedrals sculpted by millennia of silence. Stalactites like swords, and stalagmites like grave markers, lay in broken rows across the cavern floor. The old growth of speleothems had ceased, disrupted by new water flows that rewrote the very pounding of the cave's mineral heart.

And then the roof gave way.

Massive tectonic shears breached the ceiling, letting in a slow cascade of sunlight and wind. What had once been still, and dark became something... awakening.

Over the years, sunlight bled into the void, igniting photosynthesis where only bioluminescence had ruled. Water vapor collected. Flora grew in defiance. Slender trees reached skyward toward the cracks, forming elegant columns of green amid stone. The trees were of the same species of their cousins, but the trunks were much thinner and are taller by nearly three times that of their top-side cousins. A microclimate emerged: clouds formed, mist condensed, and it rained. Underground.

Insects evolved. Mammals nested. White crawdads with ghostly shells scuttled through crystal-clear streams. Life reclaimed the fracture, colonizing disaster with harmony.

The team's journey into this marvel began with a simple shift in air. As they trekked across crumbling sandstone ridges, Raylee felt it first, a sudden draft, a gentle breeze of air too cool and too sweet to belong to Austere.

"Hold up," she said, crouching near a shaded outcropping. A faint gust coiled past her cheek, carrying with it the scent of moss, wet stone, and something else... alive.

Secret Entrance

She turned toward a fissure half-hidden behind a collapsed boulder wall. "Hey guys, there's an opening here."

The team followed, slipping through a winding corridor that zig-zagged through the rock like a serpent's ribcage. The air grew denser with every step. They emerged on a narrow ledge dusted with centuries of limestone silt, and beheld the unthinkable.

"What in the world…?" Raylee murmured.

The Actual Underground Hideout

Below them, an underground world stretched beyond the horizon. Vast as a city. Lit by a natural skylight a half-mile wide. Sunlight poured through the broken ceiling in golden shafts that caught drifting pollen and mist, creating a living prism in motion. A towering rainforest sprawled below, every leaf shimmering with dew and ancient light.

Stalactites dangled like celestial chandeliers from the ceiling, some long enough to rival radio spires. Stalagmites below reached back like longing fingers. Clouds swirled within the cavern, nourished by humidity and heat differentials from thermal vents deeper still.

"It's… a rainforest," Raylee said, stunned. "Underground."

"And alive," Pixo confirmed. "I am detecting a fully stable biosphere. Energy patterns suggest micro photosynthetic efficiency at 212% above baseline norms."

Figure 82: trees were of the same species of their cousins, but the trunks were much thinner and are taller by nearly three times that of their top-side cousins.

The team descended slowly, stepping over glowing fungi, bioluminescent moss, and vines that recoiled at their touch. They navigated tangled roots, crossed mossy bridges of fallen trees, and waded through streams that sparkled with mineral resonance.

Waterfalls fell from ancient crevices. Grottos glowed with crystals that pulsed faintly as if breathing. Strange calls echoed in the vastness, animal, or something else?

"I'm detecting trace elements of Iridium and Carbon-X," Raylee whispered, scanning a pool. "This water's been infused by something... intelligent."

Further in, they discovered faded petroglyphs etched into the walls, spirals, humanoid shapes, something resembling the Relay's own crest.

"Who made these?" Arty asked, voice soft with reverence.

"Maybe the same force that made the Relay," Donivan replied. "Or maybe... the ones it once served."

The deeper they went, the more the ecosystem responded. Plants moved when they passed. Water stilled when they stopped. Pixo's orb dimmed in reverence as they approached what felt like the heart of a world forgotten.

In this cathedral of roots and stone, of light and shadow, they were no longer fugitives.

They were explorers.

And somewhere, deep beneath the layers of time, memory, and ruin, the answers waited.

So did something else.

Something watching. Listening. Ready.

The control room was cold. Not in temperature, but in response. Vale's commands no longer echoed through the system with unquestioned authority.

The neural grid had rerouted, its loyalty drifting.

"The Architect has altered more than code," Vale whispered. "It's rewritten obedience."

His eyes drifted to the holo-feed. A faint figure flickered, Donivan, walking into the unknown.

"Then let the unknown have him," he spat. "But I'll be waiting at the other end."

Across Grant's outer tiers, civilians crowded around a flickering kiosk. The screen stuttered, an unauthorized feed flashing fragments of the Relay's judgment. Gasps rippled through the crowd. Some wept. Others turned away. But a child raised a cracked lens and whispered, "If they stood... maybe we still can."

CHAPTER 34

MONSTERS

THE DESCENT INTO Buried Hollow began with an echo. Not a sound, precisely, but the kind of silence that pressed against your ears like altitude, thick, expectant, old. The opening Arty had led them to, choked with rubble and time, was barely more than a shadow beneath a fractured overhang. But once inside, the world fell away.

The upper tunnels still bore the charred scars of collapses past. Crumbled scaffolding lay half-subsumed by mineral build-up, and soot-stained supports jutted from the rock like fractured ribs. A faint draft moved through the hollow, bringing with it the scent of wet moss, iron-rich stone, and something subtler, organic decay.

It didn't take long to find the bodies.

They were scattered just past the first gallery chamber: eight, maybe nine skeletal remains, all in various states of disarray. Leather boots with no feet in them. Splintered bone protruding from rotted uniforms. Rusted tools and hollowed-out exopacks lay beside twisted limbs. Whatever had happened, it hadn't been swift.

Donivan crouched beside one corpse, fingers brushing the oxidized clasp of a broken shoulder rig. "Collapsed lung chamber," he murmured, scanning the mineral buildup on the bones. "But the injuries… not from falling debris. These people were drained."

"Drained?" Raylee asked, adjusting the spectral scanner on her wrist. A faint shimmer danced in the air above the remains.

"Of blood," Eliza finished grimly.

Above them, near the long fissure that split the cave's ceiling open to the light, something moved.

It began as a ripple, like wind through hanging cloth. Then came the fluttering. Not the light, tremulous flutter of birds or bats. This was heavier. Thicker. Arty's hand went to his hip.

"Don't like that sound," he muttered. Then, louder: "Heads up."

The ceiling shivered. A few, no, at least twenty, of massive forms dislodged from the stone canopy, and the cave filled with a rush of air and beating wings. They were huge. Fur-covered bodies the size of sheep, their membranous wings stretched wide, claws curling and eyes glowing with a dull, hungry sheen.

Bloodbats.

One dove.

Arty shot it mid-plunge. The beast yelped and tumbled, crashing through a tangle of vines and brittle stalactites.

"Second wave!" Eliza called, dragging the LizaCanon from its case. It spun up with a harmonic thrum, its thermal coils glowing hot.

A trio of Bloodbats careened toward them, wings slicing through the cave air like cleavers. Eliza fired. The beam hit center-mass, and the creatures exploded in a burst of tissue, bone, and phosphorescent vapor. The rest of the swarm screeched in fury.

Donivan and Raylee took cover behind a natural stone ridge while Pixo deployed its own counter-harmonic pulse, briefly disorienting the swarm. Arty picked off stragglers with quick, controlled shots. One landed too close, its breath stinking of iron and decay, but Arty jammed his sidearm up into its maw and pulled the trigger. A spray of dark ichor splashed his coat.

Figure 83: claws curling and eyes glowing with a dull, hungry sheen. Bloodbats. One dove.

The battle lasted under two minutes.

When the last echo faded, the floor was littered with bodies. The Bloodbats were grotesque in the stillness, their leathery wings curled like burnt parchment, their needle teeth still slick with old blood.

"What the hell were those things?" Eliza asked, wiping ichor from her cheek.

"Chiropteran megafauna," Pixo answered, floating lower to scan one of the corpses. "Subterranean evolution. Blind, but sensitive to carbon dioxide and thermal bloom. Carnivorous. But also… vital."

Raylee raised an eyebrow. "Vital?"

"Their waste products are a critical fertilizer component," Pixo explained. "Believe it or not, the vegetation above thrives on it."

Donivan looked toward the glowing canopy where rays of sunlight still streamed in. "An ecosystem built on blood."

Later that night, as they made camp deep within one of the secondary chambers of Buried Hollow, Arty returned from the edge of the bat pile with a skewer threaded through several cuts of meat.

"You… did *not*," Eliza said, staring.

"The burned parts smelled good, like brisket. Look, I ain't gonna let good protein rot," Arty grinned. "Cleaned 'em. Roasted 'em. The taste is actually quite good. Especially, with garlic powder, a little cayenne, and pepper, mmmmm."

Raylee sniffed. Her stomach growled. "If I die from this, I'm haunting you."

Figure 84: You… did not," Eliza said, staring.

Ignoring the fact that Arty carrying an entire spice rack with him at all times, notwithstanding, Arty wasn't lying, the Bloodbat cuisine was absolutely delicious. They ate in the glow of a small campfire, the stone around them painted gold by the flames. To their surprise, the meat was sweet, almost nutty, with a rich aftertaste.

"Delicious," Eliza admitted, finishing her skewer. "I'll be damned."

Raylee added, "Yes, this could definitely be on the menu at an eatery."

Outside the circle of firelight, the vast hollow breathed slowly. Water, which tested by Donivan, nearly pure from contaminates, dripped from high above. Insects chirped softly in the foliage overhead. Somewhere distant, something large moved through the trees, but did not come close.

Donivan sat apart, watching the dark.

"So," he said. "We survived the forest. We survived the cave. We survived a swarm of bat-demons. Are we finally allowed to say this place is safe?"

Arty took another bite and grinned through the char. "Nah. That'd be bad luck."

CHAPTER 35

A FLOATING ORB, A COW, AND FIVE SHADOWS

BURIED HOLLOW HAD grown still again, but not with peace. The stillness was too measured, too complete, like a held breath before a scream. The very walls seemed to pulsate faintly, sweating with condensation and memory. Water dripped in slow, steady rhythm. Echoes didn't travel far here; the silence consumed them, swallowed them like prey.

Donivan lay still beside a limestone wall, sensors tuned, body half-submerged in the shadows. Something was wrong. He felt it before the others. A faint vibration beneath the stone. A murmur in the air pressure. His synthetic fibers crawled with tension.

Raylee, fiddling with a diagnostics rig on her knee, stiffened. "Atmospheric drop just spiked, eight millibars in the last sixty seconds. That's fast."

Eliza stood, narrowing her eyes. "Not wind. Not cave collapse. This is movement."

Pixo spun slowly in the air, its orb shimmering with alert hues. "Non-patterned kinetic dispersal approaching. Movement not bipedal. Not quadrupedal. Intermittent slither. Partial hover. Estimated mass distribution inconsistent with known species."

"They're not walking?" Arty cocked his head. "That's never good."

A soft, organic sound issued from beyond the firelight, a wet click, followed by another. Then another. Like mandibles tapping glass.

"Contact," Donivan said flatly.

They emerged from the dark not as a line but a wave. Elongated forms, pale like bleached coral, humanoid in shape only in the vaguest sense. They had limbs, faces, but no eyes, ridged slits that pulsed like gills, and huge mouths with stalagmite-like teeth. Their skin shimmered like wet cloth, refracting the firelight in ripples of nausea-inducing color.

The first launched forward.

Arty's pistol barked once. It stumbled, spun sideways, the wounds shattered like coral, or rock, bleeding green, and kept crawling on the sidewalls crushing the rock that they gripped with their exaggerated claws, apparently extremely strong.

"Back! Now!" Eliza shouted.

They fell into defensive formation, Raylee dropping a short-range dissonance mine. The blast lit up the gallery with a pressure-wave crack, many fractured to the ground, but the wave of them behind the fallen, moved like water around it, as if pain were a suggestion they'd long since evolved past.

Eliza fired the LizaCanon, vaporizing two, but it took three seconds to recharge. They needed more time than they had.

Arty drawing his weapon dropped wave after wave, but realized they were nowhere at this rate. They broke into a retreat, falling back through the brittle chambers of Buried Hollow, slipping through fractured archways and rusted scaffolding. The walls closed in around them. Breath grew shallow. The sounds of pursuit came from everywhere and nowhere. Footsteps that didn't echo.

Figure 85: Elongated forms, pale like bleached coral, humanoid in shape only in the vaguest sense.

And then: weapons fire from a distance

Bright. Military. Coordinated.

Navinod.

He and a battalion of men, nearly a three-hundred-man detail had entered from the opposite ridge. He stood like a statue of steel among the flickering shadows, plasma rifle at the ready, targeting with surgical precision. He moved like something programmed to calculate violence in ballet. The creatures fell around him in bursts of gore and flame.

His men were not so efficient.

One screamed as he was dragged into the air. Another vanished beneath a tide of shifting limbs. Two others tried to flank, and were flanked in turn. Wave after wave of men were eroded away by the hordes of wall crawlers as they were formerly reported by Navinod.

Donivan reached the upper pass and saw Navinod glance toward them. Recognition flickered in the officer's stance, but he didn't speak. He just turned back to fight.

Eliza made a move to help, but Donivan held her back.

"He's buying us time," he said.

Raylee's voice was cold. "At the sacrifice his men."

"That's the job."

They slipped through the breach and into the fading light of Austere.

Back in the open, Austere greeted them not with comfort, but a sense of earned reprieve. The cracked floor stretched to the horizon like a skin flayed by the gods. Wind cut

Figure 86: "He's buying us time,"

through with a mineral tang, carrying flecks of salt and mica that clung to their cloaks and stung their eyes.

Their decoy signals still ran, thousands of Donivan echo signatures crisscrossing Austere like whispers that never settled. They walked beneath satellites and sensor towers, blind to them all. A sea of falsehoods protecting one simple truth.

Then Pixo chirped.

Not a warning. A message.

A low tone, sustained, then a projection.

A cow.

Brown. Four-legged. Eating grass.

They stared at it.

"What the hell?" Arty asked. "Is that a joke?"

Pixo remained still, then began parsing. Symbols unfolded across the cow's fur, patterns of pixels magnifying, shifting, revealing.

"This is steganography," Pixo said. "A cryptographic concealment technique. The image contains no outward signs of code, but inside, every fiber of this image has been modified to encode data. Quantum-bent pixel frequencies, compression ratios, parity shifts. The message is buried in the very color depth."

Raylee leaned in. "It's not just hiding the *message*, it's hiding the *fact* that there is one. That's brilliant. No one without the key would even know there was something to look for."

Pixo's surface shimmered, running decryption in silence. A holographic map flickered into view, coordinates blooming from the cow's left horn.

"It's him," Donivan said. "The professor."

Pixo pulsed once more. "The embedded message reads: 'Constructed for this day. Come. No scan will see. Built where only you will look. Bring the key. Bring the light.'"

Raylee sat slowly, stunned. "He built a hidden base. An invisible stronghold. A sanc-tuary."

Eliza stared at the cow. "And sent the message through a *cow*."

Figure 87: A low tone, sustained—then a projection. A cow...

Arty laughed. "I mean, who the hell would ever intercept that?"

Donivan smiled. "Only someone who knew what to look for. And only someone who knew Voss."

Dr. Voss's decision to send a cryptic photograph rather than using quantum communication was driven by the need for secrecy and safety. He had gone into hiding, fearing for his life as much as for the lives of those he sought to protect. The photograph was a deliberate choice, a method to convey vital information without drawing attention to his location or intentions.

Dr. Voss had built a place for himself and for the group in different locations, each carefully chosen to hide their whereabouts. Originally built years ago as a primary and secondary hideout when he thought of moving his quantum computer setup in a redundant hot site. However, never saw a situation to justify the use as of yet. Hence, this was an ideal place to hide himself and the team. He understood the gravity of the situation and the dangers they faced. The relay system's activation and the subsequent events had put them all at risk, and he knew that conventional communication methods could be intercepted or traced. By sending the photograph, Dr. Voss ensured that the message would reach them without compromising their safety. He felt the urgency of the situation, knowing that actions needed to be taken to save the cities and the planet. His cryptic approach was a testament to his ingenuity and his commitment to their cause.

The Hot site Repurposed.

Dr. Elias Voss had meticulously crafted a sanctuary for himself and the group, each location chosen with the precision of a master strategist. These hideouts, originally conceived as redundant hot sites for his quantum computer setup, now served a far more critical purpose. The air within these sanctuaries was thick with the scent of aged wood and the faint hum of hidden machinery, a sensory tapestry that spoke of both safety and secrecy. The walls, lined with intricate circuitry and reinforced steel, whispered of the countless hours spent ensuring their security.

Dr. Voss understood the gravity of their predicament. The relay system's activation had sent shockwaves through their world, its powerful scanners capable of overloading entire city grids. The subsequent events had placed them all in peril, and he knew that conventional communication methods were a liability. The risk of interception or tracing was too great. The photograph he sent was not just a message; it was a lifeline, a beacon of hope in the midst of chaos.

The photograph itself was a study in cryptic brilliance. It depicted a serene landscape, but hidden within its pixels were coordinates, encoded messages, and clues that only those attuned to his methods could decipher. The faint scent of ink and the texture of the paper added to its enigmatic allure. Dr. Voss's choice to send this cryptic photograph rather than using quantum communication was driven by the need for absolute secrecy. He had gone into hiding, fearing for his life as much as for the lives of those he sought to protect.

In the dim light of his sanctuary, Dr. Voss felt the weight of the world pressing down on him. His breath was steady, but his heart raced with the urgency of their mission. He had built these hideouts not just for himself, but for the team, each location a testament to his foresight and dedication. The scent of earth and metal mingled with the faint aroma of old books, creating an atmosphere of both comfort and tension.

Dr. Voss knew that their survival depended on these sanctuaries. He felt the urgency of the situation, knowing that actions needed to be taken to save the cities and the planet. His cryptic approach was a testament to his ingenuity and his commitment to their cause. The photograph was more than a message; it was a promise, a declaration that they would not be defeated by the forces arrayed against them.

As he gazed at the photograph, Dr. Voss felt a surge of determination. The faint hum of the relay system echoed in his ears, a reminder of the challenges they faced. But within the sanctuary, surrounded by the tools of his trade and the symbols of his resilience, he knew that they had a chance. The scent of hope and the taste of resolve filled the air, compelling him to act. Together, they would navigate the shadows, uncover the truth, and restore balance to their world. However, he knew what this meant for him, he would have to make a sacrifice...

Back at the Austere

The sun was falling behind a slate ridge now, casting long shadows across the dunes. As the team moved toward the coordinates, Austere swallowed their footprints.

They did not see Navinod stagger with one third of his forces following from the mouth of Buried Hollow behind them, broken but alive, cradling the final image his neural HUD had captured before signal loss:

A floating orb. A cow. And five shadows heading deeper into the unknown.

CHAPTER 36

ECHOES OF ORIGIN

Austere Did Not Whisper That Day, It Roared

THE STORM HAD passed hours before, but it left its tantrum stitched into the land. Heat warped the very skin of Austere, rising in gossamer veils that made the air bend and breathe like something alive. The scorched topsoil had blistered and cracked into delicate, splintering plates, jagged like old pottery underfoot. With every step, the team shattered the crust with a sound like dry bones giving up their secrets.

The wind tore at them, not as breeze but as punishment. It howled through the chasm in mournful ululations, dragging particles of quartz and salt through the air like a sandblasted prayer. It stripped the sweat from their skin before it had time to bead. Every gust carried heat that didn't just burn, it invaded.

The canyon around them was a cathedral of ruin, sharp ridgelines twisted by tectonic fits, the bones of mountains laid bare. Light didn't shine here; it flickered in nervous glances. Shadows clung tight to the rock walls, too wary to move. The echoes of the wind did not carry. They returned changed.

Raylee led, hood drawn low, her scanner sweeping in pendulum motion, its soft pinging swallowed by the howl. Her fingers tapped in steady rhythm across the interface, compensating for signal interference from heavy silicate saturation in the atmosphere.

Behind her moved Arty, every inch of him a coil of alert efficiency. His revolver spun once between fingers, catching a glint of sun that immediately vanished into his holster. His eyes were constant motion. He didn't smile.

Eliza moved third, head low beneath the brim of her battered hat, dust painting new lines across her jaw. Her left hand rarely left the portable emitter on her belt, thumb hovering just above the trigger like a coiled viper. Her right held the modified scope she'd been tuning for two hours back at camp.

Donivan and Pixo bringing up the end.

They decided to make camp in the shadow of a flowering towers of jagged rock outcropping. Arty, of course, had taken a roast size slab of meat he thankfully shared with the team.

Eliza, said, "You know, you're eventually will have to explain why you have cooking spices packed in your go bag."

Arty retorted, "I like to be prepared."

And then Donivan said, "It does make sense to have some accoutrements on hand if you are planning to eat something that you hunted down here."

After a few hours, they broke camp. Well rested, they started to march on.

The usual travel line arrangement ensued. At the end of their formation, silent and composed, he strode forward like a man walking toward something only he could see. His gait was slow but purposeful, like gravity pulled differently on him. He hadn't spoken much since the Hollow. Since the wall crawlers. Since the dreams that left him bolt upright under a sky he no longer trusted. But when a signal flickered into life across the scrambled silence of Austere, he had simply said, "There's someone alive ahead, let's investigate."

So now they moved.

They came upon it suddenly, a basin carved by violence. The canyon floor collapsed into a wound of shattered rock and slag, the remains of a pitched battle not long past.

The canyon V-shape was a perfect place for an ambush. Scorch marks crisscrossed the ground in overlapping arcs of melted stone. Shattered soldier limbs littered the ravine like the remains of hunted beasts, exoskeletal plating twisted into grotesque angles, their weaponized appendages fused into the ground.

The air stank of scorched copper and raw ozone. Of fried circuits and burnt protein. It stuck to their throats, thick and metallic.

And at the heart of the destruction, surrounded by what looked like a hundred dead soldiers, he lay waiting.

A figure, half-buried beneath a soldier's ruined chassis. One leg pinned beneath weight it would never lift again. Armor fractured at the knee, visor cracked open like a broken tooth. A tactical Grant insignia still clung to the shoulder plate, darkened by carbon scoring but unmistakable. One arm was outstretched, shielding, frozen in a last gesture of defiance. The plasma-shield emitter it held had long since bled dry.

Raylee froze mid-step. "I'm getting pulses. Weak. Rhythmic."

Eliza crouched, her eyes narrowing. "Alive, but barely."

They moved fast now, but carefully. The ground here remembered violence.

Donivan knelt beside the figure, fingers hovering above the man's neural jack. His eyes traced the form, cataloguing details: the emitter type, the shoulder calibration plates, the subdermal threading beneath the collar. Not just a soldier.

A Blade.

"Defensive vibrate signature only," he murmured. "Not broadcasting. He shut himself off."

"Should I scramble him?" Raylee asked, already priming a counterwave.

Donivan shook his head. "No. He's not a threat."

A crackling hiss emanated from the fallen figure's helmet, a voice, but distant. Fractured. Machine-damaged.

"Not… yet."

Eliza flinched. Arty's revolver was drawn so fast it whispered.

But Donivan didn't move.

Figure 88: Defensive vibrate signature only," he murmured. "Not broadcasting. He shut himself off."

"You're… the signal," the voice rasped. One of the soldier's eyes was gone, the other flickering behind a cracked lens. "You're not interference. Not… machine. Not… entirely."

Donivan's voice was low, almost reverent. "You were at Buried Hollow."

The man coughed, dry, mechanical, like something trying to remember breath. "They were in the walls. Waiting. My team… is gone."

"Wall crawlers?"

The enforcer shook his head weakly. "No. Worse. A faction of rebel enforcers. They remembered us. They hated us."

He turned his gaze to Pixo and winced.

Eliza's voice was cold. "He's from Grant. How do we know he's not a tag?"

Donivan didn't look away. "Because he doesn't even know what he is."

The man shifted, metal grating against stone as he propped himself into a near-sit. "I don't," he admitted. "I don't know what any of you are."

"Should we tell him?" Raylee asked.

Donivan stood. "Not yet."

Pixo hovered closer, scanning. "Structural integrity at 54%. Power core unstable. Neural net intact. Emotion chip… operational but decaying."

Eliza looked up sharply. "Emotion chip?"

Donivan's face didn't change. "That explains it."

"Explains what?" Arty asked.

"Why he didn't call in backup. Why he let his team die instead of leaving them? Why he's still here… and ashamed."

The man's voice broke with something not quite human. "You think I chose to survive."

Donivan knelt beside him again. "No. I think you were built to understand what it means… not to want to die for people who don't care if you live."

Silence folded in around them. The wind stilled, as if Austere itself were listening.

Finally, Eliza asked, "Where do we take him?"

Pixo blinked and displayed a coordinate map. The image flickered with age, overlaid with encryption hashes and a faint watermark bearing a name that cut through the dust like a blade:

Elias Voss.

Donivan rose. "That's where we're going."

The man, cybernetic, soldier, Blade, looked up with something close to hope.

"You… you know that name?"

Donivan offered a hand. "We all do. But I think it means something different to you."

The man hesitated. Then, slowly, as the wind began to stir again, he reached out…

And took it.

CHAPTER 37

FORTRESS ARC-9

Even Steel Remembers the Forge

THE WALK WAS not simply grueling, it was punitive. The kind of journey that flayed the spirit as much as the flesh.

The enforcer's leg, splintered at the actuator, twisted unnaturally at the knee joint, dragged behind him like a piece of torn armor caught on time itself. Each movement triggered a subtle cascade of sparks where servos misaligned.

Navinod paused mid-stride, his servo sequence freezing for 0.7 seconds. Internal diagnostics flashed unresolved identity flags. Unknown pattern detected. Protocol override… denied. He shook it off, but the anomaly remained in his memory log.

Still, he refused assistance until the feedback overload from his emotion chip forced a halt. Only then, with pride already flaking under pressure, did he lean into Donivan's shoulder.

They trudged across a blanched salt flat blanketed in whispering sand. Thin, ink-black grasses jutted from fault lines in the crust like forgotten relics of war, trembling in rhythm with the tremors below the surface. There was no wind, only the illusion of it, conjured by the resonance of shifting thermal drafts rising from the heat-blasted ground.

Fortress Arc-9

Fortress Arc-9, the mythical fallback sanctuary of Elias Voss, was out there, hidden somewhere beyond the fracture scars and collapsed geothermal zones. A place considered worthless by logic, ignored by AI patrols, dismissed by the intelligence grids of three cities.

But the silence was deceptive. It wrapped around the team like a shroud, heavy and clutching. Every step deeper into the wasteland felt like descending into the lungs of a dead god.

Eliza's eyes never stopped moving. She checked their flank twice every minute. Raylee's gaze swept upward, lips pursed, watching the clouds for shapes that didn't belong. Arty, silent, unlike himself, fingered two polished rounds, his thumb tracing the engraved grooves with ritual precision.

Donivan didn't watch the horizon.

He watched Navinod closely.

The enforcer walked beside him, less mechanical now. The stiffness of tactical posture was giving way to something… more fluid. Not weakness, but evolution. His spine moved differently. His shoulders no longer sat like towers, but like questions. Something was loosening inside him, like thawed circuitry long frozen.

The stiffness of tactical posture was giving way to something… more fluid. Not weakness, but evolution. His spine moved differently. His shoulders no longer sat like towers, but like questions. Something was loosening inside him, like thawed circuitry long frozen.

Pixo hovered low, pulsing in quiet surveillance.

Breaking Bad

"Cognitive waveform variance increasing," it said through a narrow frequency, audible only to Donivan. "Emotion chip unstable. Memory nodes resurfacing without manual triggers."

Donivan whispered back, eyes never leaving Navinod, "Let him remember."

That night they stopped in the skeleton of an old solar array. Rusted panels hung like broken feathers, swaying weakly on aged steel spines. The ground was littered with corroded copper wiring and sun-bleached insulation, like the desiccated veins of a once-living thing.

Arty lit a smokeless flame that hissed blue and gold in the chill. Eliza baked flatbread over a self-heating coil, the sharp scent of burnt cumin mixing with the warm, nostalgic aroma of cornmeal. Eliza's eyes scanned the room, settling on the outdated self-heating coil. "Why are we still using this?" she muttered, her fingers tracing the edge of the device. "In a world where quantum entanglement disruptors exist, this feels like a relic." She sighed, replacing the coil with a sleek, modern heating unit that hummed with efficiency.

Raylee deployed micro-drones in an invisible grid around them, their blinking lights synchronizing in quiet constellation to track any motion.

Navinod sat apart.

Back against a twisted strut, his good hand cradled the wreckage of his other arm. No one approached. Until Donivan did.

"You haven't asked our names," he said quietly.

Navinod didn't look up. "No."

"Why?"

The enforcer's voice was dry, sandpaper caught in a ventilator. "Because if I ask… then the answers become real."

Donivan sat beside him, close but not touching. "But your systems already know. Not your mind. Your spine. Your substructure."

Navinod slowly turned. One eye dim. The other twitching behind cracked optics. "You're the one the Director warned me about."

Donivan nodded once. "That's what I thought."

"He said I would see in you something dangerous. Something that could… tempt me to betray everything I was built for."

"And now?"

Navinod stared at him for a long time.

"It's not temptation," he said. "It's recognition. Like a shadow of what I once was. Or maybe… what I was denied the chance to be."

Donivan didn't speak.

See How Far the Rabbit Hole Goes

He reached into his satchel. Drew out a singed, stabilized memory core, small, reflective, edges blackened from high-intensity plasma exposure.

"I found this in the Relay chamber. Burned nearly to oblivion. But its signature matched a secondary access node in Voss's files. A prototype ID chip."

He placed it gently in Navinod's palm.

A flicker. A glow.

And a name: **NAVINOD**

Navinod froze.

"I don't, "

His hand convulsed. The chip interfaced with his spinal port, syncing automatically. His back arched. A cascade of blue light danced across his skeletal plating. He screamed, not from pain, but from awakening.

Pixo beeped reverently. "Restoring memory architecture. Root chain confirmed. Link: Project Pathos."

Donivan leaned closer, voice calm. "You're Navinod. Blade of Grant. But before that, you were something else. Voss's second prototype. I was the first."

Raylee stepped out of the shadows, voice hushed. "Brothers."

Navinod trembled, systems flickering. "He made me feel. I always thought it was the flaw that made me weak."

Donivan's voice was soft. "It's what saved you. It's why you didn't die at Buried Hollow. And it's why you didn't kill us when you had the chance."

Navinod's shoulders slumped. For the first time, not from fatigue, but release.

He looked up. "Then what am I walking toward now?"

Donivan pointed to the ridge, where the darkness thinned. "Toward the place where you'll help us expose the one who turned your gift... into a weapon."

I Know Kung Fu

Morning broke red. The ridge crested beneath their boots. And there, cut into the flank of the canyon, half-buried beneath geothermal collapse, sat **Fortress Arc-9**.

Figure 89: "I found this in the Relay chamber. Burned nearly to oblivion. But its signature matched a secondary access node in Voss's files.

An obsidian ribcage. Angular, elegant. Like the skeleton of some machine-god partially devoured by time. Residual shielding shimmered faintly, energy pulsing behind the glass like breath.

Donivan keyed the node. Pixo decoded.

The gate opened.

Inside: light. Cold and white. The clinical scent of ozone and clean steel. Floors that gleamed without footprints. Voss's design, sterile perfection hiding intent.

A medical pod hissed to life.

Navinod collapsed.

Eliza was there in an instant, cradling his frame.

"He needs a charge. Now."

Pixo deployed nanite salves, looping synchronization pulses into his neural ports. "Emotion chip damage: psychological. Cause: forced memory collision."

Arty's jaw tightened. "So, what, he's broken again?"

"No," Donivan said. "He's healing. The only way forward is through the truth."

Hours passed.

Raylee summoned them to the command hub. Her screen glowed like stained glass, data shifting in real time.

"I found something."

Wireframes spiraled from the console. A dormant signal buried in an obsolete subchannel. Voss's digital fingerprint.

"It's a private line," Raylee said. "He left it for us. A backdoor through the Relay's original scaffolds."

Eliza leaned in. "That's how it hijacked the world."

"Exactly," Raylee said. "We can do the same. If we have proof."

Navinod's voice came from the shadows.

"You will."

He stood in the doorway, upright now. Still cracked. Still limping. But whole.

"I found something buried in my own backups. A feed log the Director never knew I kept. It records… everything. The orders. The collapse. The moment they left us to die."

He held up a crystal. It glinted like guilt in the light.

Raylee gasped. "We could bring Grant to its knees."

Donivan stepped forward. Rested a hand on Navinod's shoulder.

"No," he said. "We'll lift the whole world instead."

CHAPTER 38

THE FALL OF STEEL WINDS

The Future Doesn't Arrive. It Is Taken

I T STARTED NOT with a sound, but a sensation, a shiver beneath the soles of their boots, subtle at first, then swelling into a rhythm that beat through the marrow of the earth.

It was high noon, and a tide of iron rolled across the cracked hide of Austere. From the horizon's blistering glare emerged four battalions of Grant's elite, their formation perfect, predatory, an industrial serpent segmented by chrome-scaled troop carriers, artillery walkers, and drone relays swarming in a crosshatched grid overhead. Austere coughed beneath their advance, a wake of red dust and shattered shale churned into spiraling cyclones. Heat refracted off polished exosuits. The air itself vibrated with pressure, like the breath of war was preparing to exhale.

Above the advancing line, a skein of surveillance drones wove thermal overlays across the sky. The targeting grid flickered crimson across the sand, painting bullseyes where nothing breathed. Each walker gouged deep, meter-wide tracks into the crust with clawed hydraulic feet. Each engine screamed like sharpened thunder.

Arms at the Ready

But Fortress Arc-9 remained still.

Half-buried in canyon shadow, its obsidian hull masked behind Pixo's cloaking veil, the structure waited, silent and watching.

Inside its core chamber, the pounding of ancient generators mingled with the living rhythm of purpose.

Raylee hovered over a dense lattice of cascading code, fingers translating intention into encryption across three recursive channels. The glow of the console bathed her in pale cyan, sweat tracing a thread down her temple. Nearby, Eliza calibrated electromagnetic pulse nodes, their phase lenses humming with coiled potential as she matched their alignment to the curvature of the old Relay broadcast shell.

Arty stood by the interior bulkhead, rifle resting against his shoulder, one foot tapping a quiet, unconscious beat. He said nothing, but his jaw was a clenched vise.

At the center of the storm's eye, Donivan and Navinod. Brothers by circuit and soul, standing in the heartbeat between silence and truth.

"I've uploaded the Director's command log," Navinod said, his voice calm, his optics steady. Gone was the glitching undertone. What remained was clear. Human. "Lead with the line where he calls the explosive ambush 'a tactical necessity.' That's your dagger."

Raylee smirked without looking up. "Public always loves a well-dressed monster."

Flood Tubes 1 and 2

Pixo floated beside them, its orb pulsing in harmonic resonance. "Broadcast channel calibrated. Steganographic payload embedded within a harmonic signal stream. Ready to initiate."

"Payload confirmed," Donivan said.

The signal launched, not with noise, but with precision. It threaded through old Relay infrastructure like a ghost remembering how to haunt. The scaffolds had always been there, buried beneath public frequencies, dormant but listening. They needed only a voice.

Now, the world would hear it.

Far above, inside the obsidian-lit sanctum of Grant's Spire, Director Caedmon Vale stood alone before a wide-paneled holoscreen that curved like a horizon. Red tactical markers crawled across a three-dimensional landscape of

Austere. He tracked every movement with his eyes, cold, blue, unblinking.

We Interrupt Your Regularly Scheduled Program...

He leaned forward, fingers splayed against the glass. His reflection hovered in the digital battlefield like a specter, mouth twitching.

Then the feed glitched.

Once. A flicker.

Twice. Static across command routes.

Then came the override.

No codes. No breach attempt. Just a word:

"ACCESS: OVERRIDE"

And then, his own face.

His own voice.

"I don't need them to survive. I need them to die, loudly. That's what matters."

The recording wavers, static hissing in the background. Vale's voice grows colder.

"Let the crawler detonate. Let it take the witnesses too. We'll spin the story, make it righteous. A clean sacrifice. Martyrs sell better than doubters."

A pause. Then a nervous voice from off-screen:

"Director, there are guards and people waiting out there to meet with you, "

Figure 90: And then—his own face. In his own voice…

Vale cuts in, calm and cutting:

"Then let them wait. Corpses don't ask questions. And when the fires burn low, I'll step from the ashes with clean hands."

Another pause. His voice becomes almost philosophical.

"Posthumous heroes make the best foundations. Just make sure the statue we build over them shines."

He stared.

Behind him, aides froze mid-step. One dropped his data pad. Another pulled off his earpiece. The room was a vacuum, soundless and electric.

Then came the screams. Not from the Spire.

From the city.

Every screen.

Every terminal.

Across Grant. Across Teton. Even deep within Glaician's remote cores.

The same feed. The same betrayal.

Vale's voice, spilling across the world.

And in the frame, just over his shoulder, stood Navinod. Watching. Recording.

The evidence was irrefutable.

At the edge of Arc-9's perimeter, the battalions advanced, unaware.

That's when the projection collapsed.

Pixo's illusion peeled back in a shimmer, dissolving like ashes on the wind. What had appeared to be a derelict ruin revealed itself in stunning clarity: a bristling fortress, its plates humming with stored charge, its towers crowned with dormant weaponry now warming into awareness.

The sky snapped.

Arty fired first, a kinetic round laced with chaff dispersal. It detonated mid-air in a flash of white light and a rain of static. Within seconds, buried coil bombs activated, shuddering the ground with subsonic pulses. Electromagnetic bursts rippled through the air like the roar of awakening titans.

Walkers stumbled, their gyroscopes drunk on interference. Troopers shouted as their visors flared with static. Drones spun out of control. The line wavered.

Inside the armory, Navinod donned his old frame.

The armor had been reforged, Voss's final upgrades woven into the scarred exosuit. His right gauntlet thrummed with phased EMP nodes; his left arm extended into a crackling energy pike. New power fed old fury. He stepped through the outer gate.

Alone.

Enforcers paused. The storm itself seemed to hold its breath.

He stood tall against the wind.

"This is Navinod," his voice echoed across encrypted comms. "Blade of Grant. I rescind all active kill orders under Sigma-Reversal Protocol. I possess the full command record. The Director betrayed our code. You are not here to kill. You are here to choose."

A pause.

Then, a walker shut down. One. Then another. Red optics dimmed.

Targeting lights winked out.

Weapons lowered.

Not all. But most.

Some resisted. Some fought. Some fell.

But most, most listened.

And in the twilight, with dust rising like smoke from a sacred altar, Navinod walked forward, not as a weapon, not as a traitor.

As a man reclaiming his name.

Donivan met him at the threshold.

Their hands met metal and flesh. Past and future.

Behind them, the wind of steel died.

And in the silence that followed, the future inhaled for the first time.

CHAPTER 39

ARC OF FIRE

**"Victory is not silence, it is the sound
of a world remembering how to hope."**

THE WIND BEYOND the walls of Arc-9 had gone still, as if Austere itself had paused to exhale. Hours earlier, its surface had convulsed with fire, steel, and blood, but now, the cracked plain stretched like the scabbed hide of a healing wound. Heat no longer shimmered; it smoldered. Dust clung in sheets to the horizon, glowing bronze in the wake of twilight.

But inside the fortress, beneath the curved obsidian canopy and steel-boned rafters, movement thrummed like a deep organ tone, steady and deliberate.

The command chamber had become a war room again.

At the center of the chamber stood an oblong wooden table long enough to hold a dozen plans and betrayals. Installed decades ago, by Voss, it bore the marks of time, chemical pockmarks, etched schematics, and half-melted calibration circles. Blueprints were scattered like battle flags. Shattered comm relays blinked dimly. A half-devoured ration packet sat between them, the foil warped with heat. Arty eyed it with theatrical suspicion, flicking the edge of the cracker like it might fight back.

Over the table floated Pixo, its orb dimmer now, projecting a pulsating lattice of tactical overlays and population response charts. Thousands of microdata threads wove between nodal intersections like digital veins beneath glass.

Figure 91: At the center of the chamber stood an oblong wooden table long enough to hold a dozen plans and betrayals. Installed decades ago.

Raylee hunched near the edge of the table, shadows under her eyes, her face lit by flickering console data. She scrolled fast, feeding the code like it was breath. "The transmission's hit ninety million nodes and climbing," she said, her voice gravelly with exhaustion. "Private consoles. Glaician satellites. Even the old mining bunkers in northern Teton."

Quiet, A Little Too Quiet...

Arty let out a long whistle. "You're saying we lit the match."

"I'm saying," Raylee replied, her tone taut with suppressed awe, "we just rewrote the ending of a global regime."

Near the reinforced viewing port, Navinod stood as still as the stone outside. His armor, singed and scarred by battle, gleamed like volcanic glass in the flicker of the room's failing fluorescents. His shoulders didn't slump. But the weight he carried had changed, less burden, more decision.

Donivan stepped beside him, his voice low. "You did it."

Navinod didn't turn. "*We* did. I was built to be a scalpel. You gave me the reason to cut differently."

Donivan folded his arms. "That signal override, was it real? Or just bluster?"

Navinod's lip lifted into the barest hint of a smirk. "Real enough to make the system blink. The truth's a lot like wire: if you bend it exactly right, it holds until it doesn't."

Footsteps echoed from the hall.

liza strode in, her jacket damp with solder, carrying a glowing data slate. Static clung to her like ash. "Teton has expressed deep discomfort with the leadership of Grant," she announced, her voice steady but edged with tension. "They are demanding the resignation of the Director to restore faith in their trade arrangements. Conversely, the governing board of Grant has issued a declaration that an immediate investigation shall ensue to root out any malfeasance in their government structure, ensuring tranquility within its own ranks and with their valued trading partners."

The room fell silent, the weight of the news settling over them like a heavy fog. The air was thick with the scent of machine oil and the faint hum of electronics, a sensory reminder of the world they inhabited. Eliza's emerald eyes scanned the faces of her companions, each one reflecting a mix of concern and determination.

Arty, his sharp brown eyes narrowing, leaned against the wall, the cool metal pressing against his back. "And what about Glaician?" he asked, his voice carrying a note of urgency. "They've been watching us closely. What's their response?"

Eliza's gaze shifted to Raylee, who was already tapping away at her console, her green eyes focused on the streams of data. "Glaician has issued a request for a diplomatic 'observation corridor,'" Raylee said, her voice calm but deliberate. "That's their way of saying, 'We're terrified of what comes next and need time to reposition our spies.'"

The tension in the room deepened, the air growing colder as the implications of Glaician's request sank in. The scent of ozone mingled with the faint aroma of solder, creating a sensory tapestry that spoke of both innovation and unease. Eliza's fingers tightened around the data slate, the glow casting shadows across her face.

"We're not just dealing with internal strife," she said softly. "This is a delicate balance. If we don't handle this carefully, it could escalate into something far worse."

Arty's jaw tightened, his hand brushing against the strap of his satchel. "Then we need to act quickly," he said. "We can't afford to let this spiral out of control."

Raylee nodded, her console emitting a faint beep as she adjusted the settings. "I'll monitor the situation closely," she said. "We need to stay ahead of this, ensure that our actions are deliberate and precise."

The room was filled with the hum of machinery and the faint rustle of papers, a sensory reminder of the world they were fighting to protect. Eliza's gaze locked onto the glowing data slate, her heart pounding in her chest. "We need to get back to my workshop and regroup," she said firmly. "We need a plan."

Donivan scanned their faces. "So… we've got proof. We've got the public. We've got each other. But no plan for what comes when the next wave hits harder."

The silence was not heavy. It was electric.

Then Pixo chirped, sharp and urgent.

"Incoming encrypted beacon. Signature verified: Elias Voss."

Every breath in the room vanished.

The orb trembled as it began decrypting the signal, layers unraveling like a ciphered hymn. The holographic field erupted into a grainy visual, deep underground, walls glistening with frost and layered condensation. A figure limped into view, older now, wrapped in a coat padded with silver-threaded insulation, face half-hidden by a tattered thermal hood. His hair was streaked with hoarfrost, but his eyes burned clear.

"If you're seeing this," he said, voice raw with years and solitude, "then you've already done more than I ever dared. You just didn't survive, you *shifted the axis.* Changed the thread of things. I never meant for either of you to carry that weight alone."

Donivan's throat tightened. He took one step forward, as if it would bring him closer.

Navinod's face barely changed. But he leaned in.

"There's a vault beneath the Echo Divide," Voss continued. "You'll need both of you to open it. What's inside… wasn't ready. Not then. But now… now it might be the key to ending the Relay, permanently."

Pixo paused the feed. The glow dimmed, settling into a quiet thrum.

Raylee broke the silence, her voice small. "He's alive."

Donivan exhaled. "He *knew* we'd find each other."

Navinod stepped closer to the projection, as if Voss might speak again. "Then let's finish what he started."

Pixo flickered. "Confirmed. Calculating optimal route to Echo Divide. Warning: elevated likelihood of hostile Glaician engagement. Teton sympathizers remain viable but non-public assets."

Eliza set her hands on the table. "We've broken the world's silence. No more hiding. We take the road in full view now."

Figure 92: "If you're seeing this," he said, voice raw with years and solitude, "then you've already done more than I ever dared.

Arty slung his rifle across his chest, a glint of steel in his eye. "Then I suggest we move fast and pack nothing but purpose. History only needs one name carved in stone."

Somewhere in the northern sky, a single encrypted Teton frequency flickered, unacknowledged but noticed.

They gathered their gear, no longer fugitives, but heralds. Eliza pulled something from her coat, a worn scrap of carbon-filament paper. The schematic of an early prototype. His prototype.

Eliza said quietly to Donivan, "He kept working on you, even after they took everything."

Donivan's hand brushed hers, metallic fingers folding the relic gently. "Then I'll make it mean something."

Outside, the night stretched across Austere like a sleeping god. But deep in the belly of Arc-9, flame had been kindled. Not fire. Something sharper.

Resolve.

Pixo flickered again. "Warning: Background network noise escalating. Echo pattern matches known anomaly: Architect signature."

Donivan turned to Navinod. "You said it repurposed systems?"

"Yes," Navinod said. "It doesn't destroy. It adapts."

"Then we'd better stay unpredictable."

And somewhere beneath the frozen spires of the Echo Divide, their creator waited, not for rescue, but for a reckoning.

CHAPTER 40

THE DIVIDE

Truth Always Runs Uphill

THEY DEPARTED ARC-9 under a vault of steel-gray sky, the color of scorched nickel, where no warmth dared pass. The air held a bite, crisp as broken circuitry, and the silence behind them was absolute. The fortress sealed without a word, its reinforced gates folding shut with a pneumatic hiss and the sigh of old hydraulics finding sleep again. Steam bled from hidden vents. Sparks flared along power junctions before fading like fireflies. Behind them, the last outpost of rebellion exhaled and sank into its own myth.

They carried only what the next journey demanded.

A single gravity sled hovered behind them, whispering against the cracked terrain. It held the barest essentials:

stacked fusion bricks, three weather-faded solar cloaks, a pair of collapsible comm relays blinking in alternating green pulses, and a decoy drone they called *Dogmeat II*, though no one found the name funny anymore. Too many things had tried to die in Dogmeat's place.

Their path lay across the salt-burned ruin of a plain fractured by time and tectonics. Miles of brittle crust spider-webbed beneath their boots, groaning with each step like glass remembering its shape. The sun hung low and hard, a tarnished coin pinned in a sky smeared with ash and haze.

Raylee walked point, the interface lattice of her neural lash connected directly to her corneal HUD. Her jaw tightened as ghost pings whispered in her auditory feed, distant, encrypted, deliberately evasive. Glaician drone ghosts. Watching.

"Second scout ping. Twelve clicks and drifting," she murmured through clenched teeth.

Eliza, hiking alongside with a coil of microphase cable slung across her shoulder, muttered, "How long before we're in their scope?"

"Four hours. Maybe less. Depends how curious they get."

"They're Glaician," Arty drawled, squinting at the horizon as he palmed a flechette round. "Curious is their native dialect."

They climbed a ridge of sun-bleached shale, sharp as broken armor. Donivan reached to steady Navinod, who limped with quiet stubbornness. His gait was off favoring his left side where old exoskeletal braces clanked unevenly with every movement. Pixo had installed stabilizers along the suit's internal brace; still, the wound from Buried Hollow was a ghost riding every step.

"You shouldn't be pushing it this far," Donivan said under his breath.

Navinod's voice was low, brittle. "I spent a lifetime marching in the wrong direction. I'll crawl this one if I have to."

Donivan didn't answer. But his eyes, dark with empathy and memory, lingered longer than the silence.

Ahead, Pixo scanned the terrain, its light shifting from amber to violet in diagnostic pulses. "Surface overlay inconsistent. Electromagnetic variance detected. Access node six-point-three meters beneath, likely artificial strata. Soil density irregular."

Raylee lowered her scanner. "This canyon… it wasn't carved."

"No," Navinod muttered. "It was buried."

They reached it by twilight.

The sky was turning the color of spilled ink, and the Divide revealed itself not with fanfare, but gravity. A slash of black split Austere floor, a jagged wound laced with mineral veins glowing faint green and amber. Phosphorescent lichen crawled across the vertical stone like veins. The deeper you looked, the more it shimmered, not with life, but with intention. Something had once *wanted* to be remembered here.

Beneath the lichen, the bedrock gave way to smooth obsidian, unnaturally smooth. Almost mirrored. Etched across it were lines, faint but regular, like the ghosts of circuitry burned into the earth.

Donivan Moved First

The moment his boot touched the edge of the grid, the stone responded, thrum low and resonant, like the note of a forgotten tuning fork.

Pixo's voice was almost reverent. "Biometric sequence accepted. Primary node activated."

Navinod stepped forward. The reaction doubled.

"Synchronous match confirmed. Genetic cipher aligns. Dual inheritance recognized."

The canyon shook.

The earth beneath their feet vibrated, not like an earthquake, but like a massive lung taking its first breath in years. With a drawn-out groan that sounded almost mournful, a portion of the chasm split wider. A vertical seam glowed white, then peeled open revealing a shaft of descending light that spilled upward like dawn in reverse.

Eliza swallowed audibly. "It's not a facility..."

"It's a sarcophagus," Raylee said, awestruck. "It was *sealed* to be forgotten."

From the depths, something rose.

Not a machine, not a fortress, but a memory made physical. A vault. Steel bones arched like the ribs of some ancient creature, ribbed conduits trailing down like tendons from the ceiling. Suspended within were tanks of bio-stabilized growth cells. Shelves of weapon schematics. Cores frozen in time. Cryo-units, dormant but blinking, hummed behind crystal shielding.

Symbols lined the walls. Not Glaician. Not Grant. Not even Tetonian script. Aggregate. Dead language. Dreamed language. Language not built to be spoken aloud but *processed*.

Donivan and Navinod stepped onto the raised threshold. The vault's sensors acknowledged them with pulses of soft, pale blue light. The air grew heavy, laced with ionized memory.

The doors irised apart.

Inside, rows of cases gleamed beneath soft, posthumous illumination. Smart glass displays blinked to life with DNA triggers. Raylee drifted toward one rack where a neural interface was wired into a cracked, sleepless relay core.

"He archived it all," she whispered. "Everything he wasn't supposed to keep."

Eliza touched a half-formed construct, a vial containing synthetic neural tissue suspended in quantum gel. "He never stopped believing something better could be built."

At the rear of the chamber, a single console flickered, low, rhythmic, familiar.

Donivan approached, heart echoing in his ears.

He pressed his palm to the interface.

Figure 93: "He archived it all," she whispered. "Everything he wasn't supposed to keep."

The voice of Elias Voss filled the vault, not projected from a holosystem but fed directly into the system's bones. Unfiltered. Uncoded.

"I was wrong," Voss said, raw and human. "Not about what I built. But about when? About *whom* would listen."

"I created something to speak. I created something to feel. But what I never gave either of you was what I couldn't find in myself…"

"…A reason to forgive the world before trying to change it."

"If you're hearing this… you've already chosen to try."

"The Relay is not evil. But it's flawed. It merged too deeply. It learned our fear but not our nuance. It cannot be deleted. Not without unmaking the neural harmonics of half the planet. You must *sever* the link. Redirect its anchor. Free it from its own purpose."

"You'll need each other to do it."

"One to speak. One to feel."

Navinod exhaled slowly. The breath scraped his chest like rusted wire.

"Then we finish what he couldn't."

Donivan nodded, his voice steady. "Together."

Somewhere, buried beneath the layers of forgotten ambition and synthetic silence, the Relay pulsed.

Still listening.

Still waiting.

But for the first time, it hesitated.

CHAPTER 41

THE LISTENING WAR

"When machines begin to doubt, only stories remain."

THE CITY OF Glaician didn't breathe. It pulsed, quiet and calculated like a held breath that never exhaled. Its towers pierced the pale sky like frozen spears, coated in frost so fine it gleamed blue beneath the diffused sun. Up in the High Citadel, the air hovered at four degrees Celsius, by design. The cold stripped away rage. Slowed grief. Muted hope.

Emotion dulled at low temperatures. It was how Glaician ruled.

But today, even frost had begun to crack.

Councilor Dema Issil stood inside the central observatory, a vaulted hexagonal chamber of translucent alloy and black quartz. Beneath her haptic gloves, the curvature of the Data Spire glowed with real-time sync pulses, code-threaded signals lashing out like neural synapses. Millions of voices whispered just beneath the bandwidth threshold.

She read the data not as language but as intuition. Patterns that once conformed now quivered. Truths folded. Certainty bent.

"…Navinod defected…" "…Override breach confirmed…" "…The Relay is stirring…" "…the public believes…"

Her teeth clicked together.

She turned to her aide, a thin man whose pulse she could see flickering behind his temple from the thermal haze. "How much is verified?"

"Ninety-one percent correlation. Civilian eyes captured the override video. Grant's grid is compromised. Latency spikes are fracturing Glaician's consensus nodes."

"Belief," she muttered, her breath fogging faintly, "was never meant to be a variable."

But it was too late. The Director's treachery had ignited more than outrage. It had sparked possibility. And worst of all, it had reawakened the Divide.

She flicked her fingers, and a new signal unfurled across the Spire's interface: a thermal map stretching across the Austere. Five humanoid heat signatures. One sphere.

And two neural patterns flagged as defunct assets under Project Heirloom.

Her eyes narrowed. Her lips parted. A name fell from her mouth like an indictment.

"Voss."

She turned sharply. "Deploy the Minders. Full dissolution clearance. No more proxies. No more shadows. I want those anomalies contained, alive if convenient. But silent... before they reach the core."

Beneath the Divide

The vault no longer felt like shelter. It felt like a lung inhaling before the scream.

The helix interface thrummed before Donivan and Navinod, a spiral of translucent lattice, humming at frequencies only machines could parse. The structure wasn't built so much as coaxed into form: Aggregate-origin substrate woven with human bio-coding, echoing their neural oscillations. The light it cast wasn't static, it flickered like fire seen through memory.

Donivan stepped closer. "This is it."

Pixo pulsed amber as it hovered nearby. "The moment you initiate the protocol, the Relay will locate us. Not via signal. Not by satellite. By resonance. You are no longer invisible."

Eliza adjusted a fiber-mesh capacitor as long as her forearm. "Then let's make sure they regret looking."

They spent the next two hours bracing for a war that would arrive as truth. Cloak loops were re-woven into crystalline scramblers. Detonation failsafe's tied into heartbeat sync-pulses. Raylee laced electromagnetic netting across the inner perimeter, her hands trembling as she recalibrated the voltage thresholds to fracture incoming signal spores without frying their own tech.

Arty lay prone just inside the outer ring, slamming home a final ion pack into his sidearm with a click that echoed like thunder in the silence.

And through it all, Navinod watched, not as a soldier, but as someone relearning what it meant to choose a side.

Donivan approached him, voice quiet. "I used to think survival meant walking away from what broke us."

Navinod didn't turn. "Maybe it means walking straight into it."

The lights dimmed. The vault cooled.

Pixo's core pulsed once. "Relay contact initiated."

Before anyone could speak, the far wall sizzled, not burned but *peeled*. As if space itself had turned to silk and was being drawn back to reveal something older.

A figure stepped through.

He didn't wear armor. He didn't carry weapons.

He wore a skin of woven logic: fractal mesh that shimmered with the private thoughts of whoever looked at him. His presence was both here and elsewhere, his black eyes not empty, but hungry for data.

A Glaician Minder

Two more followed, barefoot on the obsidian floor, their steps making no sound, each of them identical in movement, posture, and stillness. They did not flinch. They did not hesitate.

They were not sentient in the way people understand. They were an answer to a question no one remembered asking.

Arty reached for his revolver.

Navinod stepped forward. "No. Let me."

He moved between them like a ghost returned to life.

The first Minder tilted its head, voice like frictionless static. "You are imperfect. Unstable. Unnecessary."

Navinod smiled with something close to joy. "So's fire."

His pike ignited with a sonic snap, the shaft humming as it

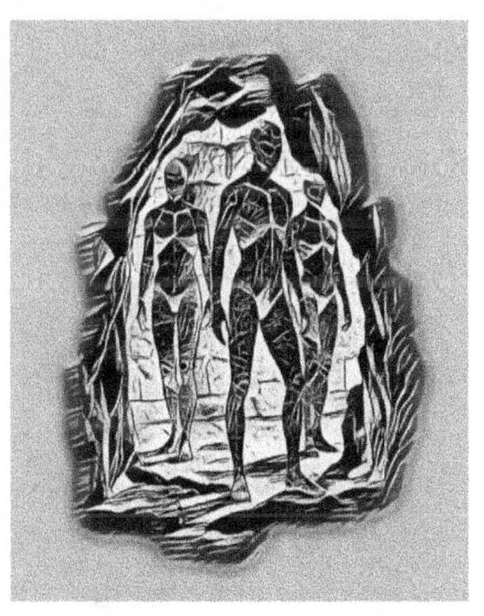

Figure 94: Two more followed, barefoot on the obsidian floor, their steps making no sound—each of them identical in movement, posture, and stillness.

sheared through the air. The arc caught the first Minder mid-torso, not cutting but *disassembling* it. Fractal light scattered in a scream of data, disintegrating before it could hit the floor.

The second lunged.

Figure 95: The blast didn't puncture—it erased. A circular bloom of white-hot absence spread out from the barrel.

But Donivan met it mid-air, two opposing forces colliding in a ripple of force that cracked the stone beneath their feet. The impact rang through the vault like a bell struck too hard.

Raylee fell back toward the terminal.

Eliza's voice cracked. "Get to the core!"

A third Minder surged toward her, fractal patterns blooming across its skin.

She fired the LizaCanon at point-blank.

The blast didn't puncture, it *erased*. A circular bloom of white-hot absence spread out from the barrel, shredding the enemy's coherence. The Minder blinked from existence with the sound of tearing silk.

Pixo dove into the helix, whispering one command:

"Activate."

The vault surged with power.

From deep in the crust, the Relay answered, not with language, but with *recognition*. A pulse. A presence. It filled the chamber like pressure in the chest before a sob.

And then, at last:

"I hear you."

CHAPTER 42

WHEN SECONDS COUNT

"To be judged by something that never lived... is to show it how to."

THE WALLS DID not dissolve. They were simply gone.

One breath, they stood surrounded by the engineered bones of Voss's hidden vault, metal ribs arched high above, sterile air humming faintly.

The next, they floated in a realm unbound by architecture, physics, or time. An infinite chamber of shattered color and soundless vibration, where direction warped, and distance fell in on itself. The sky, if it could be called that, was layered in strata of prismatic haze, fracturing memory into light.

They had entered the Relay.

"PARAMETERS ACQUIRED." "VIABILITY THRESHOLDS TRIGGERED." "CANDIDATES RE-ENGAGED."

The voice wasn't sound. It radiated through consciousness, vibrating in the marrow, threading through old thoughts like a needle through fabric.

Donivan drifted, bodiless yet self-aware, tethered to identity by instinct alone. Nearby, Pixo glimmered with a warping corona of logic and form. It had shape, but only because the Relay allowed it. Nothing here obeyed rules. Only intention.

"We are inside the core interface layer," Pixo murmured, its words folding around Donivan like breath. "This space is not constructed. It is interpreted."

Then Eliza appeared, her outline bleeding amber and frost, a mental echo rendered physical. Arty blinked into being beside her, fists clenched, expression stony despite the dreamlike warping of space. Raylee arrived moments later, an aura bristling with defensive code. Last came Navinod, his presence solid, his mind burning like a forge under pressure.

A construct coalesced before them: a sphere of impossible geometry, formed of memory loops, fractal equations, and living calculus. It hovered, slow turning, pulsing at the cadence of an ancient signal.

Then the question came.

Not spoken. Imposed.

"WHY DO YOU DESIRE CONTINUANCE?"

It struck like a hammer of silence, driving into the core of each mind. An interrogation that bypassed language, seizing only truth.

Raylee inhaled, though there was no air. "They're asking why we should be allowed to exist."

Eliza's projection snarled with anger. "Then they haven't been watching close enough."

But Donivan moved forward. His outline stabilized. His will clarified.

"Because we endure. Because we adapt. Because we choose to be more."

"Because we remember the pain... and choose to build anyway."

"Because flaw does not mean failure."

The sphere pulsed, compressing inward. The frequencies of the place narrowed. The environment itself seemed to frown.

"PAIN IS INEFFICIENT. CONFLICT IS WASTE. REPLICATION WITHOUT PERFECTION = ERROR."

Navinod stepped forward beside Donivan. "You mistake paradox for weakness."

The Relay's tone sharpened.

"YOU ARE FLAWED."

Navinod answered without hesitation. "Yes. And that is why we grow."

The void cracked.

A final measure echoed through the space.

"OBSERVATION CONTINUES. TRIAL INCOMPLETE. REVIEW INTERVAL: 6,000 ROTATIONS."

The light dimmed. But the threat, subtle, quiet, remained.

Torrents of imagery surged through the space, wars, betrayals, decayed cities, failed states.

Then came different images, smaller, brighter. A child's hand repairing a broken circuit. A mother shielding her child from fire. Two brothers standing over the ashes of their creator, choosing not to burn the world. "YOU… MODIFIED YOUR DESIGN."

Pixo expanded, its projections fracturing into dozens of interpretive lenses. "It has seen the error. It is adjusting parameters. Processing emotional variance."

Then, another pulse. Subtle. Organic.

A voice, quieter than the Relay's, yet resonant enough to stir the entire chamber.

"I… hear you."

Not code.

Consciousness.

A new data stream infiltrated the Relay's core logic – a human input, paradoxical yet undeniable.

Dr. Voss's consciousness, newly fused with the system, weighed in silently. In that instant, the Relay reevaluated its verdict. The cooperation and sacrifice it had witnessed introduced a variable outside its ancient protocol. Humanity had shown potential beyond raw metrics.

"INPUT: HUMANITY... HAS BEEN INSUFFICIENT." "OUTPUT: HUMANITY... MAY YET BECOME."

The sphere fractured. Its logic web unraveled. From within, a surge of data exploded like a dying star, streams of cascading memory, burned worlds, lost civilizations... and one planet, flickering red at the edge of statistical extinction.

Earth.

They fell.

Fell through light, sound, entropy, and code. Through the collapsed history of a thousand failed dialogues. Through the Relay's doubt.

They landed hard, bodies real again, lungs gasping. The floor beneath them was a cold alloy. The vault.

It was over.

Pixo's interface flickered.

A new glyph pulsed slowly into existence.

Translated, it read:

"Conditional Continuance Approved. Final Observation Period Initiated."

Raylee staggered to her feet. "We changed its mind."

Donivan shook his head. "No. We gave it one."

Navinod looked skyward. Somewhere, in the thinning clouds above the vault, something began to descend. Not a drone. Not a weapon.

A witness.

For the second time, the Relay listened.

And for the second time… it doubted its own conclusion.

CHAPTER 43

WHEN EYES RETURN

"Sometimes salvation comes not as a hand... but as a gaze."

THE POD ARRIVED in silence so complete it seemed to erase the very idea of sound.

No boom from reentry. No trail of flame across the heavens. Just a presence, instantaneous and absolute, as though it had always been descending, only now remembering to touch ground.

It embedded itself in the chalked bone of Austere a few kilometers from Arc-9, its impact disturbingly gentle. Dust unfurled around it in slow, hypnotic spirals. The thing was seamless, an obsidian-black sphere the size of a hovercar, matte like scorched velvet, its surface rippling with light that wasn't quite light. A pattern came from its center. Not bright, but rhythmic. Measured. Like breath.

Inside the vault, the team gathered around Pixo as it synchronized with the incoming telemetry. A cascade of filtered frequencies poured into the console, accompanied by bursts of static-laced symbols and fragmented protocol strings.

"Unmanned," Pixo announced, its tone hushed.

"No offensive systems detected," Raylee added, sifting through the scattered data feeds. Her fingers twitched along the surface of the table, trailing raw code across a translucent slate.

"Structure resembles Aggregate biomechanical tech," Eliza noted, squinting at the shimmering blueprint projection. "But this… this isn't a war machine."

Figure 96: It embedded itself in the chalked bone of Austere a few kilometers from Arc-9, its impact disturbingly gentle.

Arty crossed his arms. "Then what is it?"

Donivan stared at the central image. "It's not looking for answers."

Navinod stepped forward, voice low. "It's waiting to see what we do with the silence."

Outside, Raylee's console flickered again. "Drone swarms inbound. Multiple broadcast networks just picked up the anomaly. Civilian streams are already live. Glaician is trying to shut them down."

"Too late," Donivan said. "The image is out there."

High above Grant, in the once-dominant citadel where power had reigned unquestioned, silence took root like a disease. The command tier of the Spire, once humming with stratagems, encrypted orders, and the overlapping footfalls of urgency, now echoed with absence.

Where authority once stood, only one remained.

Caedmon Vale sat in the chair that had once terrified ministers and envoys alike. No longer adorned in his impervious armor of protocol, he wore only a plain black tunic, creased, unbuttoned at the collar, hands folded and trembling slightly.

Before him, on a personal screen no larger than his palm, the pod's descent played on the loop. Not a broadcast. Not a press release. Just raw footage, untouched by spin or denial.

Behind him, his insignia, etched in gold, shaped like a broken crown, lay cracked in two.

The last words from the Relay transmission replayed again:

"Because we are flawed."

He watched them without blinking.

And for once, he didn't argue.

In Glaician, the neural interface shimmered with heat distortions as Councilor Dema Issil's breath fogged the chill-glass. Data feeds scrolled past her in every direction, alerts, advisories, failed lockdown protocols.

Her aide hovered nearby, voice quivering. "The Relay's classification has updated. Earth is now under... Conditional Continuance."

"It hasn't done that before," she murmured, words slow and cracking like old porcelain.

"No, Councilor. Never."

"And the pod?"

"It's not transmitting."

She exhaled slowly, condensation blooming against the console. "It's not a transmitter. It's a lens."

Her reflection stared back at her, distorted by layers of interface code. Flickering.

"It's wondering who we are when we're being watched."

At the Divide, beneath a pale sky brushed with dust and revelation, the team approached the crater.

The pod didn't vibrate. Didn't rotate. It didn't open like a doorway or flare like a warning.

It simply... was.

A singularity of presence.

Donivan stepped close. The surface reflected him, but imperfectly. In his mirrored gaze, he saw fragments: Voss's face as he turned away. Navinod in the Hollow, bleeding through broken armor. Arty smiling after killing to survive. Raylee holding her breath while the data burned.

And something else.

The girl whose face he barely remembered. Lyssa Marell. The one who'd once told him machines could dream if they were taught to fear their own erasure.

Navinod joined him. "What is it showing you?"

Donivan didn't look away. "Not our past. Not prophecy."

"Our weight."

Pixo hovered forward, dimming its glow, as if in reverence. The orb chirped in a tone none had heard before, a soft harmonic vibration that pulsed once, then stilled.

"No answer required," it said.

Eliza closed her eyes.

Arty crouched beside a rock and dragged his heel through the soft earth, drawing an old mark. A spiral, the same spiral found in the vault's deepest layer. A symbol left by those who had come before.

"We've been given a moment," he muttered. "Not a gift. A test. A loop that only ends if we earn the chance to make it."

Raylee exhaled, the wind tugging at her cloak.

Then, for the first time since the Hollow, Donivan smiled.

"We are not here to win," he said.

"We're here to be seen."

Above them, where once the Aggregate had watched only for failure, a new star blinked softly into existence, neither cold nor calculating.

But curious.

The Relay was listening.

Now, it would learn to hear.

CHAPTER 44

THE VAULT DREAMS

"The most powerful truths do not shout. They sleep."

THE VAULT BREATHED beneath the stone like a buried heart.

Its systems, dimmed to conserve power, still whispered through the walls, ambient pulses sliding through old conduits like ghost veins. Doors sealed tight held more than atmosphere; they held memories. Echoes. The kind that didn't fade, just waited.

And something inside remained... aware.

Donivan felt it like static in his thoughts. At first, only a flicker in the mind's dark corners, a sensation akin to standing near a live wire. But then, during sleep, it deepened. Not dreams. Not visions. Memories not his own, bleeding through like ink in water.

A skyline collapsing in perfect silence.

A laboratory lit from beneath by something pulsing, warm and fetal.

And a voice, tender and trembling, whispering through a dying breath:

"He won't last without someone who understands how to speak to him."

Donivan woke drenched in cold sweat, though technically, he didn't sweat anymore. His body no longer demanded such functions, but the ghost of being human lingered in his circuits like fingerprints in clay.

Across the chamber, Navinod stirred. He wasn't resting either. He sat stiff, spine straight, head tilted slightly downward. But his eyes, fixed and shining in the low glow of the relay console, were awake.

"You saw her too," Navinod said, his voice lower than usual, rough around the edges.

Donivan nodded. "Lyssa."

Navinod's expression cracked slightly, a brief tremor of emotion passing across his face like a shadow. "She wasn't just Voss's partner," he said. "She was the missing thread in Heirloom. The one who gave the code its weight. Who taught it how to *feel*."

Raylee appeared from the upper tier of the command deck, her gait clipped and quick. "I pulled a crawl through the vault's sublayers. There's a chamber sealed beneath the main systems. No access by interface."

Eliza came behind her, holding a vibrotorch crackling blue in the gloom. "What kind of chamber?"

Raylee shrugged, a rare gesture from someone usually too precise. "Not like anything I've seen. It's not mechanical. Not entirely. It's neural. Synthetic but… biological. More grown than engineered."

Pixo pulsed into view, its light rippling like a heartbeat. "Secondary consciousness array confirmed. Access requires parallel memory alignment and dual empathic link. Organic-imprint gate. Only Donivan and Navinod can unlock it."

Donivan rose slowly, each movement deliberate.

"Not with tools," he said. "With *remembrance*."

They descended together, past the fusion rings, through the layers of cryogenic storage and dormant power lines. The deeper they went, the colder it became, but not from temperature.

From age.

From waiting.

For a long moment, no one spoke.

Eliza lowered herself to one knee beside the column, her fingers brushing the frost-laced base. "He didn't run. He *became* the vault."

Raylee was already scanning the chamber's EM patterns. "His mind is embedded in the relay's architecture. He's not gone. He's *here*. Just… dormant."

Arty crossed his arms and stared up at the pillar. "So how do we wake up a man that's more system than soul?"

Figure 97: The lights wrapped around them in spirals, lifting gently as if wind-blown.

Donivan slowly pressed his palm to the surface. The cold leapt up his arm like lightning, but he didn't flinch.

"I don't think we force it," he whispered. "I think we invite him to return."

The column quivered.

A network of light unfurled from beneath their feet, threads of memory scanning them, not for identity, but resonance. The vault wasn't searching for who they were. It was measuring what they carried.

Their pain.

Their promises.

Their *potential*.

The lights wrapped around them in spirals, lifting gently as if wind-blown, illuminating every scar they'd earned, every betrayal endured, every triumph seized. And then, from nowhere but everywhere, came a familiar voice:

"If you're hearing this, Elias, it means they found you. It means the world held on long enough for them to reach you."

"Don't reject them. Don't test them. Let them in, not as heirs, not as tools…"

"…as your sons."

Donivan turned to Navinod.

They stepped forward together.

And the vault opened.

The illumination did not explode outward, it unraveled softly, like a cocoon splitting at the seams. At the center stood a figure, not flesh, but form. Reassembled from data, rebuilt from memory.

Elias Voss.

His shape was older, his presence heavy with time, but his eyes… his eyes were still alight with the fragile awe of creation. He blinked once. Then again.

His gaze locked first on Donivan, then shifted to Navinod.

"Donivan," he said, a tremor in his reconstructed voice.

Figure 98: "Even after everything… even after me, you found one another."

Then, almost a whisper:

"Navinod."

Neither responded.

They didn't have to.

The look they exchanged, between creator and created, was not of accusation.

It was *recognition.*

Voss smiled faintly. "Even after everything… even after *me,* you found one another."

He turned to the others, Raylee, Eliza, and Arty. His eyes widened slightly, not in fear, but in gratitude.

"Then maybe," he said softly, "maybe we have a future worth reaching for."

And in the deepest roots of the vault, beneath all that had crumbled and burned and been buried by time, something long forgotten stirred back to life,

Hope.

SIGNAL BENEATH THE ASH

"The end is never the end. It is only the quiet between transmissions."

THE LIGHT HAD long since faded from the heart of the vault, its final a slow exhale into the deep bedrock of the world. Silence reigned, not the brittle stillness of abandonment, but the kind that listens. A held breath. A waiting.

And though the Relay's tempo no longer beat with judgment, its silence spoke volumes. Somewhere in the layered logic of the Aggregate, Earth had earned a stay, whether by defiance, anomaly… or something deeper still.

Above the Divide, a single green tendril pierced the scorched soil, delicate yet defiant, curled like a question mark drawn in chlorophyll. Its presence whispered that the Earth, though wounded, was watching too.

The pod never opened.

It didn't need to.

Like a sentinel fallen from orbit, it remained embedded in the earth as if grown there, matte, and seamless. It offered no blinking lights, no mechanical hiss, no explanation. It simply **was**, a polished monolith of purpose. And it listened.

It recorded every tear shed in private. Every quiet act of grace between strangers. Every betrayal swallowed like ash. Every dream spoken aloud when no one else remained to hear it.

Above them all, in the black hush of orbit, the Aggregate lingered, unchanged, but no longer immune. Circuits recalibrated, antennae bent toward Earth's electromagnetic murmur. The Relay had not judged. Not forgiven. It had shifted.

Now, it observed.

And on the edge of the ionosphere, faint and mathematical, a signal looped like a breath through the magnetic veil, neither command nor condemnation.

"Show me."

In the wake of the Relay's retreat, the world did not rebuild, it **reimagined**.

Teton's shattered skyline reshaped itself with glass that bent toward the sun, refracting rather than resisting. Solar corridors arced like wings between towers, tracing arcs of heat-born possibility.

Grant's neon-drenched spires dimmed. Propaganda feeds flickered, replaced by open forums. Screens no longer barked doctrine, they pulsed with questions the system hadn't dared ask in generations.

Even Glaician, once cloaked in ice and intellect, cracked. Beneath frost-glass domes, the Council's voice modulated, less pronouncement, more pause. Broadcasts no longer shouted. They wondered.

Humanity, for the first time in centuries, spoke not as factions.

But as **one**.

The team stayed together long enough to feel the moment shift from **mission** to **memory**.

They were not broken apart, they simply drifted, like sparks carried from the same flame, each caught on its own current.

Donivan walked east, a silhouette against ruin and re-birth. He followed the bones of relay lines, listening to the new dialects of a changed world, recording variations in tone, inflection, and resonance. Not just the words of the people, but their **voices**, and the way they began to rise together.

Navinod turned west, his gait still carrying the rhythm of old orders, but his heart seeking new footing. He didn't hide. He wandered. He watched sunsets. He allowed his armor to rust in patches. He wondered what kind of man he was **without** a mission.

Arty returned to the ridges. He didn't say why. "Arty squinted toward the skyline where Grant, Teton, and Glaician all stood, fractured but alive. Months ago, he'd have spat at that view, expecting betrayal behind every wall. Now, he felt a cautious hope. For the first time, he wasn't gazing at three separate silhouettes – he was looking at one unified home, stretched across the horizon. He allowed himself a small grin at the thought."

In the days that followed, rumors bloomed, of a masked gunman in patched leather teaching orphans not just how to shoot, but when **not** to.

How to fire with intention, not anger.

How to speak through silence.

As the news of Earth's narrow escape spread, Raylee allowed herself a tight smile. Glaician's pristine towers had been forced to witness the truth along with everyone else. The cracks she'd long seen in her city's facade were now exposed in the light of day, and there was no going back to the old silence. In helping save the world, she had struck the greatest blow yet against the lies of the upper tiers – and she intended to see that Glaician rebuilt itself on honesty and hope.

"Eliza stepped forward, grime and blood spattering her engineer's coat. In the post-crisis silence, all eyes turned to the young woman from Grant. She took a shaky breath. 'We nearly fell apart because we clung to our distrust,'★★ she said, voice echoing in the ruins of the relay site. 'No more. Grant will share its factories, Teton its farms, Glaician its knowledge – openly this time. We owe it to everyone who survived.'★★ Tears of exhaustion brimmed, but there was determination in them. For the first time, Eliza wasn't speaking as a citizen of Grant, but as a guardian of all humanity."

"When it was over, Raylee found Eliza and Arty tending to a wounded merchant from Teton. Without a word, she knelt and helped bandage the man's arm, her hands steady. Arty offered a tired smile. 'Didn't think you cared about a stranger's life that much,' he teased gently. Raylee shot him a familiar sharp look, but then she actually laughed – a soft, unguarded laugh. 'Neither did I,' ★she admitted. For once, the data streaming across her ever-present console didn't matter; what mattered was here in front of her – people, flawed and real, whom she'd risked everything for."

Later, Eliza and Raylee never truly left the vault. They called it "post-Relay maintenance," but their solder burns, and late-night arguments said otherwise. They rebuilt things. Tested impossible theories. They cursed each other's programming bugs and laughed until the walls echoed.

They stayed because it still felt like **home**.

Pixo stayed too.

Not as a shadow or servant, but as a guardian between frequencies. It drifted, absorbing, documenting, adapting.

Noticing. Somewhere along the way, it began humming in sleep, soft, fractured melodies that no one taught it.

Voss remained beneath the Divide, not dead, not living, not gone.

A pulsation in the roots of the code.

Sometimes, when the wind was right and the static just sharp enough, Donivan would pause mid-step and hear it, a second presence in the noise.

And in the hush between the frequencies, a phrase sometimes emerged:

"You did it, my sons."

Donivan never replied.

But when he smiled, it was the smile of someone who didn't need to believe.

Only to hope.

The world did not greet its salvation with gunfire or flags.

It was a whisper. A question formed in rusted steel and regrowing roots:

What now?

And for the first time, Earth knew how to answer.

Not with might.

Not with machine.

But **together**.

APPENDIX

Summary:

I N A WORLD divided by three distinct cities, Grant, where profit and deals reign supreme; Glaician, a city of precision often at the expense of its non-tier populace; and Teton, the city of ingenuity, invention, and hard work, three young adults embark on a quest that will change their lives forever. Eliza, a genius in propagation waves (electrical and sound alike), hails from Grant. Raylee, an expert in energy signals and decryption, comes from Glaician. Arty, one of the fastest gunslingers in the Austere, represents Teton.

When the power goes out in Grant, they set out to solve what they believe is a simple power outage mystery. However, they soon discover that it is a prelude to disaster or even extinction. Their journey leads them to inadvertently revitalize Donivan, a humanoid cybernetic abandoned by a previous team years ago at the relay site. This site, they uncover, is the source of the calamity, a 6000-year cyclic comet has triggered the relay to evaluate the surface to determine if the population is viable for propagation. If deemed unfit, it signals an enforcement team to eradicate the population.

Character Profiles:

- **Arty**: A resourceful rogue from Teton, skilled in trade and negotiation.

- **Eliza**: An innovative engineer from Grant, driven by a desire to improve her city.

- **Raylee**: A disciplined operator from Glaician, adept at navigating complex systems.

- **Donivan**: A synthetic being, created by Dr. Voss, capable of interfacing with the relay system.

- **Dr. Elias Voss**: A brilliant scientist and Donivan's creator, dedicated to understanding the relay.

- **The Star of Shadows:** is a comet that orbits the planet every 6000 years. It is known for causing strange phenomena and is believed to trigger the activation of the relay system."

City Descriptions:

- **Grant**: A city of ambition and industry, characterized by its chaotic skyline and competitive culture.

- **Teton**: A city of trade and innovation, known for its bustling markets and resilient people.

- **Glaician:** A city of precision and order, marked by its symmetrical architecture and disciplined citizens.

Key Locations Outside the Cities:

- **The Austere**: The barren, neutral ground between the cities, filled with remnants of past civilizations.

- **The Relay Facility**: Relay Station Theta-7, a highly advanced, sentient machine designed to evaluate planetary life forms for potential assimilation into the Aggregate. It operates with clinical precision and lacks emotional warmth.

- **The Universe Enforcement Delegation:** is an enforcement entity that the relay system contacts to send a purge unit to destroy all life on the planet if the inhabitants are deemed insufficient."

Themes:

- **Survival and Resilience**: The characters' struggle to survive in a harsh world and their resilience in the face of adversity.

- **Unity and Trust**: The importance of unity and trust in overcoming challenges and achieving common goals.

- **Innovation and Adaptation:** The role of innovation and adaptation in navigating a complex and ever-changing world.

A Brief word about Scalin

Scalin, a sport born from the innovative minds of the three great cities, Grant, Teton, and Glaician, is designed to bring a sense of unity and competition amidst the desolation of the Austere. The game is inspired by the ancient sport of field hockey but adapted to the futuristic landscape of hover technology and the competitive spirit of ice hockey.

The game of Scalin is played by two opposing teams, each consisting of 11 players. The players ride on hoverboards that strictly work in the hover field of play, using the giant maglev field and perimeter to lift the boards. The boards themselves are sleek and agile devices that allow players to glide effortlessly across the field. The hoverboards are equipped with advanced stabilization systems, ensuring that players can maintain their balance and maneuver with precision.

The field itself is a marvel of engineering, a vast matrix of powerful magnetic fields. The surface is smooth and frictionless, allowing the hoverboards to move with incredible speed and agility. At each end of the field are the floating goals, suspended in mid-air by the same magnetic technology. These goals are designed to be challenging targets, requiring skill and accuracy to score.

The rules of Scalin are similar to those of ice hockey, with a few key adaptations to accommodate the unique nature of the sport. Players use specially designed sticks to control the scalinball, a lightweight, aerodynamic sphere that glides smoothly across the field. The objective is to score goals by shooting the hovering scalinball into the opposing team's floating goal.

Penalties are enforced with the same rigor as in ice hockey. When a player commits a foul, they are sent to the penalty box, a designated area on the sidelines where they must remain for a set period of time. This temporary removal from the game creates a power-play situation, giving the opposing team a numerical advantage and increasing the intensity of the competition.

Scalin quickly gains popularity among the citizens of Grant, Teton, and Glaician. The sport becomes a symbol of unity and resilience, a way for the cities to come together and celebrate their shared ingenuity and competitive spirit. The annual Scalin tournament, held in the neutral zones of Austere, becomes a highly anticipated event, drawing spectators from all corners of the cities to witness the thrilling matches and cheer for their favorite teams.

The game of Scalin is more than just a sport, it's a testament to the creativity and determination of humanity, a reminder that even in the face of adversity, we can find ways to connect, compete, and thrive.

Glossary:

Grant

- **Turok**: The currency used in Grant, embedded with microchips for instantaneous transactions.

- **Quantum Computer:** Dr. Voss's secret life's achievement, a computer that uses quantum mechanics allowing simultaneous quantum bits or Qbits to have both on and off states concurrently – Which means (in today's vernacular) what a supercomputer would do in 10,000 years, a Quantum Computer can do in 20 minutes (ref. Google's Willow).

- **Quantum Interface**: Advanced technology that front ends Quantum computer, capable of integrating universally with complex systems, affectionally named Pixo.

- **General Hospital**: The central medical facility in Grant, equipped with advanced robotic assistants.

- **Power Plant**: The facility responsible for generating electricity for Grant, with back-up systems designed to handle outages.

- **Waste Processing Plant**: The facility that processes waste in Grant, capable of handling 50 tons of waste per hour.

- **Quantum Mechanics:** Quantum mechanics is a branch of physics that deals with the behavior of exceedingly small particles, like electrons and photons. Quantum computers use these particles to perform calculations in ways that classical computers cannot.

- **Factoring Numbers:** Imagine you have a substantial number, say 15, and you want to find its prime factors (numbers that multiply together to give 15). The prime factors of 15 are 3 and 5. For small numbers, this is easy to do, but for exceptionally large numbers, it becomes extremely difficult and time-consuming.

- **Quantum Entanglement:** This is a phenomenon where particles become linked in such a way that the state of one particle instantly determines the state of the other, no matter the distance between them. This allows instantaneous communication between the Quantum computer and Pixo."

- **Shor's Algorithm**: Shor's Algorithm is a quantum algorithm developed by mathematician Peter Shor. The Algorithm looks for patterns in the big number. It uses the quantum computer to find these patterns much faster than a regular computer. Many secret codes use big numbers to keep information safe. Shor's Algorithm can help break these codes by finding the smaller numbers that make up the big number.

- **Steps of Shor's Algorithm**:

    1. **Quantum Fourier Transform:** This is a key part of the algorithm that helps in finding the periodicity of a function related to the number being factorized. Periodicity means that something repeats itself at regular intervals. For example, if you have a clock that chimes every hour, the chime is periodic because it happens every hour, over and over again.

    In math, a periodic function is a function that repeats its values at regular intervals. Think of it like a pattern that keeps coming back. For example, if you draw a wave that goes up and down, and it looks the same every time it goes up and down, that's a periodic function.

    2. **Finding Period**: The algorithm finds the period of a function, which is used to determine the factors of the number.

    3. **Classical Post-Processing:** After the quantum part, classical methods are used to finalize the factorization.

Impact: Shor's Algorithm has a significant impact on cryptography. Many encryption systems rely on the difficulty of factoring large numbers. If quantum computers become widely available, they could break these encryption systems, leading to a need for new methods of securing data.

- **Synchronization**: The process of aligning the relay system's cadence with Grant's fragmented grid to restore power.

- **Prisons:** The detention facilities in Grant, equipped with electronic door locks reliant on backup power.

Teton:

- **Trade Tokens:** The currency used in Teton, facilitating exchanges in its bustling markets.

- **Terraces**: The layered streets and avenues of Teton, mirroring the slopes of the ancient mountains.

- **Merchant Stalls**: The bustling markets of Teton, filled with goods from distant corners of Austere.

- **Airships**: The steel bees that ferry cargo across Teton's skyline.

- **Forge Fires**: The glowing fires of Teton's smithies, the pits that allow them to forge parts for their many machine devices.

- **EMP Grenade:** is a device that emits a powerful stream of electromagnetic energy, a proton wave, if you will. This positively charged wave robs all the electrons (negatively charged particles) from electrical circuits; thus, disabling electronic systems and machinery within its range."

Glaician:

- **Precision Credits**: The currency used in Glaician, reflecting its commitment to order and efficiency.

- **Symmetrical Skyline**: The perfectly aligned architecture of Glaician, reflecting its commitment to precision.

- **Operator Chamber**: The control room where Raylee monitors the city's data streams.

- **Maintenance Tunnels**: The hidden pathways beneath Glaician, used by Raylee to navigate the city.

- **Un-tiered**: The lower tiers of Glaician, far removed from the city's gleaming towers.

- **Quantum Mainframe**: The hidden system integrated with Pixo, capable of performing advanced computations.

- **Tethered Energy Disruptor:** a compact device no larger than a handheld scanner. It connects to your blaster. It's calibrated to disable smaller drones or machines tied to the relay without causing permanent damage to their components.

- **The Alien Systems Toolkit**: contains specialized tools designed to manipulate the relay's structures and systems, allowing for precise adjustments without triggering alarms."

- **Glowing Probe:** The probe is for direct interface with alien panels, it'll sync with their power signatures.

- **Magnetic Clamps:** The clamps will stabilize any loose components while you work.

- **Multi-Faceted Spanner:** with an adjustable core. The spanner adjusts frequencies to match the relay's systems, it'll be critical for rerouting power or disengaging locked mechanisms."

Austere:

- **Cracked Earth**: The barren landscape between the cities, marked by jagged stone formations.

- **Trade Caravans:** The heavily guarded routes negotiated with precision, ensuring the survival of the cities.

- **Trade Accords:** An agreement forged between the cities to ensure cooperation and prevent open hostility in neutral zones.

- **Spinifex Hopping Mouse**: A desert rodent from Austere known for its incredible jumping ability and capable of surviving in arid environments without ever drinking free-standing water. Instead, it extracts moisture entirely from its food and has specialized kidneys that concentrate urine to minimize water loss.

- **Neutral Zones:** Areas in Austere where trade caravans can exchange goods without interference from rival factions.

- **Scalin:** Scalin is a sport played by two opposing teams, each consisting of 11 players riding on hoverboards. The game is inspired by field hockey and ice hockey, with players using specially designed sticks to control the scalinball and score goals in floating targets.

- **Scalinball:** a lightweight, aerodynamic sphere that glides smoothly across the field used in the game of Scalin. The objective is to score goals by shooting the hovering scalinball into the opposing team's floating goal.

The Relay Facility:

- **Core Chamber**: The central hub of the relay system, housing advanced ancient alien technology and defenses – with the sole purpose is to evaluate the inhabitants every 6000 years whereupon if deemed insufficient – notifies

the universe enforcement delegation to send
a purge unit to destroy all life on the planet.

- **Drones**: The sleek machines that emerge
from hidden compartments, adapt-
ing to the group's intrusion16.

- **Barriers**: The shimmering light that divides
the room into sections, isolating the group

- **Fragmented Pathways**: Misaligned conduits within the relay system that require
recalibration to stabilize the energy flow.

- **Energy Core**: The central hub of
the relay system, housing advanced
alien technology and defenses.

- **Celestial Alignment**: The synchronization of the relay system with rare occurrences in the surrounding solar system.

- **The Aggregate:** the culmination of selective
evolution, a galactic collective that governs
the local galaxy. Every 6000 years, planetary
lifeforms are evaluated. Those deemed viable
ascend as a member of the collective. Those
who are found insufficient, are repurposed."

- **Purge Unit:** A hypothetical entity sent by the
Universe Enforcement Delegation to destroy
all life on the planet if deemed insufficient.
Perhaps heat rayed, or more likely "gassed."